N. ANNETTE KNIGHT .

The Engine Tamer: An Adventure Novel

Manor Bjorne

To my future self: Look how far you've come. The beginning is behind you.

Contents

Acknowledgement

Thank you to this book's editor, Eric Jones.

A special thank you to Brandi Jones. Your willingness and encouragement is a bright star. My forever gratitude.

I

The World

New Victoria

II

Prologue

Darling of Smugglers

Tamara shoved open yet another door and looked in. In response, a stunning green, jewel-encrusted goblet sailed past her head, smashing against the door frame beside her. Tamara ducked.

"Who are you? Get out!" an unseen woman shouted from the room.

She scrambled to get out of the way of the next projectile aimed at her head, stumbling backward into a pile of ropes and rolled canvas. Tamara wondered if she was the intended victim of the goblet or whether she interrupted a fight.

"Fieldmarsh?! What are you doing here?" A familiar reedy voice called from inside the room in astonishment.

Barone's voice! She *knew* he was home! The "foot soldier" downstairs tried to bar her entry when she appeared at the villa's door to confront Barone. Determined to get her payment, she had snuck around the back of the house and climbed through a window in an empty room. Sneaking down hallways and opening doors led her to the near miss of the glass goblet.

Tamara heard more smashing glass. What was going on in there?

She got on all fours and peeked around the door. She saw several people gathered around a rickety wooden table in the dimly lit room. An oil lamp sat in the center of the table among piles of paper and tools that covered every other inch of it. Other, lesser participants in the smuggling ring sat on low cushions set against the walls, eating and drinking. Barone stood near the table pleading with someone in low tones.

"Barone? You haven't paid me in weeks! I'm here to collect what you owe!" Tamara called around the door, cringing in anticipation of more flying objects.

As she expected, another goblet smashed against the door, narrowly missing her cloud of hair. Tamara jumped backward again and squeaked as glass pelted her. She pulled down her goggles.

"I'm not leaving until you pay me, Barone!" She called out.

"Get her out of here!" The angry woman screamed again. A dull thud sounded against the door.

She must have run out of glass, whoever she is, Tamara thought.

She heard Barone trying to calm the woman. During the pause in the barrage, Tamara hopped about the ropes she had stepped into. Struggling to pull herself loose from a tangle of fabric, she hopped on one foot toward the door to confront Barone's guest.

"Why are you throwing things at me? I don't even know you!" Tamara called out.

Teetering on one leg, Tamara stuck her head back in. Barone was a big, intimidating man. But the petite woman who stood before him leaning in, jabbing a finger in his face, snarled ferociously about spies and his lack of adequate security dwarfed him with her obvious domineering aura.

Her hair was coloured a false black and was braided and interwoven with ribbons and scarves, rising above her skull like a tower on a rock. Her features hid behind a veil that tossed and fluttered, showing the woman's eyes behind it: Enormous. Violet coloured. Charcoal-rimmed. Insane. Those eyes narrowed into slits as they glared in Tamara's direction.

"Get out! I will make ribbons of the skin of your pretty little face if you don't get out!" The veil shook as breath came out with force as she spoke, and she raised a piece of glass to underscore her threat.

Tamara's heart thudded rapidly and she felt for the knife she kept in her waistband.

"Please, madam," Barone whined, "Please! She is just here to get payment. She entered the wrong room."

Ignoring him, the woman scrambled onto the table scattering the lamp, papers, blueprints, pens and tools to get to Tamara. The crowd in the room shrieked and scattered like the underworld rats they were. They streamed past her, battering Tamara as they clamored to escape before the gas lamp sent the room up in flames.

"*Please*, madam! I will take her out of here." Barone shouted.

Receiving a stinging slap in response, Barone winced and stepped backward. Then, with baffling speed, the veiled woman scrambled past him, swiping the dagger from the sheath at his waist. Mouth open, eyes wide, Tamara stood motionless. Her experience in fending off unwanted advances from gangsters, smugglers, and drunk flyboys hadn't prepared her for the wrath and speed of a venomous harpy intent on bloodshed.

Barone snagged the woman's clothing, ripping the veil from her face and pulling ribbons from her hair. He held on frantically.

"Go! Go to my workshop!" He yelled to Tamara. "I'll get your money! Just go before she kills you!"

Suddenly, the woman stilled. She wrested her arm out of Barone's grasp, and he put his hands up in a form of surrender, stepping away.

Tamara backed toward the entrance to the room, keeping her hand near her knife. As she backed through the door, she heard the woman's voice cut through the atmosphere thick with tension like ice, "I will tear the skin from your face if I ever see you again."

Tamara fled.

She was waiting in Barone's workshop mulling over the fracas when he walked in with heavy steps.

She observed him warily, and he glared at her balefully.

"She's gone," he said.

"Who *is* that crazy woman?" She asked, her voice taut with tension.

"No one knows exactly. She's powerful. No one wants to cross her," he said.

"Where does she come from? She has a posh accent, and she hides her face," Tamara asked, confused.

"No one really knows where she came from. She rose to power quickly, and she has far-reaching influence, even into the palace." Barone walked over to a tall steel case against the wall, glancing at her.

"And the reason she tried to assault me?"

"Who can say," he said, shrugging, "perhaps it's because you burst into a secret meeting and you weren't supposed to be there?"

Tamara nodded sheepishly, "I'm sorry about that, but I was sure you were trying to avoid paying me."

"I wasn't…," he said sulkily, "It's just been a busy time."

"Sure."

He opened the case with a key from a large ring filled with keys. He opened the wide door and reached in, pulling out a large stack of paper money and a bag of coins.

"Why do you keep all that money in here, Barone? Isn't it dangerous?"

"I don't trust banks."

"I'm amazed you trust the people you know better than you trust the banks who have security and trustworthy clerks."

"Who says I trust the people I know?" Barone asked, throwing her a glance.

"Well, you're showing *me* where you keep all your money," she replied.

"Eh, you're just a woman. You wouldn't have the guts to take it away from me," he said dismissively as he shoved the money he owed her across the table.

Even after being sought as the premier engineer and airship mechanic for all of New Victoria, no one thought of Tamara as an equal, a threat, or a worthy ally. She nodded her thanks to Barone and left his mansion, bemused.

As she roared away on the hover bike she built from scratch, she thought about the woman with the black hair and violet eyes and the threat about what she would do if she saw her again. Who was she?

III

Tamara Fieldmarsh

Chapter One

Tamara Fieldmarsh, brown-skinned and honey-eyed, grumbled and hissed in irritation. Her deft, slender fingers felt around underneath the cold, unyielding metal, searching for the bolt that fastened the panel to the engine block. Wishing she had eyes on her fingertips, she focused on her fingers reaching within the narrow opening. She pushed her hand in further and winced as the rusted metal scraped both sides of her wrist.

"Come on, come on," she mumbled.

Finally, her fingers bumped against a lump of metal, and she shouted with joy. Pulling her hand out, she grabbed a wrench and shoved it into the opening trying to grab the bolt to twist it off. Her efforts rewarded her with the wrench slipping from her tenuous grasp. It clattered down and out to the floor of the workshop.

"Bollocks!" she screamed. She was so close. She had fought with the ancient engine for days, and this was the last step she needed to complete before sending off the airship. Tamara crawled down the ladder and hurried to grab the wrench before climbing up into the engine housing again. Beaton The Cat meowed at her from his perch atop the rolling wooden tool box.

"I know, Beaton. I'm sorry I disturbed your nap. It's this wretched engine! I should have finished a week ago. They'll probably threaten to take a few points off my fee!"

Tamara usually took several weeks to repair an airship engine on her own. She thought about the new airships the military flew these days. Instead of an engine and passenger car attached to the envelope that held gasbags by riggings, the new ones were enormous, built with a hard-shell and permanently attached to the passenger car. They required enormous hangars to store them. Tamara's much smaller hangar only housed the engine and a carriage car, depending on how old it was.

Tamara climbed back up into the engine. This time, she attached a cable to the end of the wrench so she wouldn't have to make another trip down. Ignoring the pain, she shoved her hand and arm as far as she could into the opening and pushed the wrench firmly onto the top of the bolt, making firm wresting movements until it broke free from the rust adhering to it. Tamara made quick work of removing the bolt and had the panel removed soon after.

She hummed along to the tinny music that came from the small wireless radio on her work shelf as she disconnected wires, cables, springs, belts, and whatnots. She brushed her hair off her forehead, smearing oil.

"Well! The great Tamara Fieldmarsh working on yet another smuggler's airship!"

She jumped at the sound of the unexpected voice. Rubbing her head where she banged it on a crossbar, she frowned in annoyance as she turned to look down at Fillip Weathermarker. The son of a local magistrate, Fillip wasn't well-liked by anyone, but the hordes he gallivanted with exhibited an immense tolerance for his father's money. He attended the local university and showed up at various races and gambling events, throwing money around. He was tall and handsome and knew it. Tamara despised him.

She frowned as she leaned against the bulkhead of the airship."What are you doing here?" She called down.

Fillip looked up at her. It was difficult to deny he was a beautiful young man. Dark hair framed his face as he stared up at her. Bright sunlight cast a stark shadow in front of him as he stood like a storybook legend, arms akimbo, head thrown back, just inside the hangar door.

"I didn't know you were back in town. Got worried when I heard someone screaming in pain. I wondered if someone might have broken in."

"I wasn't screaming," she answered, wishing he would go away, "and I'm not sure I've ever seen you that concerned with the well-being of anyone…

or anything."

Tamara turned back around to face the engine. Pulling a wire from the top of the engine block, she prepared to test its start ability.

"You know," came Fillip's voice from below, "it's a wonder the officials haven't come to investigate what you do in here. I hope no one says anything."

Tamara's lips curled as she gritted her teeth against the veiled threat. She knew he would say nothing, but she wouldn't put it past him to drop hints to someone who would.

She looked down to glare at him, "Fillip, why do you bother taunting me so much? If you hate me, why don't you just leave me alone?"

"Hate you?"

"Yes!"

"Why would you think that?"

"Because of that night in the garden at Neridette's birthday celebration."

"As I told you before, a simple misunderstanding. Someone told me something about you, and I thought they meant something else. Besides, I was drunk."

Tamara rolled her eyes. Sure, drunk. Liar.

She pulled a series of leather straps over her head and settled it over her shoulders, tightening the clasp in front.

Fillip sauntered in further to stand by her tool boxes and work table—Beaton's fur ruffled as he neared.

"So, who *is* your protector? Is he why you said 'no' me?" Fillip asked as he rummaged around the tools on the worktable.

Tamara's mouth dropped open. She ducked her head to peer at him below the bulkhead in shocked irritation. "My protector? Do I need a reason to say 'no' to you, Fillip? How dare you!? And stop touching my stuff!"

He crossed his arms, "You wear pearls in your ears! You wear expensive perfume! You eat chocolates. Only men buy those things for women."

"Are you daft? *I* buy those things. Neridette gives me some of her unwanted things. My mother likes to send me gifts! You-!" Tamara shook her head and straightened up. She decided to drown out his voice instead of listening. She finished harnessing herself to the loops welded onto the cover of the airship's engine covering to keep her from being thrown if she miscalculated this next step. How dare he assume the only reason she rejected him was because someone else was in his place? She held a live wire from her kit above the wire jutting from the starter. She held her breath and touched the wires together. The engine roared to life like an ancient sleeping mountain dragon angered by a disrupted slumber. The rafters vibrated. Tools shook and rattled.

"Ya-hoo!" she shouted as she looked down at Fillip to gauge his reaction.

Instead, she saw poor Beaton The Cat, yowl and swat at Fillip as he bounded away. In her irritation with Fillip, she'd forgotten Beaton was there. She should have waited to start the engine.

Fillip's mouth was open, obviously cursing—although she couldn't hear him—his face distorted in pain. She saw him grab a mallet from the toolbox and lob it after the fleeing animal. Tamara saw it glance off his hindquarters, and she scrambled out of her harness, zipping down the ladder.

"You bastard!" She shouted, grabbing Fillip's hurt hand forcing his arm into an angle behind his back,

"Let go of me!" Fillip shouted back at her.

"Don't you *ever* throw things at my cat! Ever!"

"Your stupid cat scratched me!" Fillip returned, his voice faint over the airship engine's roar. He wrenched himself out of her grasp and stood cradling his hand as blood squeezed out between his fingers while glaring at her.

"Get out!" Tamara shouted.

He slouched out of her workshop, sullen.

Tamara climbed back up the ladder to the engine knowing she would have to make peace with Beaton later. She was sure he ran back home to yowl at the bakery door. The owner liked him, and Beaton loved sitting by the warm stove during the cold nights. After flipping the toggle switch to kill the engine's power, Tamara sighed and swiped her hair off her forehead. Then she realized she had just smeared engine oil all over her face and into her now stinging eyes.

She descended the ladder slowly; the altercation with had Fillip drained and depressed her, and she wondered if he might do something to get back at her. Despite what his god-like features might make one assume, Fillip Weathermarker had a reputation for pettiness.

Walking outside for a breath of fresh air, she wondered for the first time in a long time, if she should get out of this way of making her living. She looked around the towering hangar at the swinging bulbs suspended from rusty chains and the large cobwebs gracing every available spot among the rafters. How long had she been in this airship business? Three years? Five? When she had an engine to repair, she spent all of her time here: dawn to late evening. Her closest friend and roommate told her that she felt like no one else lived in their little apartment above the bakery; she saw her so rarely. Was this really the ideal life? Doing what you pleased? Letting no one dictate your every move?

Her parents wanted her to follow in their footsteps, to become a doctor. Tamara bucked against the constant expectations and left medical school during her second year after acquiring a taste for the racing circuit. The speed and aerodynamics of the hover bikes thrilled her. Her college roommate introduced her to her first hover bike, and Tamara felt free for the first time in her life. Course charted, Tamara left medical school and never looked back...until now.

She hadn't exactly meant to "aid and abet" the criminals of New Victoria. Once word spread of her skills in "engine taming" in the racing circuit, she found herself the recipient of several late night visits at her old, smaller workshop. These nameless men offered so much money on behalf of their lords and masters if she would do a little "off the books" work for them. She had no definitive proof that they worked as smugglers or in other criminal activities, but one always knew. It isn't normal to receive your payments in leather bags dropped off under cover of darkness when working for a legitimate business.

Taking one last look at the airship engine, she strolled down to the corner of Warehouse Alley to ring the messenger service bell. When the little urchin rounded the corner, she waved him down to hand him a sealed note and instructions to take it to the den where most of the furtive characters sat waiting to send and receive messages, or to operate illegal rings with impunity. She described the urchin's target and sent him off before returning to the engine in her workshop. She always wondered about these boys and their home lives. Did they have parents? Did anyone care about them?

As she finished closing up the engine, the sun dipped further behind the row of buildings, and she hoped the men came before night fell. It wasn't easy being the only woman in this area when the streets were empty of decent, law-abiding people.

Most nights, she limped up the steep stairwell to the apartment tired, aching, and longing for wide arms to pull her into a warm, comforting chest. She thought about Fillip Weathermarker's proposition at Neridette's party and how insulted she felt. Almost every man who professed an interest in her since the time she left home wanted to change everything about her. "Don't worry about being a doctor, luv. I'll take care of you." "Maybe you should try a different hairstyle." "Do you always have to wear those types of dresses when you're with me? Who are you trying to impress?" She sighed. They were all the same. Either they didn't think her capable of many things, or they didn't want her capable of anything. Tamara fought down wistfulness about her future. She guessed it would just be her and Beaton forever.

The air cooled, and she reached for her father's sack jacket. Fall wasn't far off and soon she would pass another year here in Warehouse Alley. She thought of the past five years and wondered what her life would be like if she had stayed in medical school and followed the path her parents set for her. Would she have been alone this way, too? She shook the thought away. A man would only rail against her occupation and try to force her into different work...or no work at all. She grabbed the pocket watch attached to her belt and frowned. Surely the payment should have been here by now. As she contemplated the time, a yowling motor vibrated the metal buildings lined up together on Warehouse Row. Finally.

Tamara stepped out of the hangar as two thugs dismounted a hover bike with a side seat. She was accustomed to dealing with these types of men—not to say she was comfortable with them. Most of the time, there was a glint in the eye that told her she needed to be on her utmost guard and prepared.

"Took you long enough to get here, right? Have a good drink at Melzin's?" Tamara asked, setting the tone.

The tall, wide one blinked and frowned. The small, mean one narrowed his eyes as he looked at her.

"I don't drink," he said, in a high, nasal voice, cultured and out of place in his chosen profession. "Where's the merchandise?" He asked, eyeing the hangar.

Recognizing the cues of his body language, Tamara busied herself wiping the oil from her hands with a rag and tying back her hair. She checked that her knife was in her waistband as surreptitiously as she could.

"It's in the hangar," she said, "but the order of business is payment first, and I deliver later." Her shoulders tensed as the tall, wide man inched his way around her peripherals. Backing up carefully, she ran through a mental list of makeshift weapons she could grab if she needed to fight them off.

The little man arranged himself into Napoleonic stance and regarded her steadily.

"We can take the ship *and* the money, you know," he said conversationally.

"Oh?" She answered, her blood pressure rising, "You can fly?"

He squinted at her.

"Besides," she continued, "I've built a fail-safe. None of your pilots will get this started if you steal this from me before you pay me."

She hoped they weren't well-versed in machinery as she lied through her teeth. "I'll remove the fail-safe and have it delivered...*as agreed with your boss.*" She held the man's gaze, hoping she played her bluff well.

"Come on, Jamie, stop playing around. Give the filly her money," the big man behind her said in a whining voice. "I promised that girl at the tavern we'd be back soon. At this rate, I won't get back to her before she leaves for the night. Girls like that don't wait."

Tamara held her breath. The blood roared through her limbs.

"Besides, she's got a knife," the chatterbox continued, "I can see it. You wouldn't get off so easy. Let's go!" He lumbered from behind her and climbed back into the sidecar of the hover bike.

Taking measured breaths, Tamara kept her eyes locked on Jamie's. The road that ran between the warehouses and hangars remained silent. No one entered a workshop, no one passed by, and no one witnessed her predicament. A breeze whipped her hair across her face, and swirled dust into her eyes, but she remained still. Would she have to fight for her life today?

With a dismissive laugh, Jamie pulled a leather purse from his belt, and tossed it several feet away out of Tamara's reach. She didn't move. He could have tossed a bag full of nuts and bolts to her, but payment be damned if she didn't live to find out.

Giving her a last measuring look, Jamie turned and sauntered back to the hover bike and hopped onboard. He revved the engine, flinging dirt and pebbles into the air. He roared off down the alley of metal buildings, rattling the walls and deafening Tamara. She stayed where she was until the pair disappeared around the corner to roar off back into town. Then she collapsed.

"I need to get out of this business," she groaned.

After several minutes, once her heartbeat returned to normal and her hands were no longer sweaty, she crawled over to peek inside the money bag lying in the dust. She sighed in relief. She wouldn't have to call on another smuggler to demand her payment. She stood and trailed wearily into her little office to lock it away in her desk until she could take it home with her.

Using the corner messenger bell once more, she called for another messenger and instructed him to send a telegram for her. She returned to her workshop to get the workshop ready for the transport crane.

As she turned the large crank set inside the hangar wall to slide open the roll-top of the hangar, she thought about the two thugs. She wondered if Jamie was simply trying to intimidate her for his fun, or whether he meant to cheat her. She made a mental note to avoid his boss's requests for repairs in the future. In fact, she might just close her shop and go away for a while. Neridette might enjoy a trip to see her family. The more she considered it, the more the idea appealed to her. She couldn't remember the last time she saw her parents. The last conversation they had through the post was curt and disapproving.

The transport crane arrived an hour later to pick up the engine and passenger car, kicking up dust and rattling the buildings worse than the hover bike had earlier. They were terrifying machines, as large as earth movers, volatile, and deadly. Several people lost their lives each year because of their propensity to stall and drop onto unsuspecting citizens. The emperor enacted a law restricting their travel to places outside of large cities and towns, because of the danger posed to the lives of the populace. Since Warehouse Alley stood on the outskirts of the city, she didn't need to hire another service to pick up her package and deliver it to the transport crane.

She yawned as she waited for the men to complete their work. The lamplighters passed through the streets, igniting the gaslights on the city street. The night creatures chattered and buzzed as the crew hauled their freight away to the mountains. She supposed she could have waited until the morning to have the ship delivered, but the interaction with Jamie rattled her and she wanted the airship out of her workshop. Finally, the transport crane operator came to get her signature and coins, signaling the end to her long, long day.

Yawning again, she locked up the hangar and squinted at her fob watch: nearly 10 o'clock. She retrieved the money bag from her desk as she wondered how much consternation there would be at the unexpected delivery of an antique war airship at a certain mountain hideout. Unable to think clearly around the yawns splitting her face in two, she shrugged as she locked up the workshop. She gave the door a good tug to make sure everything was secure and peeked into the small window to make sure lights were off. The weight of the money bag in her satchel felt heavier and her steps quickened as she walked down Warehouse Row to the cross street. She pulled the knife from her waist and held it in her hand just in case.

"Miss?"

She jumped. Out of the gloom, a man in the garb of a carriage taxi driver stopped just short of her, peering into her face with concern.

"Yes?" She answered breathlessly. She wrapped her fingers more securely around her knife.

"A boy said a lady might want a cab ride home? Are you it?"

Bless the little messenger boy. He must have seen Jamie and his henchmen earlier.

"Yes. I'm 'it'."

He beckoned her to follow him to the street where she saw the dim form of New Victoria's sanctioned taxi carriages., She sighed with relief and climbed into the cheery red carriage.

* * *

Tamara stumbled wearily up the steps to the apartment above the bakery. She found a note on the small dining table in the kitchenette when she went in to find something to eat.

"You don't have enough fun. Come out to the club when you get home. -Neri"

Tamara shook her head. Her roommate Neridette seemed to spend all her time at clubs, parties, and events. That life wasn't for Tamara. At first, it seemed fun: the lights, the music, the garishly colourful clothing, the men, the women. She enjoyed the exotic food and drinks that Neridette gave her. Soon, however, the sheen of Neridette's companions began to take on a brassy quality. The fun seemed forced and false. Empty. Tamara began to turn down Neridette's further invitations.

Stuffing her mouth with bread and salami, Tamara hurried through her night ritual and fell onto the narrow, rickety bed. She was awakened some time later by a fierce hammering on the door of the apartment. Heart pounding, she wondered if the thugs from earlier were trying to break down her door. She slipped her knife from beneath her pillow and crept to the door, pulling on her dressing gown as she went.

"Who is it?" She called.

"Monk, miss!"

It was the messenger boy who often delivered messages and did shopping for her and Neridette.

She tucked her knife into her night bodice and clutched her dressing gown together at the front before opening the door. She strained her eyes to see the small boy standing in the faint light of the gas lamp on the street below.

"What is it? Is something wrong?" She asked, breathless.

"Miss Neridette, ma'am. She's in trouble."

She frowned, confused, "Trouble? What do you mean? She's out with friends."

He shook his head emphatically, his wild, tangled locks shaking and bobbing.

"Not good friends. She was at the Red Room before. I saw her come out without Mr. Dane and the others and some flyboys was standing outside and got her to come with them."

She grabbed his sleeve and propelled him into the room quickly. She pushed him down onto the faded yellow sofa, her dressing gown whirling behind her as she darted to the small bedroom.

"Tell me where they went," she called as she stepped behind the dressing screen and scrambled into her clothes.

"They took her to Miss Maisie's."

That den of evil. Maisie Von allowed anyone to do anything as long as she was paid enough money. Flyboys were her favourite clients, and the ones who frequented her establishment usually had depraved intentions.

"How long ago?"

"I runned right over when I saw them go in 'cause I didn't like the flyboys' faces. My aunt got done real bad once when she was taken there when I was a youngster."

Youngster. He couldn't have been more than eleven years old now.

Dressed, she tugged her boots on. She handed the boy a silver piece.

"Do you need food?"

He shook his head and rubbed his tummy.

"I ate real good in the kitchens of the Red Room. My sister works there, and the cook likes her. If I'm real quiet, he lets me eat my suppers there."

Tamara nodded briefly.

The boy trotted out of the small apartment ahead of her.

"Thank you for letting me know about Neri. Let me know if you ever need me," she said as they went separate ways at the end of the steep stairwell. Tamara raced to the east side of town on the dark, cool street.

"Hey, girlie! Where ya runnin'?"

"Run straight into my arms for a good time!"

The catcalls of the ne'er-do-wells and alley rapists hardly registered in her mind as her feet pounded the stones of the street. She darted around a drunk lurching toward her by veering sharply to the right and onto the boardwalk that edged the closed and barred shops. The cool air whistled past her face as she ran.

The moonlight shimmered and wavered as greenish-white clouds scudded across the night sky. Tamara's lungs burned with exertion as she neared Miss Maisie's brothel at the low end of the long street. Up to this point, the street was mostly empty at almost one in the morning.

Disheveled men, deep in their liquor and beer, shuffled in her direction. Working girls called out drunkenly. Female patrons laughed, and teased thier companions. Behind them, a brothel and nightclub worked in partnership to bring society down to its basest impulses.

Tamara had never been inside the brothel, but the stories of dead or disfigured women found in this place gave her a momentary qualm as she drew closer. The entrance stood wide open, and jarring, sharp music streamed out. Silhouettes of bodies moving to and fro, up stairs, down stairs, in doors and out in the red, pink and orange lights, registered dimly. A window with a sliding glass in the blank wall opposite the entrance looked like an official registration desk and she hurried toward it.

A tall, dark-skinned man in a pin-striped suit and impossibly bright pink eyeshadow and purple eyelashes eyed her over reading glasses. Morris' *Age of Space And Reason* sat poised in his hand as he waited for her to speak.

"I'm looking for my friend! I'm worried about her!"

"Are you her moral conscience?" The man asked in a tone of questioning condescension.

Tamara stared at him uncomprehendingly.

"Are you here to…rescue her…from a life of degradation and shame?" He continued, his eyes raking over her face, hair, and clothing.

"I said my friend is in trouble! She's drunk and most likely going to be raped…by several men!"

"Girl. She may not mind."

Tamara snapped, "Fool! Where are the rooms?!"

The purple and pink-edged eyes rolled as a long, brown finger pointed dismissively toward the stairs at the front of the building. The clerk returned to his book.

Tamara sped toward the stairs, taking them two at a time to the top landing. This was going to take longer than she thought. *Gods*. The landing led to four different halls lined with doors. She growled beneath her breath. How was she going to find Neridette? How much time had passed already? Plenty of time for her to be ravaged.

Tamara heard a door open. Several male voices raised in taunting and derisive laughter floated toward her. She hurried across the landing trying to find the source of the noise.

The third hall.

A page holding a bottle stood before an open door facing a man who wore the disheveled uniform of a flyboy. Neri was there in that room. She knew it.

Heart pounding, Tamara took short cautious steps up the short hall. She watched as the room's occupant took the bottle from the page and handed over a coin. The page muttered his thanks and looked at her curiously as he passed her, saying nothing. Tamara darted to the door just before it latched and pushed it open.

The sight that met her eyes shook her. Neridette, half-conscious and muttering gibberish, writhed naked on a small, iron-framed bed in the center of the room. Several men in varying stages of undress surrounded the bed, or stood by, pouring spirits into glasses that overflowed onto the bare, wood floor. They laughed and spoke boisterously in the small room with its red window shades, red oil lamp shades, and bare walls.

Horrified, Tamara watched as two men moved to hold Neri's wrists and ankles, and a third man moved toward her with a bottle. He tipped the contents out onto her belly and bent over her.

Tamara felt her stomach clench and heave. Swallowing hard, she stepped fully into the room and slammed the door shut behind her, unconsciously trying to shield Neri from any more witnesses to her condition. Tears pricked her eyes as her friend moaned and strained against the men holding her down. What did they give her to put her mind in this state?

"Who are you?" One of the degenerates asked in drunken surprise.

Several pairs of eyes turned to gaze at her with varying degrees of intoxication of drink or the cocaine that was freely disbursed by the brothel.

"Come get on this bed, little beauty!"

"Hey-o, a brown girl for my quota!"

Tamara winced.

"You know you want this!"

A young, fresh-faced flyboy, who looked recently out of school, grabbed her arm and tried to propel her toward the bed. Tamara uttered a furious cry as she wrenched her arm out of his grasp.

"Get over here!" The ringleader of the assault on Neridette shouted, lunging for her.

In half panic, half rage, Tamara grabbed an oil lamp from the nearest table and swung it at the man. The metal object making contact with her aggressor's skull made a satisfying *whump*, but she nearly lost her grip on it as oil leaked from the lamp, covering her fingers and dripping onto the floor. The acrid smell filled the room as Tamara rushed the bed, swinging franticly. Shouting obscenities at her, the group clambered over the bed to get out of Tamara's reach. Neridette screamed in pain as the group trampled her.

"Get off her!" Tamara raged.

The lamp, slick with oil, slipped from her grasp mid swing. It smashed into the wall and clattered noisily to the floor. Free of the threat the heavy lamp posed upon them, the men stumbled about the room, searching for discarded clothes to cover themselves, shouting in confusion and calling the women every horrible name that existed.

Tamara grabbed Neri by the waist and hauled her off the bed, slipping on the floorboards slick with lamp oil. When a flyboy noticed what she was doing, he darted for her, scrabbling as he fought to keep his balance on the slippery floorboards. He snatched her blouse and hair, jerking her downwards. Tamara gasped from the sharp pain that rocked her body as she hit the floor.

"She's trying to take the girl! Help me out!" He called to his buddies.

Tamara kicked and punched, breaking his grip on her. She dived under the bed trying to think what to do. There were so many of them! A dull jab at her waist made her jump until she remembered…her knife! She pulled it from her waistband and swiped at their hands and feet from beneath the bed. She heard curses and shouts as her knife made contact with bare skin. Blood dripped down fingers and feet to mix with the alcohol and lamp oil on the floor. As they backed away, she crawled from under the bed.

Keeping a wary eye on all of them and swiping her blade intermittently, she spoke to Neridette, "Neri? Neri! Come on! I'm getting you out of here!" Spying a discarded shirt that was missed, she wrapped it around Neri's shoulders quickly.

She glanced wildly from man to man as some stood holding bunched up clothing over their pelvises, or cupped their hands over themselves. Others hopped on one foot, inspecting cuts from her knife, or sucked on the wounds on their hands. The men who were fortunate not to be naked or wounded held their hands up. Each face showed fury.

Neridette moaned and flopped to the side as Tamara struggled to hold her upright. She made her way to the door, wielding the knife as she walked backward.

"What…is…*happening here?*!" An angrily modulated voice asked from the doorway behind her.

Tamara spun around awkwardly with her burden. The brothel clerk stood in the doorway, his eyes matching the anger in the flyboys' eyes.

Stumbling slightly, Tamara growled, "I found my friend. Get out of my way."

"We paid for our time and she attacked *us*!" One of the flyboys yelled.

"They were about to do unspeakable things to her! And she was basically unconscious. If you don't get out of my way, I won't promise you that I'll keep my wrath from you either," Tamara snapped.

"She's insane!"

"Look what she did to us!"

Amidst the outraged shouts of the group, the clerk's eyes rested on Tamara thoughtfully before returning to the pathetic group of men whining behind her in the room.

"Don't let her take the girl! We paid and we're not doing nothin' wrong!"

Tamara heard a shuffle of feet and turned to swing her knife in that direction.

Too late.

The blur of a heavy oil lamp was all she saw before she felt a painful crack and felt darkness fall on her.

A while later, Tamara opened her eyes. She lay on her back in a room she didn't recognize. She heard Neri's voice muttering weak thanks to someone else she couldn't see. Turning her head, she saw a tidy little office, but she could still hear the awful music of the brothel. Groaning, she sat up, realizing she lay on a small settee somewhere in the brothel.

"Ah, you're awake."

Looking up through a haze of pain, she observed the brothel clerk turning from a blanket-wrapped Neri who sat at a small lace-covered table drinking something out of a dainty tea cup and munching on tea cakes.

"Neri!" She exclaimed in relief. Then, she took in more of her surroundings, "Where is this?" Tamara asked the clerk, gasping as pain surged through her skull.

"This is my office," he replied, his demeanor cold and detached.

"Ugh," she groaned again, "What happened?"

"You were hit by one of the flyboys you attacked. Oil lamp. I never realized they were so effective. I'll remember that the next time I have to throw someone out."

"How did you get Neri to-" she gestured helplessly at her friend.

"A little of my sweet, white powder. It's an amazing restorative in the correct amounts. I mixed it with a nice, hot cuppa. You have to add plenty of sugar, as well. I only gave her a little. It will wear off soon."

"Cocaine? But, what did they give her before to make her so, so...," again, she gestured helplessly.

"Opium, perhaps. Laudanum. I don't approve, of course. So many lives wasted away..."

"Wait, where are they?" She asked, suddenly realizing both she *and* Neri were away from danger.

"Gone."

"Did they...?"

"No.

"How did we get-?"

"I had you both carried down here by my staff."

"I see..." she said, "Thank you."

"I don't want your thanks. What I would like is never to see your faces again. You're bad for business."

Tamara's mouth fell open, "We're *what?*" She stood up quickly, regretting it immediately. Nausea twisted her stomach into a knot and she collapsed again onto the settee.

"Because of the ruckus you caused, one or two other guests in that hall lost their...ardor...and demanded refunds, or demanded better accommodation at the same price. I refused of course...but...all the same...it was a great inconvenience." He paused before continuing, "I'll have to find a way to recoup my losses for the time that room is closed for cleaning...and repairs."

"You're despicable!" Tamara spat out.

"Try a more effective insult, darling," he snarled, his top lip curling ever so slightly.

Feeling frustrated tears leaking from the corners of her eyes and rollicking pain in her skull, she walked over to Neri and helped her to her feet. This was a mindset and world she would never understand. Such coldness. Such unfeeling. How could someone stand by and profit from someone else's debauchery, or violation? It was unthinkable.

She shot a look at the clerk as she led Neri to the door. He stood watching her impassively. She turned away and heard him expel a breath of impatience.

"Don't be so horrified and judgemental, girl! We don't all find the strength to leave the environment that nurtured us."

She turned to face him.

"You are that fighting friend who came to the rescue," he said, his tone softening, "Not many of us have one. Continue fighting. There is always someone who needs it." He pushed her gently through the office doorway and closed it in her face.

Stumbling slightly in dizziness, Tamara escorted Neri from the brothel, looking her over with concern. Neri's silence was unusual. Her eyes had a glassy, childlike essence as she gazed out at the night. She clutched the blanket around her with haphazard care causing Tamara to re-adjust it several times. Tamara wondered if the opium—if that was what the flyboys gave her—had damaged Neri's mind somehow. The cool night air had a calming effect on Tamara's nerves, but she continued to seethe inside as she struggled to get Neri into a waiting taxi carriage.

Back at their apartment above the bakery, she stared down at Neri as she snored softly on her bed and wondered if her friend would remember any of this in the morning. After comforting herself with the thought of the rage she would unleash on Neri's friends the next day, Tamara collapsed into her own bed beside Neri's and fell into an exhausted sleep.

The next day didn't go as planned. She awoke late in the afternoon with a pounding head to find Neri gone from the apartment. She found a note on the little dining table:

Gone to the club. See you in the morning.

Love, N

Shock, betrayal, anger, and hurt flooded Tamara's body simultaneously. How could she?! After the way she fought off several men to keep them from ravaging her! How she took her home after her so-called friends abandoned her to such a fate! How could she?! Didn't she remember? Nausea rose to her throat. She stumbled to the bathroom and was violently ill.

Tamara's rage boiled to near solar temperatures as she made her way to the club, pushed past the enforcers, and stalked through the crowded, dark room until she found Neri with her friends.

She hadn't planned to scream about the state in which she found Neridette the previous night. She hadn't planned to call her careless, heedless, or crude. She hadn't planned to tell her she owed her life to Tamara. She hadn't planned to rail about the many ways she was thoughtless about the way she left things around their apartment. She hadn't planned to denigrate her friends to anyone who cared to hear. Yet, it's what happened.

Neri responded in kind, throwing out every infraction of Tamara's she could think of. She railed against Tamara's sense of "superiority", her rigid standard of living, her inability to see good in people, and Tamara's "stupid" belief that she was "too good" to respect her family's legacy.

Further shocked and horrified, Tamara stumbled from the club, racked with pain and dizziness. She fought off the foul-smelling embrace of an alley drunk before collapsing in the middle of the stone-paved street. She looked up at the night sky and wondered why they were spinning so quickly.

"You get her feet. I'll get her arms," a familiar voice said above her.

"No...no...," she muttered.

"Be quiet. We're helping you." The voice replied.

"What's wrong with her?" A gruff voice asked, "...she take the stuff?"

"I'm sure she's suffering from a head wound," the familiar voice replied.

Tamara looked up blearily, recognizing the face of the brothel clerk as he and someone else carried her to a waiting carriage.

"Where do you live?" The clerk asked as he settled in beside her.

Tamara told him and heard the directions given to the taxi driver.

"What is your name, girl?"

"Fieldmarsh," she replied, the sounds thick in her mouth, "Tam...ra..."

"You should see a doctor, Fieldmarsh Tamara."

"Just...Tamara..."

"Hm. Go see a doctor, Just Tamara." Then, he turned to gaze out of the carriage window and remained silent.

* * *

Two days later, Tamara felt strong enough to go to her workshop to clean up the mess she made while repairing the airship. Neri was making plans to move to her sister's house out in the country for a while. She refused to talk about what happened.

Tamara swept up the hangar floor singing to herself and felt good for the first time in a while. Neri's angry accusations ran through her mind as she thought about her life, her work, and the money she earned. She did pretty well. She had her own business, wasn't dependent on her parents, and did pretty much whatever she wanted. This was adulthood, and she figured she was doing pretty well in it. Wasn't she?

A shadow moved across the floor and she turned around to see who was there. A group of men in security force uniforms stood at the entrance. Tamara's heart thudded down into her stomach. Fillip must have reported her to the authorities!

"Tamara Fieldmarsh?"

"Yes. What can I do for you?" Tamara stood frozen with her broom in a white-knuckled grip. Her mouth felt dry. If she didn't find a way out of this, she could go to prison for years and years.

A short, rotund man strolled forward, looking around the hangar.

"This is a rather large building. Own it?" He asked, his black, curly beard and mustache hiding his lips. The other men followed his lead and inspected the area with their eyes.

"No. No, I rent it."

"Ah. What do you do here?"

Tamara swallowed, "I repair machines…sometimes, I modify them."

Movement from outside the hangar caught her attention and her eyes shifted to the tall newcomer. He wore a dark, navy turtleneck and the dark blue fatigue pants of the military airship force. He kept his hands in his pockets and strolled in quietly to stand behind the group of officers. The spokesperson seemed not to know his group had grown by one.

Tamara's eyes flicked back to the newcomer and back to the man interrogating her. He kept his eyes on hers, observing her face.

"Modify...what?" He asked, evenly.

"Uh...anything really. Farm machines. Hover bikes. I'm good at what I do."

"How good?"

Tamara shifted her weight to her other leg and swallowed again, her eyes shifting to the men beginning to move away from the group to glance over her tools and work spaces.

"I...I can't really say. People bring me their machines when someone else can't get them to work."

"Ah." He regarded her silently.

Tamara sensed she was losing control. Her breath came quicker as she tried to control herself. Her hands began to sweat. Any minute now, someone was going to go into her office and see her log of work. They would see how many large air machines she had repaired. No one, but a criminal or licensed owner would need an airship repaired, but licensed owners had to use government shops to repair them. She would be outed as a collaborator, because she kept a paper trail of her work...like a dummy.

Hoping to distract them, Tamara began sweeping again, making her way to the hangar door.

"So, what can I do for you today?" She asked, keeping her head down and making a slow and steady beeline for the door.

"Ah, yes. We are here investigating the incident at Miss Maisie's House of Pleasure two nights ago."

Tamara whipped around in surprise (was Maisie's suing her for the damage?). Dizziness slowed her down.

When would this headache leave?

"My department was distressed to hear that several of our pilots were involved in an assault upon a young woman of diminished capacity. We do not condone such behavior, and the pilots will be punished severely. However, since the brothel reported the incident, but is not cooperating with us further, we are here to get your version of the events. Ahem...a team is at your apartment interviewing the young woman in question. I am

Bingley, an officer in charge."

Opening speech complete, the man stood, hands clasped behind his back, awaiting her response.

"Oh." Tamara said, deflated for the moment. She relaxed somewhat.

The tall man who entered last, stood by her large, rolling toolbox, half-inspecting and half-listening. She felt arrested by his physique and magnetism.

She blinked and turned her gaze back to Bingley, "Well, I had to rescue her. I didn't mean to cause so much damage, but she needed help."

Bingley held up a hand to stop her, "We are not concerned with any damage caused to the brothel on your part. If there is such a complaint, that will be a different matter brought up by the business in the appropriate court. We, the emperor's counsel, are here for the criminal matter of sexual impropriety in the emperor's service."

"Oh." Tamara said still profoundly concerned about the men who continued to trawl about her workspace.

"Please," Bingley continued, "give me your account of the matter."

Speaking too fast and too choppy, Tamara described the incident beginning with the messenger boy knocking at her door, to getting Neridette back home. Bingley listened to her, eyes trained on her face, neither nodding nor making listening noises. She felt he knew everything already.

Silently, the rest of the men in the hangar gathered behind Bingley—with the exception of the tall, attractive one who showed up late. They stood looking at her as if they were Eve in the Garden of Good and Evil and had just eaten the fruit of the tree. Each looked very wise, and Tamara felt like she had just been tricked somehow.

"Thank you for your cooperation, Miss Fieldmarsh."

Tamara blinked at the smooth, chocolatey voice of the as yet unknown man who continued to hover about behind the rest of the group. An elegant thumb caressed black and white stubble on his square jaw as he regarded her thoughtfully with deep blue eyes. He looked amused. Annoyance shot through Tamara.

"Yes," agreed Bingley. He looked around once more at the hangar and its contents, his eyes resting on the shabby, wooden door in the corner marked "Private, Do Not Enter" and then her face. Desperate to evade suspicion, she bent quickly to flick away a scrap of paper and to brush away a speck of dust, rising only after she felt she was being ridiculously suspicious. Wincing, she waited for the throbbing of the three-day headache to subside.

"Are you alright, Miss Fieldmarsh?"

Her eyes shot open to see a deep, blue stare regarding her with interest. She tried to find the annoyance she felt only a moment ago, but it wouldn't come.

"Fine." She said, looking away quickly.

He nodded and strolled from the hangar. Bingley and the rest of the boy scout troop followed.

When they had been gone several minutes, she exhaled long and slow through her mouth. Then, she rushed to her little office and burned every bit of book-keeping she could find in the small incinerator in the back of the hangar.

* * *

Tamara stood at the bar of the pub on the west side on the weekend, going through her mail. She tossed aside letters from various suppliers, junk mail, and requests for donations. She stopped and eyed an official letter with the military seal stamped upon it. She wondered if this regarded the pilots involved in Neri's case. She broke the seal and opened it:

"Addressed to Tamara R. R. Fieldmarsh of Merit's Heights, New Victoria

You are hereby compelled by the Imperial Office of Defense Forces to report to service of the Sovereign Emperor of New Victoria. Compulsion toward Service within the Air Fleet requires the expedient conclusion of personal affairs. You have three days to end all civilian obligations and contracts. This compulsion overrides and supersedes any and all private matters forthwith and serves as a federal and legal release to any business and/or matters of private citizens.

Report to..."

She stared sightlessly at the missive as a faint buzz grew in her ears, gradually rising to a dull, toneless crash of sound. Then, her stomach clenched in a spasm so strong she scrambled from behind the bar to the private ministrations rooms at the back. It took over half an hour before she felt well enough to make her way back home on wobbly legs in disbelief.

Tamara Fieldmarsh, full of dread and indignation, traveled in the comfortable surroundings of a red taxi carriage to the nearest military outpost mentioned in her summons. She would get out of this. They made a mistake. She was 25 years-old, too old to be drafted! This was a mistake. It *had* to be a mistake. They would correct the mistake and tell her she could return home.

She was dropped off at the imposing stone gates of the military outpost and was allowed in once she showed the gate guards her summoning letter. They gave her directions to the reporting office, and she rushed there, believing she could somehow make things turn in her favour.

She walked up the high, wide, stone steps and opened the glass door boasting AIR FLEET COMMAND HEADQUARTERS OF NEW VICTORIA'S EMPEROR'S DEFENSE FORCES in sparkling gold letters.

She asked a passing woman where the office shown on her letter was and was directed "down the hall, to the left, keep straight, go up the double staircase, turn right, and second hall on the right".

The walk was long, and frustrating, but finally, she pushed open a wooden door with a peep through smoked glass and waited to be called up next by the secretary who asked her business. Soon, she was ushered into the office.

The woman behind the desk, looked up and regarded her over red half-glasses.

"Ah, Ms. Fieldmarsh. I was expecting you tomorrow, but today is just as well."

"Yes...er...hello, um...there's been some sort of mistake."

"Oh? Yes?" The woman said, not very interested.

"Yes!" Tamara exclaimed, relieved to be able to state her case, "I'm twenty-five years-old, and no one is drafted above the age of twenty-one. Somehow, someone mixed up my age...or...or my name, with someone else and I'm just here to-"

"-to report for duty." finished the woman behind the desk.

"No...n-no...that's what I'm saying, I *can't*. I have a life...there's a mistake... " she finished somewhat lamely.

"Ms. Fieldmarsh, there is *no* mistake. Anyone...absolutely *anyone* in the emperor's territories beneath the age of thirty-five can be drafted into the honorable service. I repeat. There is no mistake."

Tamara sunk into the seat beside her. She wanted to cry. She wanted to run.

"...how?"

"How did this come to be, Ms. Fieldmarsh? I'll tell you. Our investigations into the criminal activities of the rebel forces, smugglers, and other black market dealings showed us a commonality between them. You. You have aided *and* abetted criminals and others who work *against* the sovereign rule of our emperor and if you want to avoid prison, you *will* serve as an engine room technician...*engineer...or report to prison immediately.*"

The woman's gray eyes bored into Tamara's own with cold precision, "I suspect I know which you'll choose. You will be escorted from this base, to your home to collect your belongings and then you will be escorted back here by nightfall. Have a good day."

As if on cue, the secretary in the outer office opened the office door and held out a hand, signaling an end to the meeting. Tamara rose numbly to her feet. A mirror on the wall beside the door reflected the stunned face of Tamara Fieldmarsh, former "Smugglers' Darling", now engineer in the emperor's defense force. Dark circles framed her wide honey eyes, accentuating her short black lashes. She looked away from her reflection quickly.

Morose, she stepped out of the office, passing silently through the halls accompanied by a silent guard dispatched by the gray-eyed woman. She walked through a group of officers without noticing them, her dark thoughts holding her mind captive. One officer regarded her thoughtfully as she passed. Feeling eyes upon her, she turned and caught his eye. She recognized him as the tall, elegant man from the unexpected visit at her hangar. She knew this man was somehow responsible for her new life of forced servitude.

Chapter Two

Tamara Fieldmarsh, Engineer 1st Class stood on the catwalk that crossed between the ladder down to the engine room, across storage and up to the passenger area. A large round window at each end of the chassis afforded natural light and, as a byproduct, beautiful vistas. The blue mountains appearing in the north window look cool and inviting.

Six weeks of military training was behind her now. She almost constantly wavered between anger, resentment, and shame at her current situation. If she had been a doctor, she wouldn't have been in the situation…would she? No. She wouldn't have. Her skill working with engines and airships for criminals provided the military with the perfect setup to get her to work for them. She wondered and wondered what led them to her and what started their investigation. Did they know the whole time? All five years?

She shook the thoughts away from her head and descended the ladder into the engine room. This was a test trip on a new warship. She was in love with it already and felt betrayed by her enthusiasm. She shouldn't be excited.

The corporal below saluted her as she passed him to get to her quarters at the back of the engine room. She splashed her face with water in the small, one and a half meter wide washroom. She looked into the foggy mirror and inspected her face. Her hair was wrangled into a smooth, wavy coif that her regulation cap could sit atop, but tight curls sprang about her ears and neck, softening the effect. Her face was thinner and more angular than usual, and her frame was trim and muscular. She wasn't sure she liked the change. She wasn't sure she liked who was she was in the first place. She sighed and stepped out of her quarters and back into the engine room. She saw the corporal saluting again and was about to tell him to be at his ease, but she stopped in shock when she saw a familiar face.

"Lieutenant Fieldmarsh. A pleasure to meet you again."

Tamara activated every training sense to corral her features and reaction before they rose up onto her face and out of her mouth. She managed to salute his bars with only minimal hesitation. Before her stood the man from the hangar, the one she was sure orchestrated her compulsory service.

He stood looking at her with a bland expression on his elegant and handsome face. His dark blue eyes twinkled as he nodded slightly. She lowered her hand, then she noticed with a start that he was her captain. She tried to read his name bar slyly and saw him smile at her attempt.

"I know we haven't met officially, but I am Major Vale Brolin, pilot on this warship. We'll serve together for the foreseeable future. As you were."

He nodded once more and disappeared up the ladder.

Tamara's head reeled. What vile plot was this?

* * *

The first week after the test flight was a flurry of preparation and readiness. She had no time to contemplate her future and how she felt about serving with Major Brolin. She resented him from the start, and now she was in no position to make it known. She had no interest in a court martial for insubordination. She would just have to try to make it through. Her father tried to fight her draft in court while she was in basic training. Her mother called up every influential person in her contacts, but she met resistance at every turn. At least, this is what they told Tamara. Tamara was suspicious about how hard they say they tried.

Following their initial training, the airship crew made days-long treks out to the mountain ridges on exercises and these were difficult. Tamara noticed how different she felt about people now that she was on a rigid schedule and told what to do when. When she was a civilian, she spoke to whom she pleased, when she pleased, and rejected offers of "companionship". Now, with such venues no longer available to her, she was lonely and wished for someone to spend time with. Yes, there were young men and women her age in the emperor's service, but she was an officer due to a skill and education codicil that placed her in a separate basic training level causing her to complete her training as an officer rather than a soldier. This put many noses out of joint when during her second week of training, she was packed up and moved to the officer's training barracks.

The educated numbskulls resented a "roughneck" joining their ranks without their approval, and the trainees she entered with resented what they saw as preferential treatment where it wasn't deserved. Tamara endured a rough training period. This was made worse when she saw Fillip Weathermarker on the base in the uniform of a trainee. She couldn't say if his shock at seeing her as a trainee was genuine or not. She gave him a wide berth.

Her isolation and loneliness began to take a toll, and she experienced her first emotional blow up in her new career in the emperor's forces, putting her in a precarious position.

* * *

Desperate to get out of the barracks the weekend before her first month-long voyage, she went into the military hangar to inspect "her" engine room on the Victoria. She encountered Fillip there and lost her temper.

"What are you doing here, Fillip?" She exclaimed.

"I'll be piloting a ship like this soon, and I want to know everything about it. Nice to see you, too…" he glanced at her bars and looked back up in surprise, "Engineer 1st Class?"

She narrowed her eyes and crossed her arms, "Yes. Did you have anything to do with this?" She remembered his angry face when she kicked him out of her hangar. Did he report her?

A look of innocence crossed his face, "How could I have anything to do with making you Engineer First Class…especially since you don't deserve it?"

Not sure whether she could believe he was innocent, she changed the subject, "Why are you a trainee? I thought you were a student."

Fillip looked at her sardonically, "I *was* a student, that's why I'm a trainee. I wanted to enter as an officer."

Oh. It made sense.

"Why are you in *my* engine room? Who gave you clearance?"

His eyebrows rose, "*Your* engine room? You're serving on the *Victoria?*"

"Yes. I find it hard to believe you didn't know that."

Fillip threw his hands up, "I don't understand why you're so suspicious of me. What did I do to you?" His eyes registered some memory, "I mean, besides throwing something at your cat. I apologized for that, didn't I? Little guy alright?"

"You don't mean anything you're saying right now. Could you leave? I want to make sure my engine room is set up right for our voyage in three days." She shoved past him, hoping he would lose interest and go bother some other engineer.

"You don't deserve this honor, you know," he said quietly.

Tamara held her breath.

A noise sounded above them, but before she could investigate, Fillip continued, "You shouldn't even be here. You're not a born and bred officer. You're some girl who probably slept her way in here."

The misery, depression, resentment, and anger of the past two-and-a-half months rose in her like the rising waters in a dam and eked over the top of her resolve to get through this without mishap.

"You complete, raging bastard! How *dare* you?! My life was uprooted and ruined by my service here! Of all the utter, complete gall-," her hand searched unconsciously for something large, heavy and loose to grab. Her hand closed over one of the huge wrenches used to open and close fire and water doors.

Fillip's eyes widened at the force of anger flowing from her. He backed away slowly as the noise she heard earlier sounded again and she recognized it as a foot on the ladder rung. She stopped her tirade and reined in her

fury as Fillip's face melted into an expression of relief. She straightened
and schooled her features into a bland mask as well as she could as her
humiliation was made complete by another appearance by Major Vale
Brolin...in casual street wear.

He towered over Fillip Weathermarker in a muscle skimming collarless
broadcloth shirt tucked into trousers held up by bracers. Fillip's face paled,
and he scrambled to salute as did Tamara, her hand holding the wrench
moving behind her back.

"At ease. Good morning, Lieutenant...Corporal." He nodded to both.
"Checking on your engine room, Lieutenant Fieldmarsh?"

Did Tamara imagine it, or did he stress the word "your"?

"Yes, sir," she answered robotically.

Fillip squirmed in his boots and Vale looked over to him, "I wasn't aware
you were serving on my ship, Corporal."

"I...I'm not, sir. I..." Fillip stuttered.

"Don't let me keep you," Brolin said coldly.

Fillip scuttled up the ladder, and they both heard his hurrying footsteps
as they clattered across the catwalk on his way out.

"What do you have behind your back, Lieutenant?"

Her eyes closed in resignation, and she pulled out the large tool.

"This is the second time I've known you to grab a weapon in anger...
although once it was for good reason. Have you always had a temper like
this?" He spoke conversationally and without censure.

"No, sir...I...this is a difficult time for me and...I shouldn't have done it,
sir."

"Come out with me."

Tamara blinked.

"Out of the ship," he finished, as if he read her thoughts.

"Yes, sir."

"At ease, Lieutenant."

"Right, sir."

They climbed the ladder, crossed the catwalk, and exited the airship at the
main entrance by walking down the angled boardwalk. She looked up and

around at her surroundings again, remembering her first impression.

"This way," Brolin said and led her to a copse of trees near a pond, a ways off from the hangar and mooring docks.

Tamara often saw the families of the military personnel here. Some met for lunch here, or some brought their children to feed the ducks or to play on the wide expanse of impossibly green grass. A small refreshment stand stood on the bank of the pond that offered drinks and small-portion fried sweets to buy.

He motioned for her to sit on a curved stoned bench. He strode off in the direction of the refreshment stand. Tamara watched him, her hands clasped awkwardly in her lap. She sat ramrod straight, her chin jutted out at the correct angle, her feet placed carefully together. Nervously, she eyed the young children and adults who chatted, walked, and ran nearby. She fiddled with her nails and swallowed.

Brolin returned with two paper cups and handed one to her before sitting beside her. A scent of spiced soap and herbed oils wafted from him as he sat. Tamara looked at him from the corner of her eyes. She watched him raise the paper cup, dwarfed in his large hands, to his lips. A small smile played over his mouth. Tamara's brow creased. Why was he doing this? Not wanting to seem ungrateful to an immediate superior who may or may not have been responsible for her current situation and who must know of her criminal activities, she took a sip. It was sweet, warm, pleasant. She smiled.

"It's a tea of clove and oranges. It's my favourite and they only serve it here. Do you like it?"

He was leaning forward, his elbows on his knees, watching her reaction.

"It's very good," she said, "it's...it reminds me of my grandmother."

"Oh? How so?"

Tamara's lashes fluttered down. She felt odd mentioning family and memories in such an odd situation and she hesitated a moment more before speaking, "She was a bit like this tea, I think," she said in a low voice, "sweet to me, tart to others, brown and warm." Her back and shoulders relaxed as she remembered Granny Nessa.

She saw him smile from her peripherals. She turned to him suddenly,

"Sir...may I ask the reason...the reason why I'm here? Right now? Am I in trouble? I know I should have conducted myself better in the engine room..." she took a sip to hide her discomfort. "I know you heard me."

He looked into his cup before speaking, "Yes, I heard you, but I also heard the corporal." Brolin placed his cup on the bench beside her and turn to her. "I imagine there were some poor feelings when you were moved during training, but you should never feel that anyone is right about you not belonging here because you're a woman."

"Sir?" Tamara couldn't hold the question in much longer.

"Yes?"

"Did you...am I here because of you?"

Brolin blinked.

Tamara, finally free of the first few words, expanded on her question, "Are you responsible for me being drafted?" She looked him full in face, not sure if she wanted to know for sure.

Brolin didn't say anything for several moments and Tamara continued to watch his face. His clear, dark-lashed eyes flickered left and right over her face, and his mouth tightened at the corners. The vein at his temples pulsed.

One of Tamara's hands reached for his face, completely of its own volition. She was mesmerized by the fine hairs of his eyebrows, the deep shadow cast by his lashes...and that interesting pulse in his temple. His eyes widened as her hand drew closer. Tamara snatched her away, gasping at the temerity of her limbs acting without her permission.

"No, nevermind," she babbled, "I don't know what I was thinking. I'm sorry. Don't answer that...of course you didn't." Blinking rapidly, she raised her cup to her lips, cringing. She bit the rim of the paper cup as she grimaced and blushed.

"I..." Major Vale Brolin began, but Tamara knew she absolutely did not want to hear that he had anything to do with her being here. Not anymore. She didn't understand why she changed her mind.

"Thank you for the tea, Major Brolin." Tamara stood up and saluted. The next few moments were awkward as she stood before him saluting. She couldn't move off until he stood and returned her salute. She saw his face shutter and return to its official expression, although his eyes were warm.

"Lieutenant Fieldmarsh," Brolin said without standing, "we fly off for a month in three days. I brought you here to reassure you that you are the right engineer for this ship and that I requested you specifically…long ago. If anyone, *anyone* says otherwise to you and you feel the need to…ahem… correct them physically, come to me first."

He rose and saluted.

Tamara rushed off to her barracks confused and embarrassed.

* * *

The first time Tamara saw the military airships, her eyes widened in shock. She had never repaired a ship so large! When she saw the engine room, she was doubly shocked. She felt small and inexperienced when she thought of the work she did in her previous life compared to the bright, shiny, highly efficient surroundings now.

The *Victoria* was a brand new ship with cutting edge technology and hardware. Supposedly, only the best were to be on this maiden voyage. Tamara didn't understand why she was chosen to be here…now. The words of Major Brolin ran through her mind often "I requested you specifically… long ago…".

A party was planned the evening before the voyage. Most of the crew were new and inexperienced and looked forward to this new chapter in their lives. Tamara seemed to be the only one unsure of whether to be excited or depressed. The day after the argument with Fillip and the subsequent conversation with Brolin, she woke up late and had to eat breakfast with most of the other men and women with whom she went through training.

During training, in an act of self-preservation, she woke an hour earlier than most and ate breakfast in mostly solitary peace. She wanted to avoid the looks, comments, and "accidental" bumps from the trainees who disliked her. This morning, her stomach complained bitterly when she woke and she couldn't wait any longer to eat. The cafe was crowded, noisy, and rowdy. Her heart sank.

Tamara hesitated at the door, wondering if she could manage not to faint from hunger if she left the base to eat in the city. Then, she felt a warm, light hand at her lower back, nudging her slightly forward. Vale Brolin towered above her, smiling at her encouragingly. He nodded toward the cafe with a friendly smile. She scrambled to salute.

"At ease, Lieutenant. I woke up late and if I can survive in this den of insanity, you can, too." He said warmly before walking into ahead of her.

Tamara took a step in, looking around. Her eyes settled on the unfriendly gaze of Fillip Weathermarker. His eyes shifted between her and Brolin, who was moving toward the line at the tables of food laid out on white regulation tablecloths decorated in the emperor's military emblem. Tamara looked away quickly and followed the major.

"Hi, you're Fieldmarsh, aren't you?"

A friendly voice behind her caught her attention. She turned around, squinting at the sunlight shining through the windows at the front of the cafe and the door she had entered. A tall woman with smooth skin the hue of butter and cream stood smiling at her.

Her black hair was chopped into bangs at the front and they fringed dark almond eyes that peered out with openness and candor. Her hair was tied back into a bun above the grey collar of her fleet uniform.

Tamara returned the smile with some restraint, and answered, "Yes. I don't think we've met."

"We haven't," replied the young woman, "but I've heard *plenty* about you. I've wanted to meet you since I heard you were going to be an engineer on your own ship! *No one* gets their own ship first time out. And you're on the newest ship with the new technology! I'm so jealous!"

The ice around her heart thawed slightly. Months of resentment toward the new authority in her life, paranoia about forming enemies in her ranks, and isolation without friends began to release at the first openly friendly face she encountered since her compulsion into service.

"I'm Thorncrist. Engineer 2nd class. I'm assigned to the *Merthoy.*"

Tamara smiled and nodded, "Nice to meet you, Thorncrist."

They both turned to pick up a tray and cutlery and proceeded to choose food for breakfast. She caught Brolin's eye as she looked for him in the cafe. As a result, she bumped into a trainee as he was going the other way. Her tray shifted and the delicious-looking frosted pastry she was eager to try flip-flopped to the floor. She frowned in consternation and frustration.

"You have everything else going for you, can't stop before you ruin everyone else's day?" Said the recruit.

Tamara's temper flared, but she remembered her last flare up and didn't want Brolin to witness another .

"I'm sorry," she muttered, "I didn't see you. I'll help you clean up."

She looked down to see what the trainee dropped and looked back up at his tray in confusion. The only one who seemed to have lost an item during the collision was her. She glanced up at the young man, but he was already walking away from her muttering to his friends.

"Here, have mine," a familiar, smooth voice said in her ear.

Brolin placed his frosted pastry on her plate then turned to join a striking woman with a grey streak at her temple. She raised both eyebrows at Tamara and murmured to Brolin as they walked away. Tamara recognized her as the physical arts instructor, and her heart constricted strangely when she saw the woman place a hand on his back possessively.

Tamara glanced quickly at Thorncrist. The young woman eyed Tamara's new pastry and looked at her thoughtfully for a moment before smiling.

"Do you want to sit with me at one of those tables at the back?" Thorncrist asked.

Tamara, longing for a friendship to resemble the one with Neridette, but desperate to protect herself, said, "Um, I woke up too late to spend time eating. If you eat here at lunch, I would like to do that…perhaps?"

Thorncrist looked slightly disappointed, but smiled a bright smile and nodded, "Of course! I'll see you then."

* * *

Later, Tamara stood in front of her cot, looking down at the sleek, red dress. She wasn't sure how she felt about wearing it in front of people. It was a dress her mother had picked out for her when she wrote asking her to send her something to wear to the dance. Her mother was usually anxious for her to show off her "assets" and Tamara, although desirous of admiration, felt awkward in clothes that were meant to entice—no matter how classy. She sighed. That night, all recruits, trainees, and newly appointed crew members were to attend a mandatory dance that served as a send-off for maiden voyages. She inspected plunging back of the red dress, its barely-there shoulders, and the high slit up the front. She was sure this dress was worthy of a court martial.

Both Thorncrist and Tamara decided to at least walk to the dance hall together. Tamara felt it would help keep her "enemies" at bay, and she felt Thorncrist believed it would somehow increase her cachet to be seen in her presence.

"Why are you wearing that?" Thorncrist asked when they met at Lantern Boulevard.

Tamara looked down at her regulation jacket. Feeling self-conscious, she had thrown it over her shoulders before rushing out of her barracks room.

"It looks awful over your dress! That lovely red color! So bold!" Thorncrist exclaimed.

"Well, I didn't think it was really....appropriate to-" Tamara began.

"Nonesense! It's a dance! A celebration!"

Thorncrist skipped over to Tamara and swept it from her shoulders. The warm, night air, tickled Tamara's bare shoulders and flowed over the bare skin of her neck and back. She resisted the urge to shrink and pull her arms up over herself. She straightened her back, and looked around. Several groups of female recruits in flouncy dresses giggled and rushed down the lane to the dance hall. Male recruits hooted and catcalled dreadfully. Two girls dressed in tuxedos took a more sedate walk to the dance hall together.

"Wow!" Said Thorncrist, "you're going to have all eyes on you tonight! Maybe the handsome major will ask you to dance." She folded Tamara's regulation jacket and walked down the lane at a fast clip.

"Handsome major?" Echoed Tamara as she hurried to catch up, her suede dance shoes clipping on the smooth, crumbled stone lane.

"Yes, the one who is piloting your ship. He's seems pretty taken with you."

Tamara looked up at the tall woman in disbelief as they walked quickly, "Me? He isn't. He's in love with the physical arts instructor. Isn't he?"

"In love? Oh, I wouldn't say that. Since his divorce, he's been…here and there."

Tamara's heart winced a little.

The long walking lane lined on both sides with sphere-topped lamp poles. It was built in honor of the emperor ushering a new time of enlightenment and many couples found it the perfect romantic spot to stroll on a nice, breezy weekend evening. The light of the large spheres atop the lampposts cast a bright, warm glow down upon the freshly cut lawns, pruned trees, and ornamental bushes placed in leisurely arrangement along the lane. The perfume of the tea bushes caught Tamara's nose and her heart lifted in anticipation of the night.

"How do you know so much about him?" Tamara asked.

"Word gets around. I've seen him in the company of other women before. He's not that serious about them. Not since his wife."

Tamara pondered that for a moment. She noticed the crowd was getting thicker as they neared the dance hall entrance. Their fast clip slowed to a stroll as more recruits gathered and assembled into a makeshift receiving line at the stone steps set into the manicured hill rising up on one side of the lane. Voices chattered excitedly. Young men and women set up dances, demurred, or promised only to dance with one another.

Tamara had been to many dances when she was a girl. Most of the time, no matter how many promises were made between friends to stay together, pairs were made between dancers and couples inevitably ended up outside the dance hall rather than inside.

A tall, gangly youth crept up to Tamara and Thorncrist, giving Tamara a nervous glance.

"Hey Thorncrist," he said by way of greeting.

"Hey Maycotte," Thorncrist replied.

"Fieldmarsh," he said, nodding in Tamara's direction.

Unsure if he was friendly or not, she simply nodded at him and looked away as the two chatted with each other. She noticed several glances in her direction and knew her mother's dress selection was the reason for the interest. Several young women glanced at her dress, had a change of expression and dragged their companions away in possessiveness, or glanced down at their own attire with new eyes regretting their dress choice for its seeming dowdiness.

Several of the high ranking members of the emperor's defense force, and some who took part in their training instruction stood on the stone steps and before the dance hall doors chatting with each other, waiting for the doors to open. Sashes, medals, pins, and cuffs all signaled their ranks upon their shoulders. The pomp and circumstance of a mandatory dance fascinated her. She moved through the crowd, interested in getting a better look at her superiors in their evening's feathers, forgetting momentarily that she was dressed in becoming feathers herself.

She looked up from her place at the foot of the stairs and walked a little further past them, enjoying the rise and fall of the clipped tones of the instructors, generals, and other high ranking individuals. She placed a hand on the lamp post that stood before the left side of the stairs, a smile moving over her lips. At that moment, she felt someone watching her and instinctively searched for whoever it was in the crowd. Her eyes landed on the dark blue gaze of Major Vale Brolin. He stood facing her in a group of three, one with their back to her, and the other standing beside him. Although she couldn't see her face, she was sure it was the woman she saw with him at breakfast.

He wore the deep blue of the fleet regalia, the high collar of this regulation tunic and sash accenting the sharp angles of his face and haircut well. Remembering what Thorncrist said about him moving from woman to woman, a need to challenge and not be taken for granted rose in Tamara. She raised her chin and met his eyes in an unspoken challenge. His eyes twinkled and he dipped his head in acknowledgement. Whether he read the challenge, or was simply greeting her in silence, she wasn't sure. He returned his attention to his companions, and Tamara shrugged away the feeling that she was promptly forgotten. Feeling listless, she turned away, looking for something...anything to capture her attention.

The great double doors of the dance halls scraped open slowly and an answering thrill moved through the recruits. As she turned to rejoin Thorncrist, a hand at her elbow stopped her. For a short second, she hoped it was Brolin. Hope turned into disappointment when she found Fillip Weathermarker looking down at her with an expression of insolence and... something that bordered on admiration. She found no comfort in that expression.

"Fieldmarsh, you look well tonight," he said, in a stilted voice that reflected the formalness of the evening. His eyes traveled down from her neck, over her shoulders, caressed her breasts beneath the vibrant red fabric, and skimmed the skin that peeked through the slit of the silken fabric.

With great restraint, Tamara gently removed her elbow from his grasp, "I am well. Thank you." She took a step back.

"Care to dance with me tonight?" Fillip asked, his neck stiff within his dress tunic's collar giving him the form of a bird on a branch. He moved closer to her, his eyes taking on a possessive hue as he observed the tiny gold chain she had woven through her coily hair.

"Nice effect that," he continued, "makes you look like one of the emperor's harem lilies."

Tamara's eyes narrowed, and she turned around looking for Thorncrist. She saw her climbing the stone steps with Maycotte, and she moved off to join them. She moved quickly, reaching the top of the steps in a bit of a rush. She disliked Fillip enormously now. He had graduated past being a simple nuisance.

The high ranks lined the way into the entrance and smiled indulgently at the young people filing past. The great doors opened to a bright red carpet within, gold light fixtures, mirrors, dangling tassels, perfumed bowls of flowers, and bright, quick music. The crowd was noisy and inched forward to present their cards to the major domo at the entrance. Tamara saw Thorncrist's back, and fought back irritation that she didn't seem to be looking for her. She saw Maycotte's hand surreptitiously caressing Thorncrist's bottom as they moved along. Tamara knew that meant that at the first opportunity, they would be out amongst the trees around the dance hall. She slowed down and allowed the crowd to move her forward. There was no real reason to catch up to her now.

A hand grabbed her elbow and she heard Fillip's irritating voice, raised in an odd note, "I didn't get your answer! Are you going to dance with me tonight?"

Tamara jerked her elbow away from him and glared at up him from beneath her lashes, "Fillip, you hate me, remember? There's no reason for you to dance with me!" She turned away, hoping the crowd would separate them.

"No, no, you've got it all wrong!" He replied, pushing forward to stay beside her. "I've never hated you, in fact, I'd *love* to get to know you more. If I knew that body hid beneath those boys's clothes of yours I'dve-"

"You would have *what*, Corporal?"

They both twisted around to see Major Brolin smiling blandly down at Fillip. They stopped moving and the crowd surged around them and into the hall doors. Fillip, mouth agape, stared up at Brolin in consternation for the second time in three days. Tamara didn't know what to think. She had begun to feel that Fillip was becoming more erratic in his treatment of her and that tonight she was beginning to see illness in his mind. She also wondered how Brolin came to materialize so suddenly.

"I just meant...I didn't know she was this gorgeous, that's all. I mean, I've always liked her. I just...didn't know...."

"A woman who is, as you say, "gorgeous", is gorgeous no matter what she is wearing. Her beauty enhances what she wears, and not vice versa. Please enjoy the dance, Corporal." The major placed Tamara's right hand on his left arm and led her into the hall.

"Hand me your card, Lieutenant Fieldmarsh," he said, looking down at her.

They stood behind several people waiting their turn to enter. She pulled her card from the small pouch sewn into her Lieutenant's sash and handed it to him nervously.

"I...I don't think-" she stuttered.

Brolin grasped the card and placed it beneath his in his free hand, "You don't think what?"

"I don't think I'm supposed to enter with you," she said in a sharp whisper.

She felt ridiculously intimate with him here, standing in the fading light of the evening, the glow of the lanterns highlighting her brown skin with golden tones and illuminating the major's expressions. She felt warm and heady as if she had just drunk champagne.

"I wouldn't think too much of it, Lieutenant. You are my engineer. There is no harm in escorting you in to relieve you of unwanted company." He said, nodding backward to where they left Fillip. He turned to the major domo and handed him their cards.

"Major Vale Brolin and Lieutenant Fieldmarsh 1st Class!" The major domo boomed in his deep baritone.

Eyes turned to look at them and Tamara tried to turn away from them, but Brolin, instead of allowing her to do so, led her through the large crowd, past the refreshment tables and to the dance floor.

"I can't leave you now, not since you've been declared my 'plus one'," he muttered to her, "do you dance?"

"There is no reason to dance with me! I'm not a debutante who will face disgrace if you don't dance with me!" Tamara said, laughing derisively in her self-conscious embarrassment.

"You have no sympathy for what those in my ranks will think of me leaving my new engineer to fend for herself after than announcement?" He asked, a smile playing about his lips. "We have policies of conduct and deportment, you know," he continued.

Music played as they stood in the middle of the dance floor debating.

"Sir, I-"

"At ease, Lieutenant."

Tamara took quick glances around at her fellow recruits. Many were eyeing them with less than friendly expressions. Some were curious. Some were irritated. Some were scandalized. Feeling she was being ungrateful, somehow, she nodded and put her arms up and out in the necessary steps for the waltz.

Major Brolin took her upraised hand in his and stepped in to grasp her waist and a hot, fiery bolt of arousal rippled through her stomach and chest, threatening to cut off her breath. The exposed skin of her back yearned to feel the scorching hot hand of the major caress every inch of her. Her vision grew hazy, and she blinked rapidly to clear her vision. Heat rose to her cheeks as she felt the cool metal of the major's medals, sash, through the thin material of her dress as each pressed against her breasts. Her mother assured her the dress was not made to be worn with foundation garments, but the cut would make it unnecessary anyway since the swoop and gathering of fabric were meant to enhance the curves, rather than restrict them. Her mother seemed to be correct, but oh, she couldn't have known that *this* would happen.

"Are you alright?" Asked the major as he moved through the steps to peer down at her. Tamara looked up, unable to see him clearly through the haze of unabashed wantonness.

"Yes," she answered, surprised to hear her voice sound normal to her ears.

"Tell me Fieldmarsh, what gave you such a fiery temper? I saw the beginnings of it again tonight."

"You did? When?"

"Both times when Weathermarker was speaking to you. At first, I was mostly concerned for your well-being, but now, I'm firmly of the mind that he would come to more harm if he continues to rile you."

"He shouldn't really. I don't know why he gets under my skin so much."

The song ended and Brolin released her. Tamara smoothed her hair in a desperate attempt to distract her rioting emotions and disturbed body. She seemed to feel the fabric of her dress moving every inch across her curves. Brolin placed his hand on his arm once more and led her through the crowd and past the hard calculating eyes of her graduating class. She stared straight ahead and attempted nonchalance.

"In a way, you remind me of my brothers ," he said, leading her to a sitting area near the row of windows facing the lane of lights.

Tamara winced. She heard him chuckle in response.

"No....you look *nothing* like my brothers. I mean to say that your temper flares like my brothers'"

"Well....I...I used to follow my older brother and his friends everywhere . Perhaps that's where I picked up the fighting habit. I always wanted to be a boy," Tamara answered, looking out at the dark night illuminated by the glow of lights. When he didn't respond, she turned around to look up at him. As she gazed at him, butterflies zipped in her abdomen and her back tingled.

He stood very still and correct and no longer held her hand on his arm.

"Lieutenant, my dance with you tonight would not have been as beautiful and tantalizing if you had been. I, for one, am glad you are not a boy."

He nodded to her and turned to rejoin those in the dance hall and Tamara sat to melt into herself for a little while. What was happening to her? There were plenty of men interested in her who worked in the underworld. They had offered her mansions, closets full of expensive clothes, dinners at expensive fine restaurants, boats, and even a jewelry shop. There was so much about that life that said it would end in dissatisfaction, affairs, and even ruin when the law put an end to their endeavors, either by prison or death by firing squad.

She remembered the week of madness wherein she allowed herself to be wooed by a coed from her college days. He was good-looking and bought her plenty of things to convince her to be at his side. He promised her a large wedding in their second day together. He told her that his parents would love her, because they had always wanted a doctor in the family. At first, Tamara went along with it, believing him to be sincere and honorable. She sadly broke off the engagement when evidence of his dishonesty during exams came to light and he threatened to have his father buy the college and fire everyone one of the instructors. She returned everything he gave her.

Chapter Three

I t was customary for the crew of an airship to sleep aboard prior to its take-off on an extended voyage. The *Victoria's* crew boarded her the evening before take-off in a flurry of excitement and movement. Tamara walked up the gangplank with the other officers.

She avoided looking around as she boarded, imagining as she did that other crew members were staring at her in disapproval. She felt a gaze upon her back and smiled as she remembered Brolin's eyes on her before the dance. Trying to affect a natural manner as she walked, she turned her head to peer over her shoulder to see if she could spy him in the crowd. Who she saw was Fillip Weathermarker, Corporal, waiting to board the *Victoria*, his duffel bag in his hand. His eyes bored into hers, and she felt momentary alarm at the intensity in his eyes. She looked away and as soon as she entered the metal sliding doors. She thought hard as she took her bag through the small lobby that housed the navigation station, pilot's seat, and the doors to the passenger and crew quarters. How did Fillip get assigned to her ship? How could Major Brolin allow it knowing what he did of Fillip's harassment of her? There was nothing she could do about it, but thankfully she would see precious little of him since her duties and his—whatever there were—would keep them at different parts of the airship most of the time aboard.

The pilot was usually last to board during the eve's night, so Tamara hadn't the pleasure of seeing Brolin. She shivered from the delicious memory of the night before.

"No," she told herself, "he is the pilot, my captain, and I am only Lieutenant

THE ENGINE TAMER: AN ADVENTURE NOVEL

1st class."

Her shoes clacked along the long catwalk that crossed between the towering gas cells in the keel on the way to "her" engine room. She lowered herself to the engine room floor by the red steel ladder and walked through the engine room's various piping sections, cooling towers, and propulsion gear to get to the engineer's resting room to the aft of the airship.

She opened the narrow locker door and deposited her duffel bag on the floor of it to return to it after supper in the mess. Then, she went out to take a quick look around as she waited for her second-in-command to report. It was hot and stuffy and would be worse when the machines were running. She crossed to crank open the sealed porthole windows to allow the evening breeze to clear out the stuffiness.

She turned to gaze around her area. The various parts of the machinery were as tall as she, the steel painted a bright, vibrant red. If ever she felt like hiding out, this was the place; the room was a literal maze made up of aisles and alleys to allow the airship's crew to work on different parts of the engine if necessary. And somewhere above her was Major Vale Brolin. She felt an answering throb in her abdomen at the memory of his hand on her bare back and his chest pressed against her almost bare breasts last night. She took a centering breath and blew it out of her mouth in a long, slow and steady stream and straightened her shoulders. It didn't pay to think this way. Not when he was as good as a philanderer.

She looked at the watch fob pinned to her tunic and went to stand by the steel ladder to salute her undercrewman when he or she arrived. As she waited, she thought again about the changes to her life in the last three months. It seemed so far away and so full of danger and the threat of death. She thought about the last run-in with the thugs who threatened to take the airship without paying. She shook her head at what she thought was a daring, secure, exciting life. All her own and no one could tell her what to do with it. How very wrong she was. As she listened to the steady plod of regulation boots on the metal catwalk above the opening to the engine room, she wondered if she had been granted a new chance at life with this forced servitude to the emperor. Was she really just postponing a violent

58

death at the hand of criminals when she was a civilian?

Her under-crewman descended the ladder and once on level flooring, saluted her. Tamara was surprised to see a pleasant-looking blonde-haired corporal looking at her with guarded blue eyes and hair tied back in a loose bun at the back of her neck. A woman. She realized her fear was that Fillip Weathermarker had been assigned to her.

Quickly reading the corporal's name tag, Tamara gave her opening speech, "Corporal Vessmin, welcome to the engine room of the *Victoria*. I am Lieutenant Fieldmarsh, your reporting officer. Please, find your quarters aft the engine room and deposit your belongings. I am going to report to the mess hall. While I'm gone, acquaint yourself with the checks, lists, and precautionary measures." She returned the corporal's salute and turned to climb the ladder to report to mess for supper.

* * *

The mess hall was small and not quite a "hall". The ship would operate on a "skeleton", bare bones team during meals, but even then, the hall was too small to accommodate more than ten to fifteen people at a time in a crew of sixty.

The atmosphere was less formal than on land. Saluting was customary only upon entering the ship and the first time meeting the captain. So, the meals were taken with no regard to rank. The captain or pilot ate meals with his crew no matter their rank. Therefore, Tamara found herself eating across from Brolin as he sat beside the third mate, the most striking woman Tamara had ever seen. Her name bar read "Kerridan" and her rank was of a senior officer. Tamara feeling Kerridan's eyes on her several times, kept her eyes on the metal tray in front of her. Those seated had fifteen minutes to enjoy their meal and she hoped to get through it with little incident. Brolin had noticed her when she walked in, but had confined himself to a pleasant "Fieldmarsh", and nod as he passed by.

As she ate, she listened to the conversation of Brolin, his first, second mates, navigator, and his crew. Kerridan spoke to Brolin in a slightly thin, high-pitched voice, leaning slightly toward him in a possessive manner. Tamara resisted the urge to stand and excuse herself before her meal was finished.

"Fieldmarsh." Kerridan addressed her suddenly.

Tamara looked up into cold, unfriendly eyes.

"Yes?" She answered, sure she had a new enemy, but not sure why yet.

"I have to admit how impressed I am that you moved up the ranks so quickly. To what do you owe your success?" Kerridan's fork-holding hand stayed poised above the tin tray as she waited for an answer.

Tamara sighed inwardly. Would she ever be free of the barbs, dislike, and outright insults?

"I wish I knew. It's not an honor I expected," she answered.

Kerridan smirked, "Nor should you have...I suppose. How old are you?"

Tamara sensed Brolin's change of posture and the change in the conversations around the table. Kerridan had an audience and knew it. What Tamara didn't understand was why Kerridan didn't like her.

"I'm twenty-five," she answered succinctly. The room was warm, but the atmosphere was chilly.

"Twenty-five and mistress of her own domain on one of the emperor's newest ships with the latest technology. One would think you would have to...buy your way...here. Wouldn't you think?" Kerridan echoed Fillip Weathermarker's insult of a few days ago. Tamara's eyes flickered accidently to Brolin's face and then back to Kerridan's. The latter's eyes narrowed, and she placed her fork carefully on her tray.

"You're very young for such a placement. Do you think you can manage such a position?" The question was clearly rhetorical, Kerridan having an answer made up in her mind already. "I think there are a few places in life where youth isn't much of an advantage, don't you think, Major?" She turned to Brolin and caressed him with her eyes. Tamara looked away, trying to look busy and unbothered by the blatant sexual intimacy between Brolin and Kerridan. How could Brolin be so...so wanton?

"I think youth isn't such an advantage in the arena of *relationships*. A mature man wants a woman of mature intelligence. Don't you think so Mr.

Gray? Mr. Blackmor?" She addressed the squirming first and second mates before returning her attack to Tamara. "The major here has just celebrated his forty-fourth birthday Sunday and I can only believe that as he grows in maturity and experience, he would want someone to match him in both. But that's neither here nor there. I just mean to say that I truly hope you settle into your role here well. Don't we?"

And so, having established the hierarchy in love and war, she smiled a glass smile and resumed her meal. Tamara, remembering how Brolin came to her aid while Fillip accosted her, could not believe he would leave her at the mercy of this cow trying to scrabble over territory.

"Oh, I wouldn't know about that," Tamara said, not looking up, "I think what a mature man really wants in a relationship is not so much "old woman" as a woman who understands him. A young woman can do that well. We're much more vigorous in the amorous arts as well, if you can remember that far back. But I wouldn't imagine the major is able to handle much youth anymore. We had a rather intimate dance at the celebration and (here, she forced a feigned laugh) there were no kisses exchanged...as is the custom. I don't think he has it in him anymore." She dabbed her mouth with her napkin, gathered her tray and fork, dumped them in the cleaning receptacle. She exited the mess hall. The crew members began to chatter loudly and over-jovially between themselves.

When she returned below to the engine room, Tamara released the corporal to eat her supper a short time later. Since there was nothing to do until the morning, she sat in her resting room and boiled over with anger.

The next morning, Tamara woke up in the worst pain imaginable. The bunk was not comfortable. She would have to get used to it quickly or she would be the worst engineer possible because of sleep deprivation. The porthole in her bunk showed her a sky that was still mostly black.

She sat up, rolled her shoulders, stood and touched her toes. Attempting side bends as deep as she could in the cramped space proved difficult. So, giving up, she stepped into the even smaller bathing cylinder and used the paltry stream of water to clean herself quickly, using the rose soap she received in a care package from Neridette. She then used the bottle of jasmine oil to finger comb through her curls. Tears rose to the surface as the sweet scent filled the tiny space and reminded her of her little bohemian apartment above the bakery, Granny Nessa's gifts of colognes, chocolates, and books.

Finally, she rinsed her face and turned off the trickle of water before drying off with the rough regulation towels. Wrapping the towel around her hair, she patted, rubbed and swirled to dry her hair and then twisted it into a corona around her head. Feeling better and ready for the busy day, she dressed in the more relaxed and informal uniform of short-sleeved broadcloth blouse, soft trousers and half-boots. Then she grabbed her small transistor radio and went up to the mess hall to make coffee for herself.

Everything was dim and quiet. Suddenly, she began to feel she was breaking regulation by being up so early. Not wanting to squeak in fear now, she forged ahead and snuck into the mess kitchen to find a bag of coffee, water, and a pot to brew it in. Thankfully, everything was labeled by meal time and type and she set to work, trying to make as little mess as possible.

"You know Cook is going to be cross with you, don't you?"

Tamara started violently as Brolin's voice spoke her in the dim, quietness of the early morning. How her heart pounded! She dropped the metal mug onto the metal counter and placed a hand over heart. Brolin's hands were warm on her shoulder and arm as he steadied her and spun her around to face him. He stooped a little to get a good look at her.

"Are you alright? I didn't mean to startle you."

Tamara swallowed hard and nodded as she closed her eyes, waiting for her heart beat to slow. Brolin chuckled and released her.

"Let me do that for you...it's actually what I came to the mess for myself, but Cook knows to set some coffee making things for me....only, my way is quicker. He left bunsen burner on under a pressure pot to keep the water hot for me. See? Here." As he spoke, Tamara observed him and wondered why he was pretending her insult from last night never happened. Perhaps Kerridan was right. Maybe his age and maturity didn't care about cheap shots.

"Now," he said, continuing despite her silence, "I'll pour it into this mesh container of coffee and it'll be read in a tick."

She smiled slightly, shaken in her fright a moment ago and by being in this proximity to Brolin after so much upheaval in her mind for the past two days. She watched him retrieve two metal mugs and pour steaming, delicious coffee into both before placing two apples and a wrapped container of sweet crackers into her hand.

"Come with me," he whispered.

Confused and intrigued, Tamara carried her items and followed him out of the mess hall and to the entryway to the keel. They walked aft all the way to the end of the gang plank and they stopped at the end.

"Now, you see the large porthole here, but do you see the little hidey-hole there? It's my favourite spot on this ship."

"How do we get down there? With all this?" She asked.

"You go first and I'll hold the coffee and then hand them to you."

She climbed over the railing and dropped down onto the smaller walkway below the main catwalk. She placed the apples and crackers on the porthole ledge and reached up for both cups of coffee as he handed them down to her. Then she watched him climb down the same way.

Tamara leaned against the round window and stared out. Brolin watched her as she did. She pulled the transistor radio from her pocket and switched it on to tune it to the new channel that broadcast orchestra music for twenty-four hours a day. It was an experiment and she loved it. She hoped they would do it forever.

A waltz began to play and the tinny sound whirled around her soul and spirit, soothing her pain, her heartache, and emotions. It didn't matter that Major Brolin confused her and made her want to simultaneously rebuff him, challenge him, and pull his face down to hers in a kiss so passionate it seared their lips forever.

She held her mug in both hands and lead outward with the concave window and rested her forehead on the glass as the music washed over her.

"Did you miss my kiss at the dance afterall?" Brolin murmured, his eyes burning into her. She had wondered if he would bring up her remarks from last night, but she didn't expect him to turn the tables on her with such a question.

She closed her eyes and lied, "No."

"You believe I'm too old to kiss a breath-taking young woman like you, then?" He murmured.

Her head lay against the glass, cool, firm. "No," she whispered.

He moved closer and leaned into the window, searching her face. A sweet lilting tune with a violin melody wafted from the radio and made Tamara's heart ache with melancholy.

"Tell me," he continued in a low, intimate voice, "what *would* make you fall for an older, mature, experienced man?"

She smiled and opened her eyes. "Probably the size of his…library?" She said and glanced at him from beneath her lashes.

His answering chuckle warmed an area somewhere in the region of her heart.

Brolin placed his mug on the catwalk above and took her hand, removing her own mug, his eyes on her face. She watched him tremulously, not sure what to think, do, or say. He placed her mug beside his and pulled her close to him and his gaze traveled over her sweetly scented hair. Her rose scented brown skin. He leaned down, closed his eyes and inhaled deeply, and cupping her chin in his hand.

Her mind reacted dully, and she ignored the warning she gave herself before about resisting becoming just another one of his women.

"Now tell me," he began, his voice husky, "have you ever been kissed by a mature man of forty-four? Mindlessly? Possessing?" His voice dropped a full octave, "to abandon?"

Tamara's knees turned to water, and she grabbed ahold of his arms as they held her to him (when did they get there?) and her lips, her traitorous, traitorous lips, parted on their own, became sensitive to even the air passing across them. Oh, how she must control herself!

She shook her head.

"Let me show you how *I* kiss, little girl," Major Vale Brolin muttered deep in his throat and his chiseled face, dusky fringed eyes, aquiline nose, and perfect hair lowered to her own and his lips, firm, guiding, melding and possessive took over her own will to live. Tamara Fieldmarsh, Emperor's Engineer, Smuggler's Darling, and despiser of love was well, truly, and thoroughly *kissed.*

Tamara, in the midst of a conflux of heated emotions, felt the deluge of a cold reality that whispered what Thorncrist told her. She turned her lips away from Brolin's, and she felt his surprise. His face registered an expression she assumed was shock, and she wondered if he'd ever been rebuffed before. She was sure she was being toyed with, but didn't want to look him in the face until she could get some physical and hormonal distance away from him.

"Thanks for the coffee, Major. I'm going to get back to the engine room." The thoughts racing through her mind made a zigzagging noise across her psyche as she clambered to the catwalk above and hauled herself and her mug up to stroll nonchalantly to the engine room. She felt his eyes upon her as she reached the ladder leading down to her section of the airship, and she resisted the very pressing urge to look toward him.

Tamara busied herself running through the take-off checklist until the corporal rose and saluted her on her way to breakfast in the mess hall. There were still a few hours left until they lifted off and she didn't know how to occupy her time until she remembered her journal in her bag.

She sat in her resting room sketching the scene she saw with Brolin at the porthole when she heard a tap-knock on the metal door framing. She looked up.

"Yes, Corporal?"

"I have a message for you, ma'am."

Tamara took the message held out to her and nodded her dismissal before opening it. She read a scrawled summons to report to the Defense Force's Headquarters immediately. Her brow crinkled in stupefaction. Why would she receive a summons to leave the airship so close to lift-off? Bizarre.

As she sat in the Defense Minister's office an hour later, her face blistering in anger and shame, she realized she had certainly made an enemy.

"Therefore, Lieutenant Fieldmarsh, you are to receive a record of this reprimand and it will stay on your record for the next five years. Another infraction of this magnitude will reduce your contracted time and place you in a probationary period by which you will be remanded to the Emperor for a review of your conduct (and believe me, you will *not* benefit in this time outside of service). Have you *anything* to say to this accusation?"

Tamara fumed and spluttered, "Is-is Major Brolin to be reprimanded, too?!"

The woman's face turned red and the corners of her mouth turned down and her jaw jutted forward, "You will not ask the business of your superiors!"

"Meaning 'no'!" Tamara almost shouted. Her anger was held in check by the tiniest thread of self-awareness and self-control.

"Furthermore, your movements and activities will be monitored and recorded on your journey. Should you act in defiance-should you even *think* about defying my orders to cease all inappropriate fraternization, you will be immediately removed from service and returned here for further actions." She blinked coldly at Tamara from behind her spectacles. "Am I *crystal clear?*"

Tamara's jaw clenched. Her nostrils flared. Her lips tightened. She was outmaneuvered here. She answered simply, "Yes, Madame Marshal."

"Then remove yourself."

Tamara rose stiffly to her feet, saluted, and spun away out of the office door.

Who saw and who told?

* * *

Tamara made it back to the airship a couple of hours before lift-off. She was bruised emotionally, raw, angry, ashamed, and vengeful. She couldn't pinpoint who might have reported her to headquarters. She had made several recruits angry at her quick rise through the ranks. But, she was baffled at how anyone saw them this morning. She was positive she and the major were the only ones up and around at that time of the morning, but she was so distracted at one point that she could have missed the signs of someone approaching them.

She stopped her fast walk on the lane as the next thought hit her like an ocean wave against a buoy: did Brolin report her in retaliation for leaving his embrace? Would he be so petty and callous? The thought made her feel cold. He was handsome, magnetic, enigmatic. She remembered their dance and how it made her feel to be in his arms. Her old boyfriends of teenage-dom were young and artless, none having the sophisticated draw of an older man who has grown into his mind and body. Could he? Would he?

A chill breeze brushed over her arms beneath the short sleeves of her casual regulation uniform and she shivered. Hugging her arms to her chest, she looked up at the sky. Grey clouds sat over the mountains in the far distance, but the sky above her was blue and cloudless. Head down, shoulders hunched, Tamara crossed the catwalk to re-enter the *Victoria*. She rushed to the engine room and found a hassled-looking corporal who glanced at her sourly before schooling her features into a more respectable expression as she flipped levers, spun dials, and punched buttons. Tamara wanted to explode and tell the corporal what had happened, to cry, to find some sort of sisterhood. She resisted, opting instead for a good, long, vengeful thought of how she would get even in time. She merely nodded at the corporal and instructed her to man the communications.

When time approached the top of the hour for lift-off, Tamara stood by the messaging machine as the corporal read off the commands from the command center as they came in on the tape. Once they received the command to 'start engines', Tamara shot into action.

Tamara dived into starting the engines of the *Victoria* and soon lost herself in the rhythm and dependability of the machines. Yes, sometimes her engines spluttered, or stopped working, but there was always a logical fix. Never did engines disappoint her. She could always get an engine to run, no matter how old, or broken. She was the Engine Tamer. Her beleaguered expression melted as she set into running the machines. The deafening noise soothed her soul and muted her thoughts.

She and the corporal zigzagged through the corridors of the engine room, checking this, checking that. The engine roared evenly with no spluttering or catching. Tamara's heart soared. *This* was all she needed. She didn't need love. Love was horrible. Love was was hurtful and left all too soon. No. Her engines were all she needed.

The communications portal began a ticker tape countdown starting at 30. The corporal called out each number to Tamara as she stood before the switches and lever for the thrusters. When Vessmin got to '3', she flipped both switches and readied her hand on the lever for 'go'. Her heart pounded. This was the maiden voyage of one of the Emperor's most expensive and technologically advanced airships. *She* was chosen to be its Engine Tamer. No matter how disruptive and disheartening the call came to her, it came just the same and as hard as it was to admit it, it suited her!

"'Zero for 'go', Lieutenant," Vessmin shouted down the corridor.

Tamara pushed down the lever, and the thrusters roared into gear. She raised the ear guards waiting around her neck to her ears and smiled, big and wide to Vessmin as she gave her the 'ok' signal and Vessmin tapped confirmation into the communications panel.

She ran down the corridor to join Vessmin.

"Good job, Corporal! Now we sit and wait to be lifted to the sky!" She shouted, bracing herself as she felt the airship shudder and jolt.

Vessmin smiled, seeming unsure as to whether she could high five a superior or not. Tamara had mercy on her and held her hand up for Vessmin to 'high five' her.

Both women settled themselves in the brand new, leather bucket seats before the blinking panel of the engine room's communication module and Tamara trained her eyes on the small porthole above the panel board before them.

Tamara had been in several airships in flight, but this was the most exciting take-off she had ever experienced. The *Victoria* rose up and flitted smoothly forward toward the clouds over the mountains in the horizon, although the women in the engine room could not see the direction in which they traveled as the operations panel they sat in front was on the port side on the airship in the engine room.

Desperate to see where they were going, once they were firmly ensconced in flight with no danger of stalling, or emergency landings, she motioned to the corporal to follow her. They made their way toward the bow side of the engine room and Tamara climbed onto the shell covering the pumps and screwed open the porthole cover.

"Ma'am?"

"Yes, corporal?" Tamara replied, relishing the swift intake of clean, clear air that began to rush past her into the heating engine room.

"Is it...is it alright...that...that we're doing this?"

She turned to look down at her under-crewman, seeing the young face, wide eyes, and a face that may never see command of her own. She realized the corporal was a rule follower, and any infractions on her part would surely be questioned. Was this who Madame Marshall meant when she said "your movements and activities will be monitored and recorded on your journey"? Did she have a spy this close to her?

"Just for a bit, corporal. It's fine," Tamara replied, stepping off her perch to allow the corporal to see out of the porthole. She neededn't have bothered, because Vessmin gave only a cursory glance before stepping back down quickly.

"You can take a longer look. No one needs us at the controls right now, you know," Tamara said, curious as to why Vessmin shouldn't be interested in their destination.

"No need, ma'am. I don't need to see." Vessmin replied.

"Corporal," Tamara barked.

"Yes, ma'am?" Vessmin said, startled into attention.

"What aren't you telling me?" Tamara had a dawning realization.

"I'm sorry, ma'am, but I'm afraid of heights." Vessmin answered, sounding chagrined.

Tamara's eyebrows raised, "Afraid of heights? Why are you on an airship and not a mariner, then? Or in the army?" She asked, incredulous.

"I wanted to join the army...but my father served on airships in his career and he wanted one of his children to follow in his footsteps." She looked down at her toes, "He wouldn't listen to me when I tried to tell him," she mumbled.

An impatience for the young corporal overtook Tamara and she bit back a scathing reply. How had Vessmin made it this far with a fear of heights?

* * *

Feeling joyous in the few hours after lift-off, Tamara decided to take a moment and really see the ground whiz by below her. She told Vessmin to man the control panels as she would go for a short walkabout to clear her mind.

Vessmin gave her a dubious look before replying, "Affirmative, ma'am."

Tamara climbed up the ladder to the keel and walked slowly toward the large aft porthole. She shoved her hands into her pockets and stood looking down at the spot she occupied with Brolin in the early hours this morning. The embarrassing conversation she had with Madame Marshall and the knowledge she earned her first reprimand before her first maiden journey made her cringe. She writhed inside and almost turned away before forcing herself to climb over the catwalk's railing to drop over it to the one below. The feel of Brolin's hands caressing her face and the warm expression in his eyes assailed her memory, forcing her to squeeze her eyes shut and shake her head, trying to clear the images and memories from her mind.

She looked through the large porthole and her mouth gaped open at the beautiful scene below her. Fluffy, paint-brushed clouds passed below her in a slow, serene movements. The earth below her was decorated in squares of green, brown, purple, and red as they flew over the agricultural capital in New Victoria. She looked up and gazed in awe at the sight of clouds moving past them, the clear blue of the sky behind, and the horizon of land, homes, city centers, farms, factories, and business.

Feeling renewed, she returned to the engine room to find something to eat in her rations bag, refusing to show her face in the mess hall and risk meeting Brolin...and Kerridan. She would starve first. She hoped to sneak into the mess hall and beg something off of Cook to keep with her in the engine room to sustain her for at least a couple of days. She hoped by then she wouldn't care that she had been reported for "inappropriate fraternization" with a superior officer. She hoped she wouldn't care about Major Vale Brolin at all. She hoped she would have grown and matured past being bated by Third Mate Kerridan. Tamara hoped she would be a completely different person... in two days time.

By time the twelfth hour of the maiden voyage came around, Tamara wondered if she could sustain her meal abstinence for much longer. She couldn't live on sweet crackers and fruit forever. Her stomach reeled and gurgled as she sat at the controls while Vessmin took her allotted nap. For the seven thousandth time, she thought of Brolin. She wondered if he thought of her up there as he captained the airship. Maybe she would go up for one meal. No. She wouldn't.

By the next hour, she was desperate for food, but she waited too long and would have to wait until morning. She had Vessmin take the first watch and she went to lay in her bunk and hoped she could sleep for a while with an aching stomach.

She awoke to a desperate hand shaking her and a voice raised in urgency, "Ma'am! Wake up! The second engine! It's stalling!"

Tamara shot to her feet, her heart pounding fiercely. She stumbled over the threshold and the sounds of a lurching engine accosted her ears. The floor of the engine room vibrated and hummed erratically as one of the engines whined and choked. On what?!

"What happened, Corporal?!" Tamara shouted as she raced to the panel. "Why didn't you wake me sooner?!"

"It happened as I was inspecting a change in velocity on the readout. It was so sudden!" Vessmin replied, frightened. She watched Tamara, biting her nails, her eyes wide.

Tamara felt the entire ship buck and drop as she scrambled to open the hatch door to the second engine. She bent down to look in.

Why was this happening?

Her face was buffeted by blasts of both chilled and heated billowy air from the engine compartment as she jerked the hatch cover aside. On all fours, her head turned from side to side, looking for an obstruction, or nonworking gear. Her temples pulsed as her blood pressure rose. She could feel Vessmin's frightened energy behind her.

The engine capsule vibrated and shuddered and she felt the ship drop and buck again.

"Fieldmarsh!"

She heard the faint voice calling to her over the noise of the engine and the room's constant machine noise. Before she turned to acknowledge it, she noticed a white mist surge in through the intake vent, stream over the engine then out again. What?

"*Fieldmarsh!*" the voice called again.

"Here! At the engine!" she called back.

She heard footsteps pound in her direction and she jumped up, ready to dash to the control panel to see if her suspicion was true.

Fillip Weathermarker rounded a corner and rushed up to her.

"Fieldmarsh! What the blazes is happening?!"

Irritation crossed her face, and she shoved past him as she spoke, "The second engine seems to be sucking in some sort of vapor. It's choking it. That shouldn't be happening! It's an advanced engine!"

She dashed down the corridor to the engine panel to look at the pressure and thrust gauge.

"What do you mean 'a vapor'? Is it on fire?!" Fillip shouted back at her.

The ship bucked and all three lost their balance.

"It's not on fire, I think it's clouds! Are we in a cloud bank?" She called back as she leaned over the panel desk to peak through the porthole.

"Yes!" Fillip shouted, leaning closer to her to be heard, "It's a storm. We reached the mountains. Where have you been?!"

She ignored him and dashed back to the second engine. She leaned down to peer through the engine hatch door again. She saw the telltale vapor whip through the engine casing again. How were clouds causing this much trouble? She stuck her head into the opening and looked forward, seeing the cloud bank Fillip mentioned. It was thick.

They had to rise!

But they couldn't rise if she didn't fix this engine and she couldn't fix this engine if it continued to go into a stall when it sucked in clouds! Tamara growled through her teeth and dashed to a wall panel tool kit.

"What are you doing?!" Fillip shouted over the noise.

"I don't know! I'm just using my instincts!" She shouted back, knowing as she did that it was the wrong thing to say, especially in front of her under-crewman.

Tamara jerked out a wrench and crowbar, but instead of running to the second engine, she ran to engine one.

"Where are you going *now?*"

"Get out of here Weathermarker! This isn't your place!" She shouted back as she knelt to pry away the hatch cover for engine one.

"Brolin sent me here! So, *yes,* it *is* my place to be here!"

Gods, she thought as she leaned in to look into the engine canopy.

Then it hit her: she knew how to fix this. It was going to be dangerous and kill everyone if she didn't get this right. She pulled out of the canopy and spun to face Fillip. The engine whined behind her, trying to take up the slack of engine two. This had to be fast.

"Fillip, as long as you're going to be in my way, you're going to help me fix this! But I need make sure my guess is right."

"What are you talking about?!"

Tamara ran to the control panel and scanned the glassed-in diagram for the engine room and engines. Her index finger traced down to the legend at the bottom and she had it.

"Vessmin! Check for backup weather screens!"

Vessmin…where was she?

"I'll do it!" Fillip shouted as he dashed off.

Tamara muttered a quick silent prayer as she lifted the grid cover to the engine's emergency cutoff switch. This was going to either be their savior, or a court martial…if she lived through it. Movement caught her eye, and she glanced down at a paper ejecting from the communication machine. She knew the captain was asking for status.

"Vessmin!"

The corporal was nowhere to be seen. Tamara growled and ran to see how Fillip was doing. She saw him kneeling before a low compartment built into the engine room's wall. He pulled out a roll of delicate white screen.

"You found it!" she exclaimed, relieved, "You and I are about to take an awful gamble. Are you up for it?"

Fillip stared up at her in horror and realization.

"If you aren't, then get out and let me get to work," she snapped.

Fillip blinked as he stood. "You...you don't *have* to do this, do you? I mean, there's another way?" He sounded stiff and guarded. She assumed he was frightened out of his skin. She was, too.

"Vessmin!" Tamara screamed.

"...here...Lietenant," a faint voice called nearby.

Tamara turned to see the distinctly grey face of her corporal. Vessmin wiped the corner of her mouth weakly. Tamara understood where she'd been: sick.

"There you are. You're going to follow my orders without question for the next terrifying few minutes. When Weathermarker here yells 'cut', you flip the engine shut-off button for engine two! Do *not* question me!"

Vessmin's eyes widened. She stepped backward before stopping herself.

"When he yells 'engine's on', you restart the engine. Now get to your station!"

Vessmin ran off and Tamara turned toward Fillip, grabbing for the screening. Fillip's face matched Vessmin's, his face slack with horror.

"I'm going to crawl in and install this. When I get in, look for me to give you the signal!"

Ignoring his pale face, she knelt and crawled into the engine canopy. Even with the ear protectors on, the noise was monumental! The heat and chilled air buffeted her clothes and threatened to undo her hair. She slid carefully along the tiny ledge that led to the front section of the canopy, gripping the silky windscreen beneath her arm. The engine beside her sat nestled within a net of wires and bars that kept it suspended. The gap between the bars was large enough for her to slip through if she took a misstep. The work to get her out from below the engine would take too much time.

More cloud vapor sucked into the housing and she heard a change in the engine's roar before she felt herself suspended in midair as it bucked and dropped. Her head hit the top of the housing and she pitched forward toward the hot, groaning engine. Her heart stopped as she fell onto two crossbars stretching between the housing and engine.

Scrambling back to the ledge, she glanced back at Fillip. His mouth was open as he shouted something at her. He looked frantic. She jerked her head toward the front of the housing and continued inching her way to the front…but much quicker than before.

When she had inched past the front of the engine and reached the yawning opening of the air intake grid, she sighed and looked back at Fillip. His face was frozen in a mask of dismay. His eyes bore into hers as she lifted her hand in the signal to cut the engine. His head disappeared from view.

Tamara looked down at the white screening in her hands, and as she did, her body turned off all sensations. She heard nothing, felt nothing.

She looked up as she felt a change in the air pressure. The engine was shut off. It took precious moments for Tamara to wait for air intake to slow enough for her to move in front of it and not be sucked in. Once she was sure it was safe. She set to work. She only had a few seconds before engine one started to overheat and fail.

She opened the sheeting and began to attach the edge of it to the narrow edging along the opening. For a moment, she stood in confusion. A small torn piece of screening was attached to the clip and tie she was about to attach her screening to. Tamara jumped as a hand tapped her shoulder. Fillip stood behind her, his eyes glittering in intensity. Although the engine was off, the noise of the incoming air at this speed was still loud enough to hamper sound. He pointed at the screening and then at the bottom side of the opening. He was going to help her.

Thank the gods.

She shoved the piece of torn screening into her pocket to show to Brolin. She knew she checked for screening hours and hours before lift-off. Something was wrong. Tamara shivered. She didn't know if the deepening cold was the culprit, but as she and Fillip scrambled back out of the engine housing, she knew something had changed for the worse.

Chapter Four

Brolin stood beside Corporal Vessmin as Tamara and Fillip rounded the engine corridor corner after the engine had been restarted. Tamara didn't expect to see him and the stress of the past five minutes, as well as the fear that someone had done something to her engines, caused her to swear in surprise as she nearly collided with him at the panel.

He looked coldly in charge and without emotion. His profile was businesslike, and he snapped out questions at Tamara with brusque efficiency.

"Lieutenant, can you tell me what happened down here?" He stood with his hands behind his back, his broad shoulders filling in the empty space around him.

"Our engine was reacting to cloud vapor, sir. I was able to-er-Corporal Weathermarker and I managed to remedy that situation." She nodded slightly toward Fillip quaking at her side. Tamara looked for signs of anger on Brolin's face. Did he think it was her fault? She looked for signs of warmth, too. She waited for him to smile at her like he had before, but she clenched down on that wish, knowing it could have been he who reported her.

Brolin nodded slightly in Fillip's direction in acknowledgement before continuing, "I'm glad to hear it. The atmosphere upstairs was decidedly... tense. I'll expect your report at the end of your shift. Congratulations on a successful resolution. Good day."

"Thank you, sir." Tamara said, keeping her voice level. Was it her imagination, or did his eyes linger on her face for a moment?

Then he was gone.

Tamara hardly noticed Fillip's questions or comments as she turned away to go to her bunk and try to sort out the reason for the torn weather screening. She knew she checked. Was it faulty and did it get sucked into the engine? Was that the cause of the chaos? When they landed for refueling, she would have to crawl inside and check while both engines were off and cool. It didn't make sense that it wouldn't get coiled around the engine blades inside, however.

She sat at the panel, mindlessly checking and re-checking gauges, readouts, and compasses as her mind raced about what might come before. This *was* a brand new, redesigned airship, and things like this might happen regularly until they returned to New Victoria's defense headquarters. But, the ship was tested, wasn't it? Yes. They all were. But a storm cloud bank was new territory. Tests weren't usually conducted during anything but clear sky forecasts.

Tamara wondered if the storm would cause issues for the flight. She dismissed Vessmin, her restrained energy of exhausted fear was getting under Tamara's skin. Brusquely, she thanked Fillip for his help. Seemingly flustered, he returned to his post soon after.

Once Vessmin left for her quarters, Tamara walked around the engine room, listening to the noise of the machines and pipes, now hypervigilant for mechanical defects. All was quiet, but she went to check the wind screening she and Fillip applied to engine two. Kneeling from her place at the hatch door, she could see it was still there. So, it couldn't have simply come off easily. Could it? She would talk to Brolin about it when she gave him her report.

* * *

Tamara sat in her quarters writing her report on her bunk when she realized the temperature had dropped dramatically. She pulled out the thick, warm cashmere cloak she received from her family before she left. It was a gorgeous pale pink edged in white filigree ribbon stitched to the fabric. She smiled again as she ran her fingers over the soft, plushness. She pulled it around her shoulders and pulled up the ample hood.

Allowed one personal item, Tamara had grieved over the choice of what to bring. Books, or warmth. She went for both, by stuffing in a compilation of short stories by J. S. Bean—the new woman writer who appeared on the literary scene a year before—and this beautiful cloak. She blessed her mother for thinking of it and snuggled into it as she picked up her pencil to continue her report. Then, she remembered the cloth bag of wrapped chocolates she wrapped in her second set of regulation apparel and dug out a few to enjoy. However, by the end of the hour, the cold had stiffened her fingers and frozen her toes. She got up to check the machines, taking the report with her.

"Vessmin," she said as she approached the young corporal hunched over the panel sketching into a small book, "does it seem chillier in here to you?" Tamara rubbed her hands together.

Vessmin looked shocked as she regarded Tamara for a moment, then answered, "Decidedly so, ma'am. The storm and the mountains?"

"Yes," answered Tamara, "it's usually like that this time of year and at this altitude, but I won't lie and say I've been through it like this."

"Yes, ma'am," the corporal answered. Tamara looked over her again in impatience. Such a sensitive woman she was. It seemed the hullaballoo earlier and Tamara's insistence on obedience had rubbed the corporal's emotions raw. She sighed inwardly.

"I'm going to take my report to the Major. When I return, I'll take the first evening watch."

Vessmin nodded quickly like a nervous rabbit, "Yes, ma'am, but ma'am..."

"Yes, Corporal?"

"...should you go like...like?"

"Vessmin, what is it?"

"Nothing, ma'am. I'll do a round of checks while you're gone."

Tamara nodded and left the engine room.

Walking through the keel, the chill felt ominous and foreboding. Her boots clanged on the metal of the catwalk and she felt the movement of the keel as the airship moved through clouds. The thunder vibrated the keel and gas bags, making her pick up speed unconsciously.

When she opened the steel-and-glass gallery-style doors into the main piloting chamber, the warm air that greeted her was like stepping off a ship and onto a tropical island. From the door, she could see the expansive panelboard of flight and navigation instruments set on the other side of the room beneath a bank of observation windows. She had been up here before, but this…this view was gorgeous. The airship moved beyond the heavy, grey cloud bank and the view of the snowcapped mountains hove into view.

She took a few steps forward, a smile on her face. The windows curved all the way around the pilot deck and she got a 180 degree view of the airship's surroundings. This was beautiful. The fading light outside, and the golden glow of the lanterns and pin lights on the dash panel…as well as the warmth…created an intimate, cozy effect within. Tamara wondered if she shouldn't have become a pilot instead of an engine tamer. She put a hand out onto the chair beside her and gazed outside in rapture.

"That's a becoming cloak, Lieutenant," the familiar voice murmured nearby.

Tamara snatched her hand away from the smooth leather of the chair she was caressing as it was the pilot's chair, and Brolin was smiling wickedly at her. Then, she looked down in dismay at the ultra-feminine cashmere cloak she neglected to remove before leaving her quarters. So, *that's* what Vessmin was trying to tell her. She felt heat rise into her cheeks. No one would take her seriously now. It was already bad enough she was in this position when she had no right to it, then someone here knew she and Brolin had been together, and now she was seen flaunting uniform regulations by wearing an unsanctioned cloak.

"I didn't realize I still wore it! I-I…!" She hurried to remove the cloak.

"At ease, Fieldmarsh. I'm enjoying the sight of it. I won't tattle on you… and neither will anyone here."

If you only knew, Tamara thought.

His gaze was warm again, but he was slightly distant. She was still embattled wondering if he resented her for leaving him yesterday. She let her hands fall from the clasp of the cloak, leaving it on.

She sensed the curiosity of the others on the flight deck. Most of them she recognized from boarding together yesterday.

"I'm here to give my report," She said in a hushed voice. The torn piece of screening burned in her pocket as she wondered if she should bring up her suspicions.

"Ah, yes. The report….," he looked at her searchingly, "As if you would be here, near me for any another reason."

Tamara's eyes widened as he turned away from her as he stood.

"The lieutenant is here to deliver her report, I'll return shortly," he called to the second-in-command.

Tamara glanced at the other officers beneath her lashes, not sure if they heard his other remark. It worried her that her spy was taking notes about her proximity to Brolin. She sighed inwardly and followed Brolin to the small captain's office below the piloting deck and reached by a set of narrow, steep stairs. As they descended the narrow stairwell, Tamara's eyes traveled over Brolin's broad-shouldered frame and felt weakness attack her as he glided through the space to his office. His head brushed the ceiling, and she looked up at him as he stood at an open doorway allowing her to pass by him to go in before him.

As she moved to pass him, the heat of his body emanated into hers and she fought the haze of lust that threatened to engulf her. She paused for a millisecond too long as she moved beside him, nearly placing her head on the chiseled chest beneath the crisp, white broadcloth of his shirt. Her hand rose without her knowledge and brushed his arm before she was aware enough to pull it away. She stood trying to control her breathing as she waited for him to come into the tiny space and stand behind the metal desk bolted to the floor. Two lanterns bolted to the walls flickered their warm, orange light over the two of them. Brolin regarded her silently, his eyes deep and smoky in the jumping shadows. Tamara's gaze lowered to his lips, and she felt her tongue peek from between her lips to brush over her bottom lip. He watched her tongue dart over her lip and his eyes dilated and darkened. The electrified atmosphere heightened their awareness of each other.

The silence crushed them with the loudness of their attraction. Tamara's breath caught and released in short bursts as Brolin leaned on to his desk, bringing their proximity to unbearable closeness. Her body leaned forward, answering the call of his without her consent.

When he spoke, his voice rumbled deep and throaty in his chest, and her knees threatened to melt. She grabbed onto the desk for stability and realized dully that she was now inches from the major's face.

"Why did you leave me yesterday?" He asked, a note of hurt in his question.

She breathed in his scent of oils and herbs, her eyes closed. Her chest rose and fell deeply as they stood in that tiny space, lanterns flickering in the faint draft that moved about the space.

Tamara felt the cloak shift and fall from her shoulders. Warm hands clasped her face, caressing her jaw, her lips, her eyes. Her head fell backward in slow motion as her chin rose, lifting her lips upward, closer to Brolin's. She was against his chest, though she didn't know how it happened.

The sound of rustling paper filtered into her ears and she—paper. Paper. Paper. Her report. Someone would report her! Her eyes flew open, and she gasped.

Brolin's face gazed down at hers in a searing heavy-lidded expression of unadulterated passion.

"My...my report...!" she murmured, gently removing herself from his embrace. Somehow, she was sure he wasn't the one who reported her. She didn't believe he could react this way to her and be willing to do her harm and thus remove her from his presence. No. Someone else was her enemy. Someone who could be an enemy to them both if they sought to embroil her name with his.

"No," he whispered, "don't pull away again. Give me your report like this."

He sat on his desk facing her, a hand behind her back, holding her to him between his thighs, his other hand caressing the bare skin of her arm.

"I...I....," Tamara babbled, wanting to stay, but knowing the consequences if the spy found them like this.

"Just tell me what happened...quickly...," he murmured into her neck, the hum of his deep voice vibrating her skin and causing a reaction in her lower belly.

Gods.

81

She wanted to give in. Badly. But she couldn't! She needed to stay free as possible. She needed to serve her term and *not* go to prison. Besides, he couldn't convince her she wasn't just another notch for him to etch on a trophy.

She placed her hand atop his as it caressed her throat with tantalizing laziness, nearly crying as she pulled it away from her skin.

She took one, little step back, trying to create a semblance of distance without moving too far away from him. What should she say? *Someone saw us yesterday? I'm going to prison if I get too close to you? Someone hates me or you? There is a spy on your ship?*

Anything would be better than what she said next.

"We can't do this."

The warmth in his eyes faded, and he released her. She felt a steel door close over his emotions. She wanted to take it back and scream to him she changed her mind, that she wanted him, too! He straightened, placing his hands on her shoulders and moving her away from him. He moved behind his desk and sat in the small, metal chair, leaning back and regarded her with eyes that betrayed nothing.

"Your report, Lieutenant?" He said, snapping out the words with ice cold precision.

No! Don't say it like that!

"I think someone has sabotaged us, sir," her voice surprisingly steady.

His eyebrows snapped together, and he sat straighter in his chair.

"What do you mean by 'sabotage'?"

Tamara told him about finding engine two without screening and then what she did to correct the problem, wincing as she did so, sure she would receive a mark in her file for endangering her fellow shipmates' lives. They had accused her of being impulsive in the past, and as she stood here telling her captain she gave orders to turn off engines in mid-flight without direct permission from her captain, she feared the blaze of wrath sure to come. She looked down at her hands, fidgeting with the now sadly crumpled report.

She remembered the scrap of screening she found in the engine housing and pulled it from her pocket to place it on his desk, "I found this in the housing as I was installing the extra one."

When silence met her for longer than was comfortable, she risked a glance at Brolin. What she saw was not a face red with anger, but an expression of admiration. She raised her face to gaze at him fully, not sure she interpreted his expression correctly. She looked down in confusion.

"Tamara," he breathed.

She gazed at him.

"That's why I wanted you. Your quick thinking and resourcefulness are legendary."

This time, her eyebrows snapped together. Legendary? How?

'To have accomplished so much at your young age is impressive."

Icy water flushed her ardor and heat-filled pelvis, shaking her from the floating haze of the past few minutes. 'Young age'.

His eyes lowered to the scrap of screening and his well-formed hands reached out to grasp it. Tamara wanted to grab his hand and hold it.

"Thank you for your report, Lieutenant. The *Victoria* thanks you for your quick-thinking and for saving us from a sure end. You're dismissed."

Her heart dropped to her stomach. Woodenly, she saluted and exited the tiny office, back rigid, face like stone. She squeezed past Kerridan, the third mate, who stood on the stairs, her body language emitting guilt. Too stunned to think about it, Tamara exited the pilot's deck and retreated to her engine room to mourn in the solitude of first watch.

* * *

"Are you alright, Fieldmarsh?"

Tamara turned to see Fillip Weathermarker standing beside her at the breakfast line two mornings later.

"Why do you ask,?" she replied, returning her attention to the mug of coffee she was ladling sugar into.

"Because you're doing *that*," he replied, motioning at the fourth or fifth spoonful of sugar she dumped into her mug.

She frowned in irritation, "Just because I'm putting sugar in my coffee?

Most people do."

"Well, not just that," he said, following her to the center mess table, plunking down his metal tray and plopping into the metal chair beside her. She stared into her mug, trying not to notice Brolin and his shadow, Kerridan, seated a few spots away.

"Then what?" Tamara said, looking at Fillip for the first time.

"You've been kind of…moody? Mopey?"

She scowled at him, "Mopey? What makes you think I'm 'mopey'?"

He shrugged as he dug his fork into scrambled eggs, "I don't know. You're always a bit…dark…but, now. It's just that your…you seem different."

She scowled at him a moment longer before turning away to sip at her sugary coffee. She could feel Brolin. Ever since he dismissed her from his office so coldly, she knew where he was before she even saw him. It seemed the intensity of their encounter turned on a sixth sense for her. Brolin turned to speak to Kerridan and in doing so, his eyes brushed over Tamara before he looked away. Her heart dipped in her chest. But she couldn't blame him. She had rejected him twice.

"Nothing's wrong," she muttered into her coffee.

"If you say so," Fillip said, shrugging. "Say, everything going all right in the engine room? Find out why the screening was missing?"

"No," she growled, wishing he would sit somewhere else, but being oddly pleased to have someone to talk to. They had been on this ship for almost a week now and her soul chafed at the lack of friendship aboard the ship. Her first thought at having a female under-crewman to work with her dissipated with the complete neuroticism of Vessmin. Vessmin preferred the company of the cook and undercook.

"Oh…well…it was nice to get along for once….kinda," Fillip said.

Scowling once more, her head jerked sharply to look at him. This conversation was surreal. Not one to leave something alone, she addressed the surreality of his fresh attitude, "What's happening here? You don't *like* me."

"I keep telling you, you've got me all wrong, Fieldmarsh." He said earnestly.

Her head tilted to the side, she regarded him with suspicion and a touch of gratification. Her bruised sexual emotions felt warmer with Fillip's odd attention. She despised him deeply, but, what could it hurt talking to him? When they got back to land, she would let him know what was what.

"If you say so." She said, echoing his earlier statement.

"But...I never hear you say you don't like *me*, you know. If you did, I'd leave you alone immediately," Fillip said into his own cup of coffee, glancing nonchalantly around the room.

Tamara almost laughed out loud at his brazen attempt at unwelcome flirtation. She stared at him in amused shock.

"How old are you?" she asked.

"I'm in my twentieth year. Why? How old are you?"

"Twenty-six in two days." She pursed her lips in amusement as she looked at his profile. It explained plenty. His brashness and impetuousness. She hadn't forgotten his rudeness and condescension toward her, but she guessed an immature man feeling threatened by someone else would react so poorly. Acting first, thinking later.

"I like older women," he said, then he glanced over at her to see how his words affected her.

She shook her head and smiled sardonically. How quickly and easily he moved from one mindset to another, forgetting the pain he caused her. Well, perhaps this Fillip would be easier to bear. She would give him an infinitesimal chance and hope he didn't make her regret her choice.

"Who knows," he said, leaning over to her, "maybe we'll finally become an item once you see how likeable I am," he said, giving her a charming smile.

Amazed at his audacity, she threw back her head and laughed, turning away from him in her mirth. Her eyes glanced over Kerridan and Brolin. Brolin was glaring darkly at Fillip, and Tamara's heart found a dishonorable reason to become friends with Fillip: the desire to wound.

She turned back to Fillip smiling, "I wouldn't go so far as that, Fillip, but who knows, right?"

The next meal wasn't as lonely as the others, since Fillip found her again and squeezed in beside her. He made her laugh with jokes and funny observations about the crew, whispering in her ear. He wasn't there at dinner, and she spent the time feeling strangely bereft of his presence. Brolin sat by himself reading, and she wondered where Kerridan was.

Tamara took quick brief looks in his direction since he sat facing away from her. Her face grew morose as she watched him, wondering what he was reading and wishing she could talk to him. Prior to today, she could go ask him, exchanged small talk and no one would report her for something so innocent. Not now. Now, he hated her.

The next day at breakfast, Fillip whispered in her ear, "Boo!" and although she tried to reign herself in, she truly felt pleased at his presence. So, when she turned to greet him, her face was lit by pleasure. He looked genuinely taken aback by her enthusiastic greeting. He sat and gazed at her for a moment.

"Miss me?" He said, not without a sense of earnestness.

"Yes," she laughed teasingly, "supper was lonely last night. Where were you?"

"Oh…uh…I had work to do," Fillip replied, turning to tuck into his breakfast.

"Oh," Tamara said, expecting him to elaborate. When he didn't, she shrugged and looked around the room. It was a habit to look for Brolin whenever she was out of the engine room. She caught sight of him as he walked out of the mess hall and her heart dropped.

She turned back to see Fillip's gaze upon her. She smiled instinctively and asked him a nonsensical question about something unimportant as she dropped into moodiness in the absence of Major Vale Brolin.

When she returned to the engine room, she went to her quarters to splash water on her face and stare out her little window for a while, to gather her emotions back together. This time, it strained the meal with Fillip. She was feeling her impulsiveness in agreeing to a pseudo-friendship with him was a mistake. He grated her nerves with his forced cheerfulness and she left earlier than intended.

"Tamara."

Her heart lept.

She turned slowly and saw Vale Brolin leaning against the steel cutout opening of the entrance to her quarters, one arm thrown above his head, one hand casually in his pocket as he gazed at her through heavily guarded eyes.

"Major Brolin. What can I do for you?" She said cooly.

She moved to stand before the tiny bunk sink attached to the steel wall beside the shower entrance. She gripped the sink with both hands to steady herself as she looked at Brolin.

"I dismissed Vessmin to the mess hall, Tamara."

"Oh." She said, suddenly flustered. Bothered. Aroused. Confused. Lustful. Upset.

"I'm leaving the ship for a period," he said.

Tamara's eyes widened in disbelief.

"I'm being called away...on...other business," he continued.

The small anchor of constancy in Tamara's world crumbled and blew away in the wind of injustice.

"But why now? In the middle my...our...the *Victoria's* maiden voyage?"

"What can I say? When the emperor calls, I must obey." His face was immobile, expressionless.

Inside she screamed with frustration. Brolin had become a rock in her sea of uncertainty. He was the constant presence she counted on from the very beginning of her unexpected career change. She remembered what he said about her skills being legendary. Had he always been there? Someone in the shadows? Always aware of her? Keeping tabs on her? Why did he have to leave *now*?

"What am I...I mean, I..." her voice trailed off as she realized what she was about to say.

"Yes, Tamara?" Brolin's eyebrows rose sardonically, as if he understood her unasked question.

The air between them snapped and crackled with magnetism and chemistry. She watched his eyes as they traveled down to her lips, settling there for several warm moments. Her lips trembled and her nose flared as she inhaled heavily and tortuously, wanting to tell him how much she wanted him to come in. Her imagination, with its ability to create scandalous, heat-filled scenes, flashed images of the cold interior of the tiny shower, space filled with broad shoulders, muscular thighs, and generous hands, her legs around his waist, skin against yielding skin.

"You'll be fine, Tamara…"

She blinked as his cold tone crashed down on her daydream.

"…Weathermarker will be here to keep you company in my absence." And with that cruel taunt, Vale Brolin, Tamara's heart and soul stalked away from her to leave her alone on the *Victoria*.

Tamara collapsed onto the small bunk and stared straight ahead, hearing nothing, thinking nothing until Vessmin came in asking excitedly whether she had seen the small craft that hovered near the ship and picked up Brolin.

Tearing herself away from her stupor, Tamara stood, feigning interest in Vessmin's conversation. She sighed in relief when Vessmin asked to be relieved of duty to go to the mess hall early. An hour later, she screamed long and hard into her bunk mat when her thoughts refused to stray away from the major and her work had slowed down considerably.

* * *

"I have some news for you….but don't tell anyone I told you first."

Fillip and Tamara stood at the window in the keel; the same spot she and Brolin stood in two weeks earlier. Tamara turned to look at his eager face with interest.

"Oh, yes? What news?" She asked.

"We're returning to base early."

Tamara's browed furrowed, "Really? We've only been out for two weeks!"

"I know," Fillip replied, "I saw the callback on the readout tape before Kerrigan got it and took it to the second mate."

Tamara shook her head, "You'd get in real trouble if it gets out you gave someone information before the acting captain, silly."

He laughed, "Aw, no one knows we're here. No one can hear us."

Tamara laughed at his impulsiveness, "Well, I know for a fact that-" She stopped. She realized she was about to tell Fillip someone had seen her and Brolin in this very spot!

"You know for a fact what?" Fillip asked eagerly.

The blood drained from her face as she realized her very near mistake. She tried to cover her flub, "Er…nothing. Just, I know for a fact that…anyone can be watching…anytime." She knew her statement ended lamely, and she avoided Fillip's curious gaze as she looked out the window.

"I wonder why we *are* turning back," she mused.

"Maybe the ship isn't as skyworthy as thought?" Fillip guessed. "It's the maiden voyage meant to iron out the kinks afterall."

Tamara shook her head, "Well, not really. Testing is meant for that…but… the screening…"

"What about the screening?"

"Oh, I'm sure its nothing. I just saw ripped screening at the engine housing when we were putting it up. I've been wondering about it."

"Oh."

She glanced at Fillip. He was looking at her thoughtfully. Remembering his fear of that day, she put a hand on his arm to reassure him.

"Oh, I'm sure it's nothing, Fillip. Just a mistake, most likely. It probably got sucked into the engine. I meant to look for it when we landed for refueling, but now I guess I won't get the chance."

Fillip nodded silently. She smiled and patted his arm. He looked down at her hand on his arm and covered it with his own. Then, he leaned forward and kissed her forehead in a strange fatherly way. Feeling at odds with such a gesture, she pulled her hand from his and turned to the window.

"I guess I'll get back to the engine room. I guess we'll see what happens, hm?" She said.

"Yes." Fillip said. He watched her climb the railing and when she turned back before disappearing down the catwalk, she saw him staring after her with an odd thoughtfulness on his face. Unnerved, she descended the ladder to the engine room to run the routine checks on the machines. He was so strange at times.

* * *

Tamara woke up with a start that night. She sat up sweating and breathing raggedly. She coughed and rubbed her throat. *Gods.* In the dream, someone was choking her, asking for secrets. Blasted Fillip and his "news". It gave her nightmares.

She reached up and turned up the wick in the lamp so she could see and stood to splash her face with the paltry stream of water from the tap.

The airship was to begin its return trek in the morning, the official news having been sent down to the engine room by communique a couple of hours after Fillip told her.

She wandered out into the engine room. It was dim, the lanterns being turned down for the night. She was careful not to wake Vessmin, the two taking an informal approach now that they were soon to return to base. They each slept with their bunk doors opened to listen for warnings, instead of taking watch. She rubbed her face and looked at her fob watch in the dim light of the lamp. It was just after midnight and she was starving. She remembered the first breakfast she had on the ship with Brolin and her heart zipped about in her chest at the thought of him. Where was he? Why did he leave?

Tamara decided to run up the mess hall to grab some fruit and crackers before trying to sleep again until morning. The dark was like black ink in the keel, forcing her to feel her way to along the railing of the catwalk—lanterns and any type of heat source being banned in this area. Halfway through, she felt she couldn't bear the eery blackness of the walk and ran, boots clanging loudly, until she reached the steel doors to the lobby and rushed through them like some hapless soul being chased by all of the spirits of Hell.

The night lanterns glowed softly at intervals about the level, making her feel cozy and safe. She padded softly across the carpeted floor to the mess galley, but stopped when she heard a muffled voice. She looked around confused wondering where the voice was coming from. She spun around to find the voice, but whoever she heard stopped speaking. She stood still, listening hard. There it was again. The only doorways nearby were to the piloting deck and the mess hall. The mess hall was gloomy, but someone was on duty at all times at the piloting deck when it was airborne, so perhaps it was the second, or third mate, or navigator. Curious at what the operation looked like at this time of the night, she crept up to the door.

Just like the rest of the airship, the helm was dim and quiet. Peeking through the top glass of the doors, she stood on tiptoe, peering in. The spotlight attached to the outside of the pilot deck lit their way through the skies, but she could see nothing from her vantage point. As she strained to see inside, she heard the voice again clearer, but she still couldn't discern to whom it belonged.

"The target is off-ship. Unknown location." A staticky sound replied.

"Affirmative. Suspicions of subversion on the ship." The static sounded again.

Whoever it was spoke on a radio transmitter. What was this about "subversion"?

"Affirmative." The still-unknown voice replied, "Ship designs gained."

Static again.

"Affirmative. Captain to be disposed of at his return. Over and out."

Tamara ducked down out of sight of the windows. What had she just heard? Tamara's instincts screamed in her head. What she heard was wrong. Very wrong. And she shouldn't have heard it. Working quickly, she tugged her boots off and ran hell-for-leather for the engine room in her socks on the catwalk. Her feet hit silently as she ran on her tiptoes. Tamara knew now that she had just heard an assassination plot. A plot to assassinate Major Vale Brolin!

IV

Vale Brolin

Chapter Five

Major Vale Brolin strapped himself into the small, steam powered craft that pulled away from the *Victoria*. His eyes strayed to the engines...and the area he knew its engineer would be right now. The wind that entered in through the sides of the steam craft buffeted his face and hair as he turned to watch the *Victoria* move further and further away....carrying Tamara Fieldmarsh away from him.

The small craft's pilot chattered happily in his ear, but he heard not a word, his mind instead replaying the conversation with Tamara wherein which it took all of his strength and training not to rush into her small quarters and remove her uniform, thread by thread until the only thing between their skin was sweat. The expression on her face was so clear and obvious to him. For the first time in his life, he knew exactly what a woman wanted without her saying it. Somehow, he felt he ruined everything, reacting out of her consistent rejection of him.

He shook his head. The last time he acted like this, he was a teenager: lovesick, wounded, and full of petty motivation. He was no longer a young man, but his behavior and attraction to Tamara Fieldmarsh belied this fact. She was so much younger than him, how could this be? He had assumed his romantic life would forever be with his wife, ending in death. How wrong he was.

He felt ashamed. This was no way for a man of his age to behave. He was a high-ranking officer in the emperor's defense force. He was a man of responsibilities and action. He was depended upon to make decisions for an entire army prior to his return to active pilot status. How could he act so stupidly? Tamara Fieldmarsh was a jinx. What a tantalizing, beautiful jinx she was. Her skin glowed golden, brown and red with the firmness of youth and health. The full curve of her waist and bottom in her casual uniform caused her body to sway and twist in such a delicately arousing manner that Brolin found to be difficult to pull his eyes from. It was difficult to stay away from her without agony.

When he saw her in person for the first time, defiant and strong-willed in her rented hangar all that time ago, his heart lurched and jolted in his chest. He put it down to the tenseness of the situation, or the lunch he ate, or the fact that he had little sleep. When he saw her again at the Defense headquarters, her face full of rage and shock, his heart lurched again. He was fully aware of her mood and emotions. *He* was shocked.

She was a child. An opening flower. He was past his prime...he thought.

He encountered her rage again as she crossed words with Fillip Weathermarker in the engine room that Saturday morning. The rioting life and red-bloodedness of Tamara Fieldmarsh got his own blood surging within him. The seething undercurrent of her liveliness, and brazen beauty and youthfulness, claimed him forever when she reached for him. His body, full of the tenseness of the duties of the past seven months, strained toward her. He knew everything would melt away when she touched him. When she pulled her hand away in embarrassment, he wanted to jump up and place her hand on his cheek, to continue whatever magic her presence had begun in him.

When he received the communication from the palace to leave the ship immediately, he fought the impulse to delay returning, to tell the palace he would be there in a few days. His first thought was that he wouldn't be able to see Tamara at meals, or to observe her walking about the ship on her own, the sway of her hips, and the tilt of her chin leaving their indelible impression in his mind. He wouldn't be within kissing reach anymore.

He closed his eyes, attempting to erase the memory of their assignation in his office. How she looked, standing so still and petite and alluring in her quarters as he told her he was leaving. He had to see her before leaving, to drink in the sight of her, to create an indelible memory to take with him as he was forced to be away from her.

This had to stop.

Perhaps this time away would cure him of the psychological disorder that painted the essence and being of Tamara Fieldmarsh all over his mind and body.

As the lightcraft drifted further away from the *Victoria* and the fierce young woman who crept surprisingly into his heart, Major Vale Brolin suddenly realized he had taken to calling her by her first name, rather than the correct, regulation family name. And it felt good.

* * *

The lightcraft landed at the palace's designated landing pad for small aircraft, and Brolin realized the emperor had sent for him in his personal craft. He wondered what mayhem required his services this time. Ever since he allowed the Emperor to convince him to cross the border and be recruited into their enemy's service, Vale found himself becoming disillusioned that the part he played was valuable. The emperor wouldn't have called him away from an active airship unless it was important, however. He knew whatever came next would be.

The palace landing pad was luxuriant and surrounded by exotic plant species, stone masonry, flowing fountains, and statues honoring past emperors and statesmen. Surrounded by the walls of the palace, the landing pad was completely setoff from the outside world and meant to provide the emperor with a safe escape; any attempt to take over the landing pad by enemies requiring them to either scale the outside wall, run over the expansive roof to descend the other side into the area, or a rush from the main entrance to the palace and past the thousands of guards within to reach the landing pad.

He crossed the pebbled path from the craft toward the massive stone doors leading into the palace. One of the emperor's top advisors stood before them, waiting for his approach. She gave a welcoming smiled tinged with pleasure.

"Vale. You've come." She said, her voice low and intimate.

"Assandra, so nice to see you again," he said as he reached her at the doors. He smiled down at her, noting the glow of her deep-toned skin and the highlights on the sharp angles and planes of her face. He noted her hair and skin and how similar it was to Tamara Fieldmarsh's. His heart skipped a beat. Their heritage was different, but he was sure he was more likely to compare any woman he met now to Tamara.

Her eyes flicked appreciatively over his full military garb, lingering at his broad shoulders and chiseled chest. She turned and beckoned him to follow him into the airy expanse of the palace. Cool air flowed consistently through the palace rooms and meeting places through hidden horizontal columns above the halls, and by the use of breezeways situated at strategic points through the palace. During the warm months, the large doors were flung open and closed only during poor weather, or for security.

He walked beside Assandra Marananth, taking shorter steps to accommodate hers. She spoke as they walked.

"Sylvanus is worried about news he's been given," she said in a low, cultured voice, "in fact, he's alarmed by it."

"Alarmed?" Brolin echoed.

"Yes. To be frank, I'm alarmed as well, although my brother tries to pretend things aren't as serious as they have potential to be. You know him."

"But that doesn't mean he downplays, or is careless with the information." He said, looking curiously at Assandra, not used to seeing her this concerned for her brother.

"No, no, you're right. That's not what I mean though."

"Is he worried there will be a successful attempt in the future, or something like that?" He asked.

"He won't really say. Hopefully, you'll find out. To be frank, I was surprised he called you in. Pleased...but, surprised..." She glanced at him from the corner of her eyes.

For the first time since his divorce, Brolin found himself disinterested in a personal alliance with an attractive woman. Assandra and he had flirted on the outskirts of an outright affair for a while, but his friendship with her brother held him back. Now, the idea, although pleasurable, didn't interest him.

"Yes, I was surprised, too. And a bit alarmed. He's never called me away from active business before."

They turned to walk down a wider hallway with a low, wide ceiling decorated with gilt designs and filigrees. Four guards, two at the entrance of the hall, and the other two looking into the hall from the outside, stared blankly ahead as they passed. Gold and glass tables, placed at even intervals below large painted portraits, lined the hall walls. The lamps on each table, shone a warm light downward, heightening the sense of secrecy and circumstance. Brolin's boots sank into the plush, red carpet that led the way further into the hall before lining the wide, short staircase before a large, glistening gold door. This hallway led to the throne room, High meeting places, and the emperor's personal quarters... one of several, depending on the security level at the time.

Two guards sat a lounge table in an alcove to the left of the door. They played cards. Four firearms and several bladed weapons sat in holsters behind them on the wall, ready to be accessed at any second. To the right of the glistening door was another alcove, this one empty. Set deeper inside the shadows of this alcove was the hidden entrance for guards in the guardroom within the half floor below the throne room.

This was top secret knowledge and Brolin, being part of the emperor's top circle wasn't sure if Assandra Marananth knew of it. For the protection of the emperors in centuries past, this knowledge was provided only to specific members of the top circle by the top security personnel, to prevent takeovers and coups by disgruntled family members.

The guards stood at attention as Brolin and Assandra neared the throne room door.

Assandra laid a hand on his arm, "I leave you here. I was up late with him last night, and I'm due a rest this afternoon. He'll meet you in his private parlour, rather than in the meeting room." Her smile deepened, "Call on me if you have time before you are off on your next assignment, won't you?"

Brolin looked down into wide, purple-hued eyes that were fringed with long, gold-tipped lashes, below perfectly shaped eyebrows and felt...nothing.

"I will if time permits. Enjoy your rest, Lady Marananth." He clipped his heels as he bowed and turned from her to enter the doors that were now open by guards on the inside of the throne room.

As he entered the outer room, he turned to trod sedately toward the emperor's parlor, wondering vaguely if he had gone slightly insane. Assandra Marananth was a seductive beauty who had no qualms about enjoying herself with desirable males and leaving them once she had tired of them. There were no "strings attached". He could do as he wished, with no need for attachment, responsibility...or guilt. Yet, there was no real desire to engage. He was confused.

* * *

"Vale!"

Brolin grinned at his old friend's enthusiastic greeting. He clasped the arm of the emperor, but Sylvanus Marananth, Emperor of New Victoria leaned forward and pulled him into a bear hug.

Brolin laughed, "Sylvan, I'm pleased to see you looking so well. 'Sandra led me to believe you were in a poor state of mind!"

The portly man with greying temples grinned, dimples creasing his laugh lines, "She would, she would..."

"Tell me," Brolin said, sitting in the deep-cushioned leather chair the emperor motioned him into, "why *have* you summoned me. It must be rather important."

Sylvanus settled into his chair, picking up a half-smoked cigar and resumed his pastime, "I received some intelligence thirty-seven hours ago and held it until we could figure out if it was true or not." He looked at Brolin from the corner of his eyes in the manner he and his sister had. "We knew this might happen with the new ship and you in the command."

Brolin stared at him, "So...sabotage."

Sylvanus stared out toward the enclosed garden beyond the windows, "Yes."

"Well, your call came in time, since I—and my engineer—suspect the same."

The emperor turned to look at him, an eyebrow raised. "What's happened aboard my new ship, Vale?"

Brolin outlined the report he received from Tamara, leaving out his shameless plea for her to remain in his embrace...as well as her rejection of him. What was it about the woman? How did she do this to him? He swore this time away from her would purge him of all his desires for Tamara Fieldmarsh.

Sylvanus sat puffing his cigar, lost in thought. "Hm," he said finally, "Seems you were right about her. Young. Skilled. Instinctive."

Brolin restricted himself to a nod.

"You're very silent, Vale. Anything to add?"

"No, Your Highness."

Sylvanus turned quickly in his direction, cunning appearing in his eyes. "So formal, all of a sudden? Why is that? Do you not approve of the woman?"

"No, sir—Sylvan. I approve of her just fine."

Sylvanus' eyes narrowed as his eyes flicked over Brolin's face. Brolin kept his expression neutral.

His Highness heaved himself to his feet, tapping the cigar into the ashtray before leaning it against the side. He strode toward the large marble and gold office desk a few feet away and shuffled a few papers as he spoke.

"Did you know her father serves on my medical advisory panel?"

Relieved he was no longer under scrutiny, Brolin relaxed in his chair. "No, I didn't," he said, "did you know before you signed her order to serve?"

Sylvanus was quiet for a moment, "Her family name isn't common, but...I didn't put two and two together until I received her family information just before you visited her with Bingley."

"Ah."

"Her father thanked me, you know."

"Oh?" Brolin faintly shocked.

Sylvanus tapped his fingers on the marble top of the desk in a distracted manner, grating on Brolin's consciousness. He could see the emperor was considering something.

"Yes. Apparently the girl had written to her parents asking them to do something to get her out of service."

Brolin felt a momentary pang of sympathy for Tamara, "Did she?"

Sylvanus' eyes narrowed in on Brolin again, then he turned away to busy himself with a file as he answered, "Yes. I believe he and his wife gave her various answers and reasons why they weren't successful."

"I'm…I'm surprised parents would be please by..er…a child's military draft….to be frank."

"Ohhh, yes, yes. You would, you would," Sylvanus breathed as he strode back to his chair, "but you know her work was dangerous for her…and illegal. They wanted her out of the business and safe…by certain standards. The child is fiercely stubborn and possessed of more than her fair share of independence…for a woman."

Brolin's eye twitched, and he glared down at the intricate patterns woven into the floor coverings in the room. "All due respect, Your Highness. She is past being a child and, as such, is quite entitled to her stubbornness and independence."

Silence greeted him and he was concerned his old friend would see him escorted from the room demoted.

He shot a look at the ruler of New Victoria and for a moment, wondered if he had seen a smile hidden behind the hand holding the cigar. The emperor's eyes were twinkling.

"M-my apologies, Sylvanus! I don't know what-" Brolin stammered.

"I don't know what you're blathering about, Vale….anyway, I want you to come to the state dinner tonight. You'll meet Fieldmarsh…the father. Ah, and I want you to cross the border tonight and find out what you can about the attempts of sabotage on my ship. I'm catching wind of another assassination plot, too. Find out, eh?" Sylvanus stood, and offered his hand to Brolin, signaling the end of the meeting.

* * *

Brolin looked around the table, noticing the richly dressed men and women and listening to the conversation that became increasingly louder, sillier, and in some cases, bawdier. The emperor, his sister, and other high-ranking individuals were not yet in attendance and since only spirits were available, almost everyone was drinking alcohol on empty stomachs.

The lighting from the chandeliers above each table cast a hectic, glittering light down onto the diners. Gold and silver tiaras waved and twinkled. Men's monocles, bars, and medals caught the light and reflected light onto diners. Women's tunic sashes edged with metallic ribbon flashed, earrings, diamonds, and ceremonial cutlasses winked in the candlelight. Brolin, feeling a headache forming, downed his entire glass of water. He noted he was in attendance without an escort and prepared himself for a long, boring evening ahead of his departure into the next territory later that night. The image of Tamara Fieldmarsh in a second-skin dress the hue of fiery passion and the warmth of bronze dewy skin pressed against the fabric of his dress tunic at another dance not so very long ago flashed in his mind. A profound sense of longing assailed his mind, and he decided to drink something stronger.

"Gentlefolk, Officers, Officials, please stand to welcome His Highness Sylvanus Marananth, Lady Assandra Marananth, Lord Medical General Fieldmarsh and Lady Medical General Fieldmarsh, Lt. Major Doveneck, Captains Von Pek...."

Brolin allowed his thoughts to wander as the majordomo rattled off the names of the highest ranking individuals arriving late to the dinner. The wish that Tamara Fieldmarsh was by his side washed over him again. He wondered how she was faring on the ship without him. He remembered her look of entreaty before they parted. He hated himself for that stunt, for being desperate to see her reaction to his leaving, to see if she would miss him. To see if she loved him. His eyes widened at the thought that crashed through his mind.

"What a treat, Darling Vale," A low, svelte voice whispered in his ear, "I had *no* idea you would be seated next to me."

Assandra Marananth stood beside him, gazing at him beneath heavily made up eyes, and gold foil brushed eyelashes. Her dress, a velvety mustard yellow that hung on voluptuous curves as though they were smooth boulders lying beneath a lazily pouring river of succulent streams of water, draped negligently over breasts that were on display for the evening. He didn't recall if her breasts were always this size, or not.

He choked on the last dregs of water from his glass as he greeted her, "Lady Assandra. It's my pleasure to see you."

She smiled a full-lipped seductive smile as she lowered herself onto her chair and the footman pushed it in.

"Vale! So glad you could come!"

Brolin wrenched his eyes away from Assandra's jiggling chest, his face reddening in embarrassment at Sylvanus catching him with his eyes on his sister. He stood to bow to his emperor and then noticed two people standing beside him.

"Meet the good Doctors Fieldmarsh! I told them their daughter's senior officer would be in attendance tonight and they begged to meet you! Janus, Riette, your places are in front of the good Major. I shall see you all later tonight!" The emperor sailed away, ceremonial robes catching the breeze and flying out behind him.

* * *

Brolin yawned as the hover bike roared in the night. The flickering gas light attached to the bike illuminated the road dimly, as well as his companion sent to assist and guard him. He wished he could have waited until the next day to cross the border, but night was a mercy. It had to be now.

* * *

Brolin's heartbeat raced as he sat in the dingy back room. What did the man say?! His palms sweated profusely, but he resisted rubbing them on his trousers to dry them. If they thought he was nervous, they would likely slit his throat just out of suspicion and without evidence.

The barkeep entered the backroom yanking in a blindfolded man behind them. The man sniveled quietly, his hands tied behind his back. Brolin wondered what he'd done, but he wouldn't ask. He strained his ears to hear the voice coming through the wall behind him.

"Get the girl." A deep muffled voice said.

The door creaked open as the barkeep pushed it open to tow in his hapless prisoner.

"What's the name again?" A squeaky, nasally voice asked.

"Fieldmarshal, or something like. Odd name, what?"

'Yeah."

Brolin clenched and unclenched his hands. Tamara's face flashed before him. He had to find out what was going on! Taking a gamble and hoping he wouldn't lose his life for it, he jumped up and rush past the door just as the owner of the squeaky, nasally voice came though it.

"Hey! Watch yourself, dummy!"

"I was just standing here, idiot. You're the one who came crashing through." Brolin said, wary of the man's hands.

"What did you call me?"

"What's going on out here, Neely?!" The barkeep roared, appearing behind the man called Neely.

"He rushed out the door without seeing if anyone was here!" Brolin said, trying to peer into the room surreptitiously. "I'm looking for a job anyway, heard you guys need to find someone? Need me to do it?"

"Get outta here," Neely screeched, trying to shove past Brolin. Brolin stepped aside and then stuck out his foot, catching the man midstride. He jumped backward into the room in a dramatic movement as Neely whipped out a blade in anger.

"Get out of here!" A man roared from inside the room. Brolin assumed his was the other voice he heard telling Neely to find someone named Fieldmarshal.

Neely whipped past the barkeep at the door and rushed at Brolin, swinging the knife. Brolin ducked and dodged left, bumping into the rough wooden table. This prompted the big man sitting there to jump backward, shouting. The barkeep screamed out the door, demanding someone to come get Brolin out of the room. Meanwhile, Brolin ducked, dodged, jumped, and rolled to stay out of reach of Neely.

"You did that on purpose! You'll pay!" Neely yelled, swiping and swishing in a haze of rage.

Brolin kicked over the table, sending the ink wells, papers, and boxes flying. Neely lunged at the table, trying to stab at Brolin. The big man and the barkeep hopped around trying to stay out of Neely's way, while simultaneously trying to grab Brolin and harness Neely.

"Alright! Alright!" Brolin shouted from where he crouched, "I'll get out if you'll just put the knife away!"

"No!" Neely screamed back. "You tripped me and you'll pay with blood!"

"Enough!" The large man roared.

Brolin jumped and Neely shut his mouth in shock. The hand holding knife went slack as he stared at the large man.

"Who *are you?*"

Brolin kept an eye on Neely as he stood carefully. He addressed the man, "I'm Carper. Just looking for a job. Haven't had one in a while and I need to eat." His head beneath the wig itched. He wondered if it was infested with nits.

The large man snickered, "Must not be very good if you haven't worked in a while."

Brolin crossed his arms, now graced with a myriad of tattoos. "Prison." He said. "Let me help with that. Sorry I knocked it over." He knelt to right the table, keeping well away from Neely who looked like he was gearing up for another burst of energy.

"What work are you looking for?"

"I find people. Need anyone found?"

Neely uttered a whine.

"Shut up, Neely," the man growled, then turned to Brolin, "How fast do you work?"

"Depends. Where you trying to find them?"

"New Victoria."

"I've got people there. How soon you need 'em?"

"Yesterday."

"This is *my* job, Jakob! I'll hunt him down and kill him if you give it to him!" Neely erupted, causing everyone in the room to flinch.

Brolin put up his hands in surrender. "Fine. Fine. No hard feelings. I'll earn my beer somewhere else." He made a dramatic and obvious show of avoiding Neely by walking in a wide circle around him toward the door. "Sorry for butting in. I'll be off."

Once through the door, he continued walking backward, every sense on high alert in case Neely made another rush for him, or in case the barkeep or the other man refused to let him go, but they were already berating Neely about his bloodlust and terrible temper. They scolded him about always trying to fight people without good reason.

Brolin walked through the main bar area, avoiding serving maids and drunk patrons until he was out the door. He walked down the front of the buildings until he rounded the corner into the first alley. The shadow of a man loomed up in front of him. Brolin put a hand behind him, reaching for his back holster.

"It's me."

His bodyguard stood in the alley, smoking a pipe.

Brolin relaxed momentarily. "Nord. I just found documents with a list of people of assassinate. My engineer is on it. We need to head back over the border *immediately!*"

Chapter Six

Brolin's trek back to the palace in New Victoria was painted with anger and anxiety. She was just a new recruit! Why did those fools want Tamara dead? How in the blazes did they know about her? He knew he was being stupid. Tamara wasn't a newly-born innocent child. In truth, she was an aider and *abettant* of the underworld prior to her service in the defense force. Dark forces must want her dead before the secrets she knew got out. But what did Tamara know that the palace didn't know already? There were plenty of spies, turncoats, and double agents on both sides. It seemed everyone knew everyone's secrets…things just depended on who knew it first and who did something about it before the other side did! What did Tamara know?

He and Nord raced through the mountains on the six-hour journey through the mountains, stopping as infrequently as possible. They arrived in New Victoria shortly before dawn to arrive at the palace by early morning.

The sun peeked over the West Mountains, casting golden light over the valley. The palace's gold capped towers glittered, heralding the wealth of the empire. The scattered scarcity of the outer lands morphed into emerald greenness of trees, lawn, the richly hued natural pools, and the cool groves evenly spaced in the acreage leading to the palace doors.

He and Nord raced to the Poor Town residence to change into their military attire and send a messenger to the palace major domo announcing their return and to request an audience.

As they waited for word from the palace, Brolin paced and his mind raced. What he and Nord learned across the border was troubling. All secret work could be classified as "troubling", but in this instance, his heart was troubled. The new airship was in danger of sabotage, and his heart in the engine room was on a list for assassination.

* * *

"We *must* call the *Victoria* home! All the soldiers on that ship are in danger of their lives and the secrets of this great empire are in danger of being leaked to our enemies! We can't allow it!" Brolin gesticulated wildly as he paced hecticly before the emperor who was seated in his silk-lined chair in the meeting room.

His trip not only produced the information of the eminent attack upon Tamara Fieldmarsh, but also news that the enemy installed spies at the Defense Force training grounds and upon the *Victoria* herself! Vale's anger increased as he realized the laxness of their security policies. How could spies simply waltz into training and onto the Victoria!

When Tamara handed him the piece of screening for the engine, he assumed the sabotage was enacted prior to the ship's ascendance and they could resolve the problem with future attention to security and changes. However, now knowing that Tamara was aboard the ship with the saboteur… he fumed. His jaw worked, sending a thick red vein pulsing toward his temple. His blood pressure rose. Sylvanus pondered him thoughtfully.

"Vale," the emperor said quietly, "I, too, am aware of the dangers to our soldiers, but you…you seem on the verge of a breakdown. Is there more to this? Are you keeping something from me? I've never seen you this… shaken."

Brolin sat down with an effort to control himself. He avoided looking at Sylvanus. His hands felt wet against the cool, smoothly laquered tabletop. He wiped his hands on his trousers and took a deep breath in, then out slowly. He felt calmer and more centered.

"Brolin, what is it?"

Brolin glanced at his emperor, trying to shutter his emotions before Sylvan's probing gaze. He looked away again and slumped backward against his seat.

"I was shaken at the level of cutthroat ruthlessness which created this plot. I was rattled by the efficiency of the plan to steal our airship's secrets and destroy anyone who got in the way," he answered softly. With his imagination flashing images of Tamara's possible fate and the destruction of the airship and its passengers, he traced the pattern of the wood grain in the tabletop. He felt helpless here on land. Sylvanus seemed to be moving slowly. Unnaturally so!

"Sylvan," Brolin said suddenly, sitting up in his seat and addressing the ruler of New Victoria with a lack of deference, "I believe Tamara Fieldmarsh may know something about a plot, or a dark secret our enemies are determined to keep quiet. And I don't think she is aware that she knows."

Sylvanus raised his eyebrows, his cigar-holding hand poised in mid-air, "Oh?"

"Yes," Brolin said, palms on the table, leaning forward.

Sylvanus regarded him steadily as he stabbed his cigar into the ashtray.

"Why are you so convinced?"

"I also discovered a plot to have *her* assassinated."

Sylvanus crinkled his brow and dropped the cigar into the ashtray in surprise. Brolin noticed this curiously. He knew why he felt anxious, but he wasn't sure why Sylvanus would.

"You discovered a plot..." Sylvanus began.

"...to kill Tamara Fieldmarsh. Yes." Brolin finished for him.

Sylvanus stood thoughtfully, his hands steepled in front of his massive stomach, "I agree with you Vale. These plots can't succeed!" His eyes darted hither and thither, his head lowered to his chest, and jaws clenched and unclenched as he paced.

Pleased to see this change to urgency, Brolin was nevertheless puzzled over this change in Sylvanus' posture. He stood, eyes trained on the pacing monarch, waiting for the call to action. His fingers tapped impatiently upon the tabletop and his free hand clenched and unclenched.

"Call the *Victoria* back." Sylvanus muttered. He trod over to his desk and rummaged around through the drawers before finding a ream of silk paper.

He snapped out a sheet and dipped the gold pen into the inkwell, scrawling his name to the bottom of it before handing it to Brolin.

Brolin bowed swiftly at the waist, "Your Excellency!" He exited the doors of the meeting room and raced—as decorously as he could—through the palace halls.

Nord met him at the outer room of the palace's entry and matched his long, quick strides.

"What did His Excellency command, sir?" Nord asked.

Brolin, eyes forward, answered tersely, "The *Victoria* is to return." He handed the officially signed paper to Nord, "I received the *signatural* paper. Write the order upon it."

Nord nodded and pulled out his pad to scribble into it as he hurried alongside Brolin.

"And order a watch detail on each crewmember upon the *Victoria* when it returns. Ah, and send an order to the Defense Force Training grounds. I want to have a watch set up there."

"Yes, sir."

"They won't get away with this," Brolin growled.

Nord looked at him and lost step for a moment.

* * *

Vale returned to his usual quarters at the court-sanctioned property not far from the palace gates. Serving so high in the ranks came at a personal cost, but the compensations were admirable and comfortable.

His home was one of several villa-styled houses situated picturesquely in a royal garden. Although categorized as a villa, they were smaller, but the privacy was adequate. Manicured lawns, sculpted bushes, fountains featuring individuals at a loss for clothing, and small fruit tree groups where the fruit never seemed to drop, surrounded the homes.

These homes were guarded less vigorously than the palace although it was essentially adjacent, but Vale never felt his safety compromised here. He stood in the enclosed private garden outside of his living quarters, sipping the piping hot coffee his houseman brewed for him the next morning. He knew the *Victoria* was on its way back, and he tried earnestly to remain neutral, guarded, disaffected, and in control, but his fingers dropped everything he grasped, his eye twitched at every unfamiliar sound, his heart thudded at the sound of quick steps in his direction. He dreaded the news that he failed to protect the airship. They had to make it safely home!

Later that day, he instructed Nord to plan a mandatory state dinner at the training grounds so the quarters of the trainees could be searched. He was determined to find evidence of sabotage or spying. This would require a monumental undertaking. First he would need to move a large number of security personnel to the training grounds over the next several days, the dinner would need to be planned, a file of everyone in training within a specific two-month period needed compiling, a background search of each trainee… Brolin was glad he had delegates.

* * *

Days later, Brolin stood on the second-level balcony of the building of offices at the training grounds. Arms crossed, he surveyed the buildings sprawled about the acreage, stopping at the barracks further in the distance. He traveled down from the palace to oversee the search for spies and evidence of sabotage during the state dinner. The plan was to attend the dinner for the first hour then excuse himself to receive any news from Nord about the searches.

Missives of the mandatory nature of the dinner reached each unit with those who were sick or injured told to report to the campus hospital for the night. Warnings of punitive action added gravitas to dissuade anyone who planned to ignore the dinner.

A firm knock sounded on his office door. Brolin walked back into his office from the balcony and called, "Enter!"

"Sir, I'm sorry to bother you, but can I speak to you a moment?"

Brolin blinked, taken aback at seeing Fillip Weathermarker peering around the door. He had forgotten about the young idiot. "What about?" He asked, with the usual bit of short patience whenever he saw him.

"Just about the dinner, sir?"

"Are you trying to get out of it, Weathermarker? As you should be well aware, all-"

"No, no, sir! Not at all. It's about something else...may I come in?"

Brolin waved an impatient hand toward one of the chairs in front of his desk. Fillip entered and lowered himself discreetly into a chair, prompting Brolin to further dislike the man. His air of false humility toward his superiors in light of what else Brolin knew about him grated his nerves.

"Well?" Brolin asked.

"I...forgive me if I'm being impudent, sir, but...I was thinking about the opportunity the mandatory dinner affords you, sir."

Brolin blinked, but remained silent.

"Er...I just mean, I've heard that there are enemy agents on the emperor's soil and maybe even here! I wanted to suggest that you conduct a search of everyone during the dinner. It's the perfect time for it. Sir?"

Brolin felt his face heat and grow red with anger. This idiot boy would dare to come to his superior with a 'suggestion'! He was further incensed with the understanding that his thinking and...this idiot boy's...aligned in the same manner. He didn't want there to be any favourable comparisons between himself and Weathermarker.

"Weathermarker."

"Sir?"

"You *are* being impudent."

Fillip's face blanched, but he charged on, "I'm aware of that, sir. I apologize, but we have to protect the empire at all costs! Everyone should be searched! Even...even me! Even *you*, sir....for good faith!"

"You trod upon shaky ground, Corporal," Brolin purred dangerously.

"Yes...I'm sorry. But will you, sir?"

"Young man, I would hardly tell a mere corporal my plans. Now leave my office and don't return with any suggestions for improvement. It isn't your place." He held Weathermarker's gaze as the young corporal, hiding signs of gratification, saluted and shuffled out the door.

Brolin tapped his fingers on the desk. He didn't like the boy, and this conversation didn't improve his estimation of him. Eventually, he pushed Fillip out of his mind and left the building for lunch. He walked down to the campus cafe, hoping there was something particularly delicious on offer.

He passed the pond with the ducks, families, and children cavorting about. His mind transferred to the pleasant memory of drinking clove and orange tea here with Tamara Fieldmarsh. He stood in the sunlight, the sunlight warming his skin and relaxing the tense muscles of his neck and shoulders. Hands in his pockets, he continued down the wide walking path toward the cafe.

Glancing at the people standing around the opposite bank of the pond, he slowed as he saw Weathermarker in an urgent conversation with a female corporal. From this far, he couldn't hear the conversation, but it seemed intense. The young woman gesticulated feverishly, her movements causing her long black hair to swish about in the air. Weathermarker passed something to the woman, and she grabbed it quickly, shoving the item into her pocket before turning to walk swiftly away. Irritation with how easily Weathermarker seemed to harass his female peers crossed Brolin's mind. He moved along the path, promptly forgetting about what he'd seen.

As he ate at the reserved table on the raised platform behind the others in the cafe, he caught himself reacting to every svelte, brown-skinned recruit that passed through the cafe doors, expecting each to be a young, intense engine tamer. Then he saw her. The warm light from the sun shone behind her through the glass doors, highlighting the curls in her coif wound tightly at the nape of her neck. A halo of light outlined her slightly tilted shoulders, her bare arms, the deep curve of her hips and the shape of her legs beneath the regulation gray of her uniform trousers. She didn't look his direction, instead she perused the offerings of the cafe, choosing this, then that.

He regretted the way he left her those weeks ago. If he had paid attention to his senses, and simply left to do his duty, then he could simply walk up to her and greet her. He could lightly discuss her lunch options and give recommendations. He could ask her to join him at his reserved table. She would smile that beautiful smile and say, 'I'd love to, but please, I *must* have my dessert, Vale darling!' and Brolin would laugh joyfully and kiss her on the cheek as she bent down to view the selections. And he would view her particular selections as she... Brolin shook away his thoughts as Tamara smiled at the sweet desserts offered at the end of the buffet cabinets. Brolin smiled at her delight. Then he frowned.

Fillip Weathermarker joined Tamara at the buffet and leaned in to whisper in her ear. Knowing Tamara's disdain of Fillip, Brolin half-stood, ready to rescue her yet again. Instead, Brolin's frown deepened as he saw Tamara laugh and turn to look up into Fillip's face. She slapped his arm playfully and gestured toward a few empty tables nearby. Brolin's mouth fell open.

Movement behind them at the door caught his attention. The young woman he saw arguing with Weathermarker on the way to the cafe walked quickly over to them, gave Weathermarker an enigmatic look and then beamed brightly at Tamara. All three moved to a table and sat down. Brolin didn't know what to think. How had Tamara suddenly become close with that stupid, impudent young man she so despised? Who was this woman he saw arguing with him and now seemed to be friends with all three? He looked the newcomer over, noting the delicate Eastern features and black long hair. Where had he seen her before today? He wasn't able to ponder her face once they sat since she and Weathermarker sat facing away from him and Tamara sat across from them affording Brolin a good vantage point.

As if in a trance, Brolin's eyes drifted over Tamara's face as she chatted with her companions, looking down at her fork trailing lazily on her plate. She rested her chin on her hand, her delicate fingers framing her jaw. The distant melodies of a song from a long-forgotten era trilled through Brolin's mind as his eyes rested on Tamara's beautifully formed mouth, laughing, smiling, giggling. His memories of his mouth on hers quickened his pulse as her tongue flicked tentatively over her lips. Her deep, black lashes framed her large eyes and his heart skipped a beat as they flickered over each companion's face, threatening to still on his lurking figure well within her line of sight.

A group of officers interrupted his view of the trio as they looked for a free table. He felt a profound sense of loss and longing and stood abruptly to leave. As he placed his plate and glass on the discarding table, he took one last look at the young people. Tamara was standing, preparing to leave as well, but she didn't look in his direction. Instead, her eyes seemed to search the raised platform reserved for high-ranking officers. His heart thudded as he wondered if she searched for him! Not seeming to find for whom she searched, she bent to retrieve her items. Brolin moved along the space toward the exit. As he moved, he got a better view of Weathermarker and the other young woman.

As Tamara walked toward the discarding table, he noticed the two in a strange byplay of signals and whispers before they straightened up and went to join Tamara. The still unknown woman slung her arm around Tamara's shoulder and gave her a hug. Tamara laughed. Weathermarker kissed her cheek and Brolin's face darkened in anger. He disappeared through the door of the cafe and walked briskly to his office.

* * *

Brolin stood in front of the large, heavy, gold mirror in his bachelor living quarters in the sanctioned dwellings just off the training grounds. His formal deep blue suit sat crisp, straight and without wrinkles on his broad shoulders increasing the sense of unyielding stoniness in his figure. He straightened his formal sash and pondered his face. He glanced over the fine lines at the corners of his eyes and the grey at his temples. His fingers brushed the thick hairs of his finely cropped beard. The hairs trimmed closely to the jaw made it looked square and uncompromising.

I'm getting old, he thought. Now why did he think that all of a sudden? He didn't recall any close attention to his age until recently. As recently as... His heart beat rapidly as he realized the reason for his newfound awareness of his forty-four years was to be at the state dinner. He remembered the picture the three young people made as they walked from the cafe. All three were young, seemingly ageless, their skin glowing with health. Their steps quick, their movements agile. He should be ashamed of himself. He had no business longing for the bronze, firm flesh of Lieutenant Fieldmarsh!

There were plenty of mature, accomplished women of a comparable age that he could spend his time with. They understood him. They understood the passage of time and attainment of experience...and wisdom...and...age. Brolin slumped on the nearest chaise longue, creasing the back dreadfully. Would this longing never go away? Would it only find satiation when he melted into the warm caresses of the object of his affection? How could he ever rid of himself of this obsession if she never submitted to it? He jerked out of his stupor some time later as the grandfather clock struck seven. He left to attend a state dinner with a heart heavy with depression.

*   *   *

Brolin listened with half an ear to his companion's prattle. Dyva Windcage was a beautiful bore. At no time did her conversation become scintillating, interesting, scandalous, or otherwise questionable. Her interests remained confined to second-hand observations of observations she heard from others and the food served here tonight.

He had seen Tamara enter and Weathermarker's move to sit beside her. From then on, he resisted seeing her again lest he descend into a black pool of depression. He couldn't wait for Nord to give word for him to leave the dinner. He was glad to be leaving before the dancing began, because he couldn't bear the thought of seeing Tamara on the arm of Weathermarker knowing what pleasure that young idiot would have. He stared down into his glass of sherry willing time to pass quickly.

A tap on his shoulder made him look up, and it was with relief that he spied Nord standing over him.

"Yes, Nord?" He asked.

"If I could have a word with you, sir? It's important," Nord replied, keeping to the script.

"Oh...," Brolin said, mustering a flustered tone into his voice as he looked apologetically at his companion, "I'm sorry Dyva, darling, but duty calls. You understand?" He didn't hear her or see her in his haste to be away. As they walked through the ball room doors, they dropped the pretense.

117

"Everything went underway without a hitch?" He asked Nord as they trotted down the stone steps of the lawn to the lane below. The cool night air was a refreshing change from the heat inside.

"Right, sir. They've been at it for about forty-five minutes. We should have some returns soon."

"Right!" Brolin exclaimed shrugging out of the constricting dress tunic and tossing it over his shoulder as they picked up speed.

"Did anyone try to remain in their quarters, Nord? The recruits are usually excited about balls and parties, but since we know we have…er…others on our campus…."

"I haven't heard word of anyone attempting to stay indoors, sir, but I instructed the searchers to fabricate a reason they were in recruits quarters if they encountered anyone. Did you have someone in mind?"

Brolin pulled the brass key from his trouser pocket to unlock the outer doors of the office building in the alley as he spoke, "I can't really say I do, but something isn't settling right with me."

"What isn't, sir?"

The door swung open and warm stale air rushed past them from inside eager to get out into better climate.

"I don't know how to describe it really, Nord. It's something involving the young engine tamer….Fieldmarsh…" His voice trailed off as he tried to place where he had seen the young woman with long dark hair before. "I don't know," he continued, distractedly, "there's something about her that I just can't…can't…" He shook his head as he turned up the gas lamps on the wall in the narrow hallway leading to his office.

"Are you saying you think she's in league with the other side?" Nord asked.

"I hesitate to say so. It's a serious offense."

"Right, sir.

"It may just be a love triangle. Perhaps that's it."

"Love triangle?"

Brolin opened his office and crossed to throw open the windows. He looked up at the bright moon above and listened to the faint music coming from the ballroom. The dancing had started. He turned around and shrugged at Nord, "Ignore me. Just….love on the mind, I suspect."

He could see Nord's face as he nodded in complete confusion.

"Well, sir, I'll leave you here and return to my station. I'll bring word as soon as the search is complete." The muscular young man saluted.

Brolin nodded and Nord left.

Nord returned an hour later, his face beaming with success. A young security guard stood behind him holding a long narrow crate.

Brolin stared at him from behind his desk, "Something was found, man?"

"Yes, sir!" He turned to gesture the woman holding the crate. She stepped forward briskly and set it on Brolin's desk. The words *DEFENSE FORCE - PARTS* and a serial number was stamped on the lid beside a stenciled image of an airship engine.

Brolin dragged the desk lamp nearer to the box and lifted the lid. He stared down at the wad of flimsy material inside the sawdust in astonishment. "Where did you find this?" He asked Nord.

"In Fieldmarsh's quarters. In the bottom of her trunk. My soldier knew she shouldn't have this in her quarters and alerted me immediately! Your instincts were correct! She's obviously working with the enemy. That's why her name was on the list to be—."

"Nord! You fool! You're dismissed!" He barked the last at the security woman who jumped in astonishment and scuttled out the door. Nord stared at him in surprise, not understanding what he had done wrong.

Brolin looked down at the white filmy material and spread it out quickly, his heartbeat growing rapid. His fingers searched for what would be the edge and finding it, ran his fingers over the length of it, searching….searching. He found it. Under his fingers was a section obviously torn, a gaping bit of it left behind somewhere. He and Tamara knew where. She had given him that torn piece on the ship.

"Sir? Shall I go arrest her now?

"She's been framed!" Brolin roared.

Nord blinked and took a step backward. His face settled into lines of disapproval, but he said nothing.

Brolin shook his head as he stared at the monumental judgement against

Tamara Fieldmarsh. The surefire way to get her to a firing squad. The most positive way to get her dead. He knew now that the enemy was working its magic to kill Tamara. What did she know that had her marked for death? If they simply wanted her dead, they would have succeeded by now. They needed more than that. They needed a scapegoat.

Tamara needed protection! She needed *his* protection!

"Nord," he said tersely, "I wish to apologize for my earlier…outburst."

Nord stared at him impassively in the dim light.

Brolin continued, "This is not evidence of espionage in itself. It's evidence that agents of the enemy are trying to cover up *their* actions, by framing the Lieutenant."

"How do you know it's a frame-up, sir?"

"Because she found the missing piece from here on the ship and gave it to me aboard. She told me she believed someone sabotaged the ship before take off as she had inspected the ship twice before."

"Oh." Nord said and retreated into silence.

"Someone knew we were conducting a search and placed this in her quarters."

"Oh." Nord said.

Brolin watched his face and saw when the dawning realization took over.

"Oh!" Nord said, "Sir! Someone knew!"

"Yes. There is a spy in our ranks."

Nord shook his head and rolled his eyes toward the heavens, "Sir, this… this is going to take some work…finding the mole, I mean."

Brolin nodded as he shrugged back into his dress tunic, "Yes! It will!" He said, buttoning the gold buttons. "And I know you'll do a fantastic job discovering the culprit. I have faith in you." He replaced the engine screening in the flat crate box and covered it with the lid. "I'm going to lock this in the safe at headquarters. No need to accompany me."

"What will you do then?"

Brolin turned down the lamps, and opened the office door, "I'm headed back to the ball. The person who wants to kill Tamara Fieldmarsh must be there tonight. I'll stake my life…er…my job on it."

"Major?"

It wasn't often Nord addressed him by his rank, and Brolin turned to him in mild surprise. "Yes, Nord?"

"What is so important about this young Lieutenant? By all accounts she's just a criminal trading prison for time in the emperor's army."

Brolin regarded the stocky, powerfully built man who assisted him in many of his dangerous missions. He wondered what to tell him. Did he say he loved this woman and wanted to save her life? Would he understand that? Did he say she was 'destined for greatness'? He said none of those. "The enemy wishes to encroach on this sovereign soil and dispatch whom ever they wish. I won't allow that." Then he turned and walked pensively down the hall to the exit a floor below.

* * *

Upon his return to the ballroom, Brolin searched the dancers for Tamara's trademark mass of barely-contained hair. He nodded at recruits and other dinner attendees who greeted him as he walked across the dance floor, looking for her. He looked for the elegant posture that held up a defiant chin. He looked for a red dress with a plunging back that reveal bronze skin with deep golden highlights. He stood spinning among the dancers, growling in frustration, and feeling like a fool.

Unable to find her, Brolin walked off the dance floor into the small hall beyond it. The lights from the walking lane outside shone into the space through the wall of windows, hiding nothing. He heard low murmurs of the young assignees whispering sweet nothings to each other. He found himself peering into annoyed and angry eyes as he tried to figure out surreptitiously if either of the women were Tamara here in the dim light.

He picked up the pace, all manner of paranoid thoughts crossing his mind. What if the saboteur didn't want to stop at merely waiting for a firing squad to do its business. What if they meant to kill her *tonight* at the ball when everyone would be distracted. His eyes roamed over the heads in the hall and he headed toward the doors leading to the back garden. The cool air was once again a welcome change from the heat inside.

Voices murmured here and there under the glow from the gas lights shining above the garden. He heard a familiar voice. It was Weathermarker. His voice had an odd quality to it that made his hair stand on end. He disliked the man intensely, especially when he saw him in his office offering his suggestion of a search. Brolin paused. Weathermarker wanted a search conducted during the dinner. Brolin paled. He remembered seeing Weathermarker in a deep argument with the unknown woman across the pond before handing her something wrapped in paper, and then he saw them again later with Tamara. Tamara, whose quarters were later searched for items of espionage. Tamara who had warned him of sabotage a few weeks earlier. Tamara who had been on the airship without him for almost two weeks...*with Weathermarker.*

Suddenly, he remembered where he had seen the woman with Weathermarker earlier. She was lurking around the cafe one day. Her name was Thorncrist. She looked like she was waiting for someone. He saw her later in the cafe with Tamara. Alarm bells clanged in his head and he lurched forward to barge into Weathermarker's conversation. He stopped abruptly in shock as he stood not three feet away from Tamara Fieldmarsh in a passionate embrace with Fillip Weathermarker.

Jealousy overtook him with such force Brolin clenched his fists reactively. With intense effort, he pushed his emotions into the background, remembering Tamara was a pawn in a plan involving Weathermarker and the other woman, he was sure.

"I wondered if you were coming back to me, darling!" A high-pitched voice reached him from behind: Dyva. He knew Weathermarker and Tamara heard her and heard a low intake of breath....most likely from Tamara. A scuffle behind the bushes told him they had pulled apart and moved away. He growled before turning around.

"Vale?" A small hand tugged his tunic sleeve.

"Dyva, forgive me for not letting you know I had returned," he said insincerely...to her notice. She frowned at him.

"Come with me! We'll join the younglings in their sport!" She pursed her lips together while attempting to drag him into the same bushes recently vacated.

"Oh...I don't know, Dyva. I-" He heard another gasp, but it wasn't from Dyva.

"Oh, my god!" He heard someone whisper. He heard a frantic scratch of movement nearby and the beautiful glowing face of Tamara Fieldmarsh peered around the tall column of greenery before him. His heart lept in his chest as her wide-eyed gaze landed on him. His heart in his eyes, and soul in his arms, he reached for her as she took a frantic step toward him.

"I've been looking for you! I have to tell you something-" Her frightened whisper was cut off by Weathermarker laughing loudly and pulling her away forcefully and Dyva grabbing his arm in a vice grip and pulling *him* away. Angry and frightened for Tamara, he pushed Dyva aside and darted around the bushes to get to Tamara. The spot she stood in only a moment ago was empty. He charged in the direction he believed Weathermarker took her. However, after several minutes of re-tracing his steps, he saw neither Weathermarker, Thorncrist, nor Tamara.

I've been looking for you. I need to tell you something.

I need to tell you something, too, Tamara Fieldmarsh.

* * *

The next morning, Vale Brolin awoke to the worst news of his current life.

Nord stood in his room, pulling back the curtains and holding his morning coffee on a tray instead of his houseman. He handed him the warm mug.

"What the devil, Nord?" Brolin said blearily as he took it.

"Good morning, sir. I regret to tell you that Tamara Fieldmarsh has been arrested for treason."

Brolin threw the mug, splashing the dark brown liquid against the wall.

V

Tamara Fieldmarsh

Chapter Seven

As Vale Brolin spoke to the emperor and traveled over the border into enemy lands, Tamara Fieldmarsh worried, feared, and paced. What could she do? An unknown enemy agent served among them all on this ship! She squeezed her eyes shut multiple times trying to discern some familiarity into the voice she heard. Was it a man? Was it a woman? The voice was low and quiet. It was too difficult to tell! Should she tell Fillip to see if he knew anything? She wasn't sure about that idea. She didn't completely feel at ease with him. He also had a pattern of spilling secrets. She would have to take solace because Brolin was off the ship and safe from the spy for now. She supposed she would have to be patient until they returned to base to take action.

The return trip took three days. The atmosphere aboard was even more informal than it was at take-off. She found Fillip in her engine room often, and once or twice she went to seek him out when her nerves got the better of her. Sometimes, when she sensed Fillip's growing infatuation with her, she tried to put some distance between them. Somehow, he got around her defenses. He was just so insistent. Vessmin was no company, being so unsure of herself, and slightly unpleasant with Tamara.

It was with relief that Tamara disembarked the *Victoria*. She planned to leave her things in her room and then try to get a message to Brolin.

"Hey!"

Tamara turned around as she walked down the path toward the quadrant housing the barracks. Fillip bounded after her with his bags. She fought down a groan as she spied his beaming face. She said nothing, waiting.

"Hey, why didn't you wait for me?" He said, slowing down as he reached her.

"I didn't hear you ask me to wait for you," she replied, wishing he wouldn't grab her arm that way. She increased her walking speed to disguise the way she pulled her arm from his grasp.

"You know, I can't figure you out," Fillip said.

"What do you mean?"

"I mean we got along really well on the ship. I figured you and I would be an item by now, but you just leave saying nothing to me?"

Tamara, never failing to feel thrown off by his manner, stopped mid-stride and looked up at him askance, "You what? Why? How? Just because we've become...friendlier?"

"Well, yeah! I mean, I like *you*, so...it makes sense."

"But it *doesn't*, Fillip," Tamara's hands flapped around helplessly, "people can simply be friends for the rest of their lives, you know. People do it all the time!"

"Not me."

She stood before him trying to see into his mind and his motivations. There was something off with Fillip Weathermarker.

"I always get what I want. I want you, so..." Fillip's eyes bored back into hers. Dark. Impassive.

Tamara's heart skipped a beat. Not in pleasure. She felt warning tingles light up the back of her neck. A sudden smile flashed across Fillip's face and he laughed.

"You should see your face. I think you thought I was a rapist for a second."

"Just don't say things like that. It's not that pleasant to hear," she said, frowning. She started off toward her barracks again.

"What? I thought you women loved to hear that sort of thing from men!" He said.

I'd love to hear that from a certain man, she thought. She said nothing to Fillip, and he trotted beside her quiet for once.

"Yoohooo!" a voice called behind them. She recognized Thorncrist's voice and turned to greet her.

"Hello!" She said, smiling at the exuberant woman. She expected Fillip to introduce himself in the usual overbearing, overtly flirtatious manner he had, but he said nothing.

Thorncrist gave her a tight hug, "I saw the ship as it returned to base! I was so surprised! Your ship wasn't due for return for several more weeks, right?"

Tamara agreed and chatted amicably with her friend as they walked toward the barracks. Curiously, Fillip excused himself and wandered off after she half-heartedly introduced him to Thorncrist. She looked after him confused. She wasn't sure she could handle much more of Fillip Weathermarker on land.

After Thorncrist left, Tamara sat down in the hard chair by the window to think. How was she going to talk to Major Brolin without someone reporting her? Could she get a message to him? She would have to try that. But how did she know someone wouldn't see her message before it got to him? Paranoia took over, and she went for a walk to clear her mind.

As Tamara walked and thought, she realized her steps took her in the pond's direction. She guessed the urgency she felt guided her there since it was one spot she spent time with Brolin. Tamara sighed. Even in his absence he influenced her.

She sat on a bench opposite the tea stand and let the sounds of voices wash over her. A tap on her shoulder startled her.

"Is it all right if I sit here as well?" A soft voice asked.

Tamara spluttered an apology and moved further to the edge of the bench to make room. The newcomer was an older woman with greying hair pulled back in a loose bun. She wore a full blue pleated skirt with a plain white blouse, and she carried a paper shopping bag. Not sure what to do, Tamara gave a slight smile and looked out across the water.

"Enjoying the day, hm?" The woman asked.

"Yes. It's nice here," she replied.

"Hm, it is," came the pleasant reply.

A minute passed, and Tamara wondered how soon she could excuse herself to find a spot where she could be by herself. Then her companion spoke again,

"May I beg you to be wary of Corporal Thorncrist? Or would you consider that much too impudent seeing as she is a dear friend of yours?"

Tamara's mouth dropped open as her head jerked around to goggle the woman beside her.

"Ex-excuse me?" She exclaimed.

"I know, I know. This is out of the blue and... you have no reason to distrust your friend."

Tamara couldn't figure out what to say first.

"I'm sorry, but...I don't know you, but I know Corporal Thorncrist-"

"Well? Do you know her well?"

Tamara stood up, prepared to walk away, unsure if this woman was insane.

"Stay for just a moment, please."

"I don't stay to hear people speak ill of my friends."

"But *is* she a friend? How did you meet her? Did she come to you?"

Tamara frowned, "Well, yes, but-"

"This makes no sense to you at all, but just remember my words. It will make sense as time goes on." The woman watched Tamara with calm, grey eyes.

Tamara plopped back down onto the bench, "I don't understand all this! Why do I have to be wary of her? Who is she? A spy?" She laughed as she said this, struck by the ridiculousness of this entire conversation. But the woman didn't laugh with her.

"I can't give you such information, but you are in a position close to power and we can't allow anyone to use you for nefarious reasons." The woman said. She patted Tamara on the shoulder before standing and strolling away.

Tamara gaped after the woman in astonishment until she disappeared, then looked around to see if anyone was staring at her. Did she really have this insane conversation? Thorncrist? A *spy?* What an impossible thought! Spies were moody. Secretive. Unfriendly. Thorncrist was none of those things. Tamara brushed off the woman's question about how the two of them met. Thorncrist had said she had heard of her. That's all. Lots of people did. They didn't like her, so they noticed her.

But no one but Thorncrist came to speak to you.

Tamara ignored the old bat. There's no way what she said was true! She returned to her quarters.

The next several days were full of training procedures, classes, check-ins, and appointments to brief the generals about her time on the airship. No one she served with on the airship could tell her the reason for the airship's shortened journey. She had her suspicions. Only she and the major alone knew about the sabotage on the ship. Perhaps he told the emperor. It made sense.

Eventually, as time passed, the message she overhead that night on the ship faded into a dream. She was glad she said nothing to anyone, because surely she must have been mad. There was no news about the major, so everything must be fine. She must have misunderstood. The news that everyone was attend a state dinner within a few days proved a welcome thought distraction for a while, but that changed the day of the state dinner.

Tamara, feeling restless, sought out her friends. It felt like weeks since she had time off. She realized she didn't know where Thorncrist bunked, so she went to look for Fillip. He had told her which barracks he lived in at some point, so she headed in that direction. She considered it odd that he didn't seek her out after she and Thorncrist left him the day they returned to base. She felt sure he would have come to her to demand she allow him to be her escort. She shrugged away the thought. She didn't want him to seek her out...did she?

Hands in her pockets, she stood in front of the barracks plaque listing the names of the occupants in the different wings looking for Fillip's surname. Finding it, she marked the corresponding barracks number and strolled along the paved walk. She allowed her eyes to roam around the structure, noting the recruits standing around outside the lawn, or above on the balconies, speaking to friends, or waiting out the day. She raised a hand when she saw Fillip standing out on one balcony, but he was looking away from her in the opposite direction. Tamara followed his line of sight to the form of a young woman hurrying away from her ahead. Tamara recognized her.

"Thorncrist! Thorncrist!" she shouted to the woman, pleased to have found her.

Thorncrist turned around, an expression of surprise on her face, "...Oh....Fieldmarsh. Hi." She said, a noticeable lack of her usual upbeat friendliness in her demeanor. Tamara's feet slowed, unsure of her welcome.

"I...I didn't know you lived here, too. I was looking for both of you today."

Thorncrist's face seemed to undergo a considerable reigning in of emotions as she stood waiting for Tamara's approach. Tamara at once wanted to turn around and leave. She felt uncomfortable and unwelcome.

"Oh, I don't live here. I'm on the other side of the base."

"So...you and Fillip...you're here to see him, then?"

"I didn't know he lived here," Thorncrist said, but her eyes flicked up and over to the spot Tamara had seen Fillip standing a moment ago. She felt an odd tingle at the back of her neck.

"But," Thorncrist continued, franticly, "I just realized this morning he lived here. I was here seeing someone else."

Tamara nodded wordlessly.

"A shipmate," Thorncrist added.

"Oh."

They stood staring at each other awkwardly. Tamara, annoyed with the old woman and her words, and annoyed at her willingness to believe something bad about someone who had befriended her without strings attached, forced a bright smile.

"Well, I'm just out for the day. Maybe I'll see you at the dinner tonight." She turned around to continue her walk to Fillip's building. She looked up, surprised to see Fillip still standing on the balcony. He watched her approach, but she couldn't read his expression from this far away. She raised a hand in a tentative wave. He returned her greeting with a brief nod.

"Wait!"

It was her turn to stand irresolute to wait for Thorncrist to catch up to her. Her face once again wore the familiar bright, cheeriness Tamara knew.

"Why don't we all hang out today! It's a Saturday and I have nothing else on the agenda til tonight!" She said, her voice carrying and bouncing off the brick of the barracks. She linked arms with Tamara and looked up with a vague expression. Tamara too looked up, and saw Fillip looking down at them both.

Tamara shrugged, "Ok. You guys haven't actually really met except for that one time."

Tamara deemed the meeting the oddest she had ever experienced. Fillip acted strange. Thorncrist forced cheeriness. They stood in the interim hallway of the barracks—the opposite sex not allowed in each other's rooms—and made small talk. She felt the twinges of regret about her impulsiveness.

"Let's go to the cafe," she blurted, "All I had for breakfast was a cup of tea."

She turned around, not waiting to see if her companions agreed. All she wanted was a different focal point. Perhaps food would make them relax.

"You two go on," Thorncrist said behind her, "I'll catch up. I have to drop something off at my room."

She heard Fillip fall into step beside her and they walked to the cafe without a word.

They entered the crowded cafe and waited in line at the buffet, most people being there for the low prices at the end of the breakfast period. As she moved along the line, choosing items to add to her plate, she thought about Brolin, again worried about his safety. Why hadn't she seen him on the base at all? She listened to Fillip make suggestions about what she should try. She thought about Thorncrist. It was ridiculous that anyone could think she was a spy. Spies were secretive, and odd. Thorncrist was friendly. Even in her work with the smugglers, she didn't think a spy would be audacious enough to work in the Emperor's defense forces. Would anyone be so foolish? She decided that later she would see if Fillip knew anything about spies on the base without letting on about what she heard about Thorncrist.

Thorncrist joined them a short while later. As they sat, Fillip seemed to relax, and he began telling silly jokes. To her surprise, Tamara laughed helplessly several times. Why couldn't he always be charming and funny like this? Why couldn't he just be easygoing?

"This is why I want you to be my girl. When you laugh, your beauty just blows me away. Everyone will stare at us tonight."

Tamara sighed, "Gods. Fillip. Please...I-"

Thorncrist looked back and forth between Tamara and Fillip, "Wait... you guys? You guys are an *item*?!"

Fillip looked startled. His face turned red. His mouth opened and closed a few times.

"No. We're not." Tamara mumbled, all taste for the day leaving her.

Thorncrist looked scandalized as she stared at Fillip. The young man avoided Thorncrist's gaze and fidgeted. Tamara stared at the both of them in confusion. Why was Thorncrist so upset? Was that what she was? She never knew Fillip to experience embarrassment over anything. However, he was suffering from embarrassment now, certainly!

This day turned out to be too strange.

"Well, I'm ready to go," She said, standing up. As she did so, she looked over to the tables reserved for the upper ranks, wondering again where Major Vale Brolin could be. For the second time that day, she left her companions without concern over whether they followed her. A thought formed at the back of her mind, a thought that wondered if Thorncrist and Fillip knew each other. Tamara wondered if they pretended not to know each other for her benefit. That cursed old woman! This was her fault! For the first time in a long time, she wished she had never let those men into her hangar. She wished she had never left college to pursue her love of mechanics. She wished she obeyed her parents and became a doctor the way they wanted.

Her mind raced, and she hardly noticed Thorncrist's arm link with hers, or Fillip's odd brief kiss on her cheek.

Tamara desperately wanted to leave this base.

She surprised Thorncrist and Fillip by telling them she needed to shop for a dress for the night instead of hanging out with them until evening. Depression hounded her while she was with them, making it necessary for her to get some distance from them. Her thoughts ran around her head in a muddled mess. She hadn't planned to wear a fresh dress, planning instead to wear the one she wore at the last one. She needed an excuse to get away, and she found it.

* * *

Having had trouble finding the right dress in the shops, Tamara returned to the base later than she intended. As a result, she had to race to the ballroom through empty pathways while the enormous bell tower rang the hour. She felt grimy and out of sorts from dressing hurriedly and wrangling her hair into a semi-presentable coif. She raced with the train of her dress looped over her arm hoping she wouldn't receive a reprimand for being half an hour late. The crackling blue dress she wore reminded her of the super hot blue fires in the gunsmith's near home (how she missed home). As she ran, her mind sorted through her memories of Fillip's and the major's reactions to her when she wore the red dress. Would reactions to this one be the same? And where *was* the major? She needed to see him!

The walking paths from offices, barracks, and other buildings were all but empty since the administration mandated everyone who lived on the base to the dance. A few times she frowned curiously at a glimpse of someone slipping into a building just before she passed. Odd. She twisted around, unease slipping down her back. Looking around, she wondered if people were avoiding being seen. No one spoke. No one showed. She continued down the lane.

No one waited outside. She hurried in.

All was quiet as the voice of the base commander droned on inside beyond the curtain. The major domo frowned at her disapprovingly as she passed through the door. He pushed her urgently into the room where the dinner was being held. Eyes followed her as she picked her way to her assigned table. She avoided the stares, sitting gratefully in her chair, waiting for everyone to stop looking at her. Looking around as surreptitiously as she could, Tamara recognized a few recruits sitting at her table, but no one with whom she had ever had a conversation.

The man sitting across from her stared at her with blatant admiration. She noticed a motion at a table nearby and saw Fillip waving to catch her attention. Without waiting for acknowledgement, he moved around her table, whispered to the person sitting to her right and dropped into the seat they vacated.

"You look a treat tonight. Even more drop-dead gorgeous than in the red dress. Be mine!" He whispered, his voice carrying in the silence.

"Shh!" She hissed, feeling equal parts gratified and annoyed.

She looked around the room hoping to see Brolin sitting with the other high-rankers. But Fillip grabbed her hand and tugged it to his lap interrupting her perusal. She tried to pull her hand away, but he held it with both hands, grinning into her face mischievously.

"Fillip!" She hissed.

"You're mine tonight, even if you're not tomorrow."

Knowing that fighting his advances would serve only to increase his ardor, she stilled and waited for the right time to move away from him. Half-hearted applause filled the room as the speaker finished his speech and the dinner commenced.

"Fillip, I-"

"Don't reject me *again*, Fieldmarsh. Not tonight." Fillip wheedled.

"Fillip, I need to ask you something. I'm *serious*."

He allowed her to remove her hand and leaned in to listen to her hushed voice as the attendees chattered and moved about the tables to greet friends.

"I...," she took a deep breath, sure he would laugh her to derision once he heard her out. She took the plunge, "I need to talk to you about...," Still believing herself to be acting ridiculous, she took a different tack, "What do you know about espionage?"

Fillip watched her face as emotions flitted across it. He sat rock still. Finally, he spoke, his voice lowered, "Espionage?"

"Yes. I've heard some things."

"About *me*?" He asked, his face going pale.

"What, you? No. Someone else."

"Who?"

"I don't want to say. I just want to know if something that like could happen here at the base. I didn't think it was likely."

Fillip sat back and regarded her thoughtfully. Tamara was impatient, wondering if he knew something and he was hiding it. Did he know something, too?

He nodded slowly, observing her, "I know for a fact it's happening here." He sat still, giving Tamara the impression of a snake gauging its prey. "You'll never guess," he continued, "who I think the spy is."

Tamara's eyes narrowed, believing he was about to do as he usually did and pretend to know more than he did.

"If you know something, you're duty bound to report it." She said.

"I couldn't do that. They wouldn't believe me."

"Why not?!"

"Because he's a high-ranking individual."

Tamara looked at him surprised. She didn't expect him to say the spy was male, nor did she expect him to say it was someone of rank!

"*Who*?!" She hissed.

"I don't know if I should tell you. You're pretty close to him."

"What? I don't know anyone who ranks us who could be a *spy*! You're full of-"

"It's Brolin." Fillip hissed.

"Now I *know* you're just talking out of your arse!"

"How crass you are! It's why he left the ship! He always disappears on secret trips that no one knows anything about! Someone in the aircraft tower told a bunk mate of mine he has a special light aircraft he uses that they allow no one to discuss!"

"Of, course, you idiot, he's most likely on missions for the emperor. "

Fillip's eyes grew cold and hard, but he smiled, charmingly. "Let's dance," he said as he stood. Tamara was sure her barb caused the change in her demeanor.

"I'm sorry, Fillip. I shouldn't have said that. It's just that I can't believe Brolin is a turncoat."

Fillip merely looked down at her as he stood beside her chair, his eyes moving over her face rapidly. The old feeling that Fillip wasn't quite right crept over her again.

"I...I don't think I want to dance...Fillip," she mumbled, turning to look out over the crowded dance floor. She the couples who tried to disguise their amorous advances and those who slipped out of the various doors of the ballroom.

"Just one dance…to say farewell."

Tamara's eyes jerked back to Fillip's face in surprise, "Farewell?"

"Perhaps." He said, not providing more information. His eyes remained cold and his smile was tight and drawn.

Tamara, remembering his grip of before, wanted to see if she could find out what was on his mind, or to slip away unnoticed later.

"Okay, Fillip. I'll dance for a little while."

The music playing was mostly the same as the previous state dinner, there being little imagination in the minds of the military goodwill committee. Tamara wished for the music she heard on the new 24-hour classical music station from her little wireless. She wished for a tall, powerful body to move her sensuously across the dance floor. Fillip danced silently, his eyes thoughtful, darting here and there whenever she dared look up at him.

They remained on the dance floor for several musical selections, Fillip heedlessly keeping her well within his grip and remaining on the dance floor. Finally, begging a break, she moved to the refreshment table, hoping to lose him in the crowd. She was beginning to feel alarmed by Fillip Weathermarker. As she sensed his approach, without turning to meet him, she raised a hand in delight, shouted 'hello' and rushed happily out the ballroom and through the hall of windows to the garden in the back.

Once outside, she dropped her pretense of seeing a friend and slinked into the darker recesses of the garden so she could think. Armed guards stood at the exits, ensuring no one left the area. She watched an amorous couple whisper and gesture as a guard turned away from a little garden gate. She couldn't understand why there was security at a state dinner barring anyone from leaving. Something was going on. Was it about the spy? As she walked around the garden, she thought about Thorncrist…who she hadn't seen all night!

"There you are."

She groaned as she heard Fillip behind her.

"Where's your friend?" He asked blankly.

"She had to go back to… her other friends." Tamara muttered, looking around, searching for anyone else. She didn't see a guard nearby, and she was in the middle of a 'intimacy garden' that was all the rage now in New Victoria. Tiny inner gardens surrounded by tall, shaped shrubs, and shrubby trees, stood within larger gardens, creating the feeling of intimacy and seclusion. She realized no one would be able to see her if Fillip tried anything here.

"So, Fillip," she began, wanting to get control over this odd situation she was in.

He interrupted her, "I just want to say 'I'm sorry', Fieldmarsh." He stared down at her in the mute darkness, the far light of the lane and firelight of the lanterns glittering in his eyes.

"Sorry for what?" She asked, not at all calmed by his statement. Her eyes darted around in the darkness, looking for someone. Anyone.

"Sorry, for everything."

"Fillip, what's going on?! You've been acting strangely all night."

He shook his head, "…I just wish things could have ended differently for us."

Tamara stood frozen for a moment, then she began carefully sliding one foot behind her, and then the other. Fillip moved toward her in a flash and her alarmed yell was smothered beneath his lips. Fillip was kissing her. Passionately. Frozen in shock, Tamara bent painfully backward as he crushed her with the force of his kiss. Her mind blanked. Then, it screamed at her to stop this kiss, to get out of this embrace. Her salvation came in the form of a voice nearby. She pushed at Fillip until he released her.

"Fillip, stop!" She hissed, grunting as she stumbled backward. Tamara lurched out of the intimacy garden, hoping to see whoever had spoken, to grasp them, to keep them by her side for the rest of the night.

Through the bushes, she could see the light from the open door of the ballroom. A nearby lantern shone directly onto the beautiful, chiseled face of Vale Brolin. She gasped. Her heart sang at the sight of his face, and relief that he was alive warmed her body; Fillip Weathermarker existed no more. All that mattered was Vale Brolin. Hurrying around the bushes, she rushed toward him, desperation to speak to him, to touch his face, overcoming her.

"I've been looking for you!" She whispered. Her steps quickened as his arms reached for her.

A boisterous, unhinged laugh erupted behind her, and Fillip jerked her backward into another painful embrace. Tamara yelled in fury, shoving herself away from him. Fillip stumbled backward into the bushes, and a snarl marred his handsome face as he rushed to disentangle himself from the shrubbery. Tamara saw madness in his eyes as they glinted dangerously in the lantern light. Her breath came quickly as she moved backward among the trees and shrubs, keeping an eye on him while looking for the major. Sharp leaves of bushes and trees tugged at her dress and hair slowing her progress.

Under her watchful gaze, Fillip lunged to his feet. Tamara fled, returning to the spot she had seen the major. He was gone. The only thing for her to do was dart back inside the ballroom and try to keep clear of Fillip.

She hurtled to the ladies' coat room once inside. Sitting in one of the resting chairs, she listened idly to the chatter of the ladies who flitted in and out. A young woman she recognized from her training days came in to adjust her rouge, and Tamara sidled up to her.

"Hi. I'm not sure you remember me," she began, wondering if this woman was one who hated her.

"Sure, I remember you. Lieutenant First Class, right?"

Tamara nodded, "Could you do me a favour? I'm in a bit of a predicament."

The woman turned full toward Tamara and looked her up and down, "Are you hiding from someone in here, honey?"

Tamara felt heat rush to her face.

"Don't worry about it. I've had to hide a time or two before. These boys can be awful. What's the favour?"

"Could you tell me if Major Brolin is out there?"

The woman's eyebrows raised to her impossibly red hair, "Is *he* the one you're hiding from? He's every woman's dream! He's chasing *you*? Are you impaired?"

Tamara raised her hands to stop the stream of incredulity from continuing, "I'm hiding from someone else. But I'm looking *for* the major. You understand?"

"Oh, I see. You want me to look for him? Give him a message?"

Relief flooded her, "Yes! Please!"

"What do I get out of it?"

Tamara's heart dropped, "Oh, I...I don't know. It's...terribly important."

"Tell you what, you think about it while I go see if he's out there. What's your name?"

"Fieldmarsh." Tamara answered.

"Fine. I'll be back." The woman left.

Tamara returned to her seat to wait. She fiddled with the flounces on her dress and avoided the curious looks of the women entering and leaving the room. After a while, she felt her messenger decided not to return when she saw the familiar flaming red hair.

"I'm sorry, doll, but he's not here."

Tamara's face fell, "You're sure?"

"Yes, I'm sure. Looked inside and outside. Kept interrupting lovers' trysts in the hall and the gardens. Was kinda fun. I guess you don't owe me nothin' since nothin' happened. Anyway, good luck with whoever is pursuin' you." And with that, she disappeared again.

Tamara slumped against the back of the chair and stayed there until the major domo announced everyone could return to their quarters. She found a group of women from her own barracks and begged them to let her walk with them.

"Sure. You all right, duckie?" One girl asked, concern on her face.

Another woman, linked arms with her and peered into her face.

Tamara nodded, keeping an eye out for Fillip, "Yes, thank you. Just avoiding someone. That's all."

The women giggled.

"I know that feeling! You never get the ones you want, eh?"

The group strolled toward the barracks. The girls were pleasant and once they returned to the barracks, one of the girls suggested they have a drink in Tamara's quarters to help her wind down. Tamara had heard of the moonshine the recruits brewed on campus and was curious about it. A few sips was all she needed before she felt all was well in the world. The girls noted how sleepy she was and left her to rest for the night. Tamara smiled sleepily, a feeling of wellbeing coursing through her.

A few hours later, the emperor's guardsmen kicked down her door to arrest her for treason. Thus wrenching her from a delightful, rosy dream that featured a sensuous dance with the handsome major.

Chapter Eight

Twenty-four hours later, Tamara stood on the steps of the base jail blinking into the sunlight. Tired and dizzy from the lack of sleep and hunger, she descended the steps shakily. She had spent the night full of terror that her time on Earth would end with her being shot by firing squad for treason. She paced the tiny room asking herself over and over what reason they had for believing she committed treason while in His Highness's service. No one spoke to her. No one gave her any information. Then, quite suddenly, the iron door was unlocked and the guard brusquely informed her she was free to go.

"Why was I held here?" She had demanded.

The guard stared passively down the corridor as he stood beside the open door. Tamara grabbed her shoes and tried to jam them on her feet, but the night of pacing caused them to swell, giving her the step-sister complex.

"Am I out on bond? Do I need to see a magistrate?"

"Do you want to leave, Lt. Fieldmarsh?" The guard intoned.

"Yes!"

"Then do so before I just as easily swing the door shut again."

Tamara scurried past him. After several wrong turns down passages that looked identical, she found herself at a series of barred doors that led to the outside. She gave the guard in the cage her name; he looked at his files of releases for the day and opened the next gate. She did the same at the subsequent cages until being essentially locked out without so much as a "Good day, miss."

She stumbled up the steps of her barracks to her room when she reached the barracks, pleased to see that no one was in the building. That or everyone was still asleep. But it was Monday morning. Wasn't it? She couldn't be sure how long she was in locked up.

After a hasty bath, she pulled on a fresh uniform and wolfed down a stale pastry she saved from breakfast a few days ago. She ran out of the barracks to the administrative offices in the headquarters, determined to find the major's office.

Instead of using the front door, she looked for an alley door, hoping to catch someone exiting or entering. As luck would have it, an adolescent office boy was loitering on the steps, playing with a worn deck of cards.

"Don't you have work to do, boy?" She asked, affecting the air of someone in command, and striding up to him quickly.

Startled, the boy jumped up, shoving his cards in a pocket and brushing off his hands.

"I was just taking a break, ma'am. Lost track of time!" He said, saluting.

"Well, open the door for both of us. I don't have all day."

"Yes, ma'am!" He said, pulling a string of keys from his coat pocket and shoving one into the keyhole of the alley door.

"Thanks," she mumbled as she brushed past him, hoping he wouldn't put up a fuss having never seen her before. Would he know she didn't have access to the building? However, the boy grateful not to be reported to his superior, said nothing more to her and hurried down the hall in the opposite direction.

Tamara hurried through the halls, losing her bearings several times. She slowed to a sedate stroll, avoiding the eyes of the people with legitimate business inside. She remembered the first and second times she was here. The second time, she saw Brolin and she assumed he worked in this area. She searched for a name plaque at each hallway. She finally found success on the plague for the third floor offices!

Commander C. Lace-Baggadoor Office Unit 300B

Squadron Commander V. Carmandy Office Unit 301A

Major V. Brolin New Project Control Office Unit 304C

Brig. C. DeMille Defense Force Committee Office Unit 306

She found a separate set of stairs set near the back of the building. She figured using this one, rather than the crowded wide staircase at the front of the building, would allow her to slip around the building unseen and less likely to be questioned on her business here. The carpet on the stairs was a depressing brown and the walls a dull white. Small dirty windows placed above, leaked sunshine in small amounts, making the staircase shadowy. Several deafening squeaks sounded under her boots, causing her heart to thud noisily.

At the top of the stairs, she stood still, listening. Several typewriters *clicked* and *clacked* behind closed doors. She heard an imperative female voice calling to someone in an office. A cabinet drawer scraped further down the hall and a young voice discussed the day's lunch order in another office. Tamara's heart dropped. Anyone could hear *any* and *every* thing! She took the bull by the horns and attempted to walk casually through the hall. The floor answered her attempt by declaring every step she took with a squeak or a thud.

Tamara's hands felt clammy. Brushing them on her trousers, she eyed the plaques on the door and groaned inwardly. It seemed the plaque downstairs only boasted the names and offices of the important building personnel. The hall was long with more offices than she expected! Some doors were open affording the individuals inside with a good view of Tamara the interloper. Suddenly, she realized she was being stupid. No one here knew she *wasn't* supposed to be here.

"Excuse me," she said conversationally to the young man in the fashionable haircut and suspenders who stood over a desk in the next office.

"Yes, Lieutenant? Good morning. May I help you?" He answered pleasantly.

"I fear I've spent a good time trying to find a Major V. Brolin's office. Am I on the correct floor?" She asked, hoping he wouldn't note her nervousness.

"Oh! Yes, it's just down a few more doors."

"I thought I might have ended up in the wrong place. Thank you."

"You're welcome. Good day." He turned away and continued his work.

Tamara continued on her way, but for a moment, she lost her courage.

What would he say to her when he saw her? Would he be glad to see her? Would he still be angry with her? Their parting seemed so long ago! Would he even care anymore? Had he moved on to a new woman? She shrugged away the thought. Tamara tried to plan how she would greet him and what she would say about her news.

Soon she stood staring in consternation at a half-open door to a gloomy office. The window shutters were tightly closed in Vale's office.

"Are you lost Lieutenant?"

Tamara turned to see a woman in a Squadron Commander's uniform standing in front of a desk in the office across from the major's.

"I seem to have made a mistake. I'm here to see the major," Tamara said, her eyes returning to the dark office.

"Oh, I see," the uniformed woman said, stepping toward her, "Yes, I would say there's a mistake. He's off on another one of those trips of his, Lieutenant."

"...another...?" Tamara said, despair closing over her face. She missed him? By a day?

"Yes, he takes them often. You should double check your information with whoever sent you to him. I'm sure you have the wrong day."

"I could swear I was to see him today. Will he return soon?"

"Well, it's possible. His trips vary in length. He left last night according to his houseman who came to retrieve something. I'm sorry you had to come all this way for nothing." With that, she turned away and closed the office door and began speaking to her assistant.

Tamara, rooted to the spot, stared into the dimness of the office and pondered how awful life had become.

* * *

Fifteen minutes later, Tamara rushed around her room, throwing items into a duffle bag. She tried not to think of how this may cost her freedom. She observed the effects of sabotage on a royal airship, overheard an assassination plot against Major Brolin on the same airship, had been told her friend was as good as a spy, someone somewhere set her up as a patsy for treasonous activities, and now she was going AWOL. Tamara could see no other way to move forward. Either Major Brolin would die, or she would… in the firing squad. Her heart shuddered at the thought of him dying. Yes, her heart shuddered at the thought of her death, but somehow, this wasn't so important.

She felt a million years older. She felt a million years stronger. Half-a year ago, she thought working among the fringes of society was true life. Her life was her own! No one could tell her what to do or when to do it! Today, as she shoved items into a duffel bag, she realized, authentic life was the willingness to sacrifice your own so someone else would live. She was willingly breaking a law in the emperor's service to save Major Brolin's life.

Crossing the room to the back window, she raised the sash and leaned out. The sound of faraway voices flitted to her through the air. Birdsong ebbed and flowed. However, no one was in sight. Tamara knew she was taking a huge risk, but she darted back to her cot and raced back to the window. After taking one last glance around, she shoved the duffel bag out of the window, hoping no one noticed in the rooms below hers. The bag landed in the bushes below with a *whomp!* Tamara withdrew into the room, lowered the sash and lay on her cot to nap.

* * *

When she opened her eyes again, the room was inky. She listened hard for the sounds of movement in the hall, outside her window. Silence. She sat up quickly, feeling for matches on the table beside her bed. She didn't expect to sleep so long. Finding the book of matches, she struck one on the flint and held the lit match to the wick of the lamp. The room glowed with orange light. She quickly turned down the wick, hoping no one could see a glimmer of light below the door or through the shutters.

She looked at her old pocket watch. It was nearly midnight. She had slept too long! She took a hasty glance around the room. She shouldn't leave it too tidy, although heaven knows she had very little. If it looked like she left on a planned absence, the law would be on her tail quicker than if it looked like she was just out for too long. She assumed. Sighing, she turned down the wick more, leaving things almost too dark to see and tiptoed to the window.

She held her breath as she raised the sash once more. No squeaks. Things are inordinately louder at night, and it petrified her that any noise she made would be heard and noticed as suspicious by anyone below or beside her. She carefully threw her legs over the window ledge, tensing her muscles against falling. The night was pitch black and the lane lamps extinguished. Her heart pounded. Clammy hands slipped as she extended her legs down the wall and turned around to lean on the window ledge with her forearms. Breathing tensely, she reached up to pull the window closed. Then, she let go and landed in the bushes below her. Tears pricked her eyes as the pain from the sharp branches and leaves plunged themselves into her skin. Her mind screamed. Breathing hard, she moved gingerly. It hurt, but she felt she hadn't broken any bones. Whimpering, she felt around for the duffel bag. Fear clutched her heart when she didn't find it.

"Oh, no! Oh, no!" She whispered frantically under her breath. Hands rustled the rough branches and limbs, pointy leaves pricked her fingers. Rough fabric met her searching hands, and she almost yelped with relief. Tamara threw the duffel over her shoulder, tightening the strap, and vaulted into the night.

* * *

Tamara snuck behind her old garage, ensuring no one was around to see her. Only the criminals and malcontents were out at this time of night, making it the worst time for Tamara to except not to be seen. She stashed her bag in some trash piled up in the alley by a restaurant. The owner was still inside whistling to himself, readying supplies and cleaning up before the day began in a few hours. Abstractedly, she wondered how the man did it. It must be a horribly constrictive life living a life around one place forever until one died.

She moved past it and scurried further into the alley, keeping an eye out for men sleeping rough and other belligerent and drunk members of low society. The smell was horrible and it was with relief that she emerged on the other side of the alley to cut down to the street behind her old rented hangar.

Darting across the street before a group of men standing further down in a group saw her, she ran silently to the row of hangars. Behind her hangar sat a smaller metal building she used to store odds and ends she didn't want inside. She wondered if the landlord had tried to rent it out in her absence. She was paid up for the year and expected to be able to return to clear it out. Her departure for training was abrupt and limited her time to sell all her things.

Pulling out her key, she stuck it into the padlock by feel—alleys not graced with the presence of streetlights. The pale moonlight provided some illumination. Finally, she had the padlock opened. She pulled the aluminium door open and squinted in the darkness. She could see the slight outline of her hoverbike. She sighed with relief. She rummaged around for the petrol can and poured what was left in into the hoverbike tank. Pulling the bike out of the little shed, she tested the engine. It roared to life. She closed and locked the padlock, hurrying to mount the bike to ride out of the alley before someone found her here. Then she was off.

She roared through the alleys, left and right and then took the path to reach the travelers road at the end of town. When she made it, she sighed with relief. She knew she wasn't completely out of trouble. It was possible someone saw her go and reported her. She revved the engine and roared off into the night.

The terrain before the hover bike bounced and swayed in the light of its headlamp. Chill winds played with edges of the kerchief tied over her nose and mouth. Her forehead grew cold in the space above the goggles and below the leather helmet shoved over her burgeoning curls. Beneath the thick woolen insert of the leather riding jacket, Tamara's heart pounded and thudded. She dared not look back. Surely no one had detected her absence as yet. She calculated she had been off the base for four hours. She hoped no one would assume she was AWOL until the next evening. By then, she would be at her destination. She felt alone and vulnerable as the hover bike sped in the chilly dawn hours. The terrain spread open and bare before the mountains. Tamara hunkered down on the bank and shifted to make herself comfortable. She was in for a very long, dangerous ride.

* * *

Noticing the sky brightening just a bit on the horizon, Tamara felt safe. Staring straight ahead, not looking back for the entire ride away from the base kept her anxiety at bay. Now, feeling she would reach her destination safely, she took a glance back. She was fine. She would make it. She took another look and her hover bike swerved to the left. She righted herself quickly, breathing hard. Someone was behind her. Whoever it was stayed far back enough to escape recognition. It couldn't be the base guards already!

Eyeing the petrol level gauge, Tamara squeezed the accelerator and felt the hover bike pull forward. She would run out of petrol at this rate! After several minutes of increased speed, she risked another glance backward. The shadowy rider remained at the edges of detection. Tamara gritted her teeth and squeezed the accelerator once more. The engine vibrations sparked her hands and travelled up her arms. She would not be taken this close to her destination! Tamara lowered herself til her torso touched the instrument panel and her nose touched the plate glass of the wind shield in front of her. She heard nothing. Thought nothing. The sun rose higher by degrees as Tamara Fieldmarsh and her unknown pursuant raced against time and speed.

The tense chase lasted for several more miles. To Tamara's consternation, her pursuer did not give up. Yet he didn't gain and he didn't lose.

Immense relief flowed over her at the sight of houses dotting the landscape. The bare, sandy brown of the interim desert lands grew more fruitful in sight. Greens became darker and more emerald. She saw more foliage. More greenery and more homes meant a nearby city. Then, without warning, a dip in the road revealed a road travelling down into a luscious, colourful valley lit up by the morning sun! She made it to the emperor's city at last! She tossed one last look over her shoulder. Bolstered by the nearness of more people and buildings, Tamara's brow furrowed in defiance and she sped down the mountain road into the city.

She could see the palace set in the northwest quadrant of the city from here. She quickly mapped out the way there through the slums of the city, into the middle-class neighborhoods and finally into the richer suburbs nearest the palace. Once she descended into the city, her bearings deserted her. Tall buildings blocked out the sun and further east, the mountain range seemed to keep part of the city in pre-dawn darkness. How did she think she could lose her pursuer easily in a city where only the marketers had risen? She eased up on the accelerator once the streets became narrower, shorter, and ripe for collision. Should she leave the bike and run to the palace on foot? She would lose precious time and possibly end up in the clutches of whoever chased her! No, she had to stay on the bike for as long as she could. She took left turns when she glimpsed the gleaming towers of the palace.

Finally, she felt alone on the streets of the city. She may not have outrun her pursuer, but she hoped she put enough distance between them to get her to the palace before they arrested her! Once she reached the richest neighborhood of the city, she slowed, knowing patrols and paranoid dignitaries kept watch for persons who didn't belong.

She saw milkmen delivering bottles of milk, delivery boys from grocers scurrying through side alleys to deliver the day's orders to the cooks of the wealthiest houses. Young menservants stood staring agog at the rider of the hover bike. The machines weren't common here, horses remaining the chosen transport. Tamara knew she needed to make it to the palace before word of a machine rider spread to herald her arrival.

Finally, she passed a well-kept road leading into a manicured tree-lined lane. A towering iron gate, gleaming in the early morning sun stood just beyond. The palace! Tamara cringed. How else did she expect an entrance to the palace to be? She looked for a disused alley, somewhere she could hide the bike.

Spying a mansion with a lane leading to the road she sat on, she noticed a work shed on the property with scrap lumber and old rusting farm equipment built up around it. She put the hover bike into the lowest gear and crept the bike up to the shed. Stashing her duffel bag beside it, she covered the hover bike hastily with light materials and scraps of heavy burlap cloth. She would return for it later if she could. Then, she scampered across the road to the lane leading to the towering gate.

She crouched close to the ground, peering around the grounds before the stone wall and iron gate. The morning was pleasantly cool. Dew lent a pleasant scent to the air. The trees held on to their shadows in the early morning, and Tamara hugged the ground as she crept closer to the tall stone wall. It was strange being here as a deserter on a strange mission. Nothing about her surroundings suggested intrigue and espionage in the emperor's defense force. The day seemed perfectly normal.

When she reached the wall, she crept over to the iron gate. Lying flat on her belly to peer through the iron bars. No movement. How secure was the emperor's palace that no one considered a patrolling guard on the grounds? The grounds housed a series of outbuildings with covered walkways leading through a garden to the much larger palace in the center.

Where does a Nobody enter the palace, she asked herself.

She stood halfway, trying to find the primary gate to the palace when she spied movement at the corner of her eye. Thinking a small animal was searching for its breakfast, she turned to see. A figure stood in the shadows of a tree further down the lane. Tamara froze. Also clad in riding goggles, helmet, jacket and boots, the shadowy figure didn't move as it watched her. She knew without a doubt *this* was her night ride pursuer.

Not stopping to think about what she was doing, she scaled the gate, slipping twice, and propelled herself over the top before dropping painfully to the other side.

"Hey! You!" She heard a commanding voice call to her.

Aargh! I assumed because I couldn't see them they weren't there!

Fright fueled her flight to the cottage-like outbuilding nearest her, praying someone who wouldn't turn her away was inside. Shouts erupted on the ground and she lowered herself closer to the ground for aerodynamics and sprinted *past* the cottage and further into the garden surrounding the palace. Her breath was strained and shallow in her ears. This behavior was bound to get her shot, and she heard the furious voices behind her tell her so. She couldn't stop now. She had to take her chances.

Tamara vaulted small bushes, circumvented fish ponds, toppled over low stone walls, and zigzagged through flowering trees and trellises. Her steps faltered as she felt her strength ebbing. Her chest hurt with the pain of exertion.

She reached a circular inner garden before a tall, golden door, when it swung open. A tall, bearded man in crisp, flowered robes stepped out of the door, held up a hand, and uttered a single command, "Stop!"

Rocks and pebbles sprayed from beneath Tamara's feet as she skidded across a rock path. She slid to the ground and stared up at the man before her.

Thundering footsteps vibrated the ground as all of her pursuers converged upon her.

"Who are you, young man?" Asked the man before the golden door, "Why would you attempt so dangerous a stunt when you can see how close you've come to death?"

"I...," Tamara choked on air. "I made it...this far...!" she wheezed.

The man's eyebrows rose, "You're a woman?"

Tamara coughed up a lung there among the pebbles, "All my life."

"And are you an assassin?" He asked, odd humor creeping into his voice.

Breathless and with no more tolerance for sharp wit, Tamara lay back on the pebbles, closed her eyes and answered, "No...I'm trying to stop one..."

"...stop one..."

"Yes," she gasped, "My captain. Major Brolin...someone trying to...kill him...!"

Silence met her declaration. She opened her eyes and stared at the mugs of the stony-faced guards. They looked terrifyingly ready to kill her. She closed her eyes again.

"Bring her in," The man intoned.

Rough hands—made rougher by the chase Tamara took them on—grabbed her shoulders and legs. The guards moved in unison to carry her into the palace.

"Okay! Okay, I can walk. Just…*choke*…give me a minute," Tamara said, pushing them off her and leaning forward with her hands on her knees, wheezing.

"Are you an asthmatic, young lady?"

"No…I just…it's more exercise than I've ever needed….running for my life…" she said, righting herself slowly. She slowed her breathing and stood with her eyes closed, letting the world calm. She made it to the palace. She actually made it. She didn't die.

Tamara held out her hands so the guards could see she held no weapons and walked toward the golden door.

"What is your name?" the man asked her.

"I am Tamara Fieldmarsh, Lieutenant First Class in the emperor's defense force."

"Ah. I am Felix de Maldane. I am considered the major domo of Emperor Sylvanus' household."

"Why are you letting me in?" Tamara asked, wary of the invitation.

"Let's just say I know of you. And Major Brolin is a close friend of the palace."

Tamara blinked and her hands dropped to her sides, but at a suppressed growl from a guard behind her, she raised them again and continued up to the golden door.

de Maldane turned to lead her into the palace and as Tamara entered, her eyes widened. She was an absolute fool. Guards, five men deep, stood just inside the door, weapons raised and aimed at…*her*.

de Maldane turned to look at her, "You wouldn't have succeeded if you *were* an assassin, young woman. You were very foolish. However, your heart and determination are a credit to you. You placed yourself in grave danger to save another. If I had not exited the doors to speak to you, you would have died there in the palace garden and no one outside of this palace would have ever heard of it. It wouldn't be the first time." He turned away to continue down the magnificent hall. The understanding of the magnitude of her stupidity overwhelmed her, and she swayed momentarily.

"In here, Miss," de Maldane said with an arm outstretched toward an open door off the main hall.

Tamara peeked in, hands still up in a show of surrender. The plushest of couches and armchairs, the poshest of tables and wall coverings, the plummiest of rugs and carpets graced the room. She walked inside slowly, unsure of why she was in here.

"Sit anywhere."

Tamara made a beeline for the overstuffed sofa in the center of the room and felt her eyes close immediately as the exhaustion of her journey caught up with her.

"Er, not just yet, Miss. You need to explain yourself." de Maldane glided into the room and seated himself across from her in a delicate white and gold armchair.

Tamara's eyes shot open, "Oh, yes. Yes, of course. I'm just exhausted, you understand."

"Tell me all," the major domo said, a sympathetic expression on his face.

Tamara unburdened herself. She had held secrets for several weeks and midway of the telling; she wondered if she was making a mistake. What if she couldn't trust de Maldane? Who *could* she trust? She suddenly felt more foolish than before. She was a former engine tamer who aided smugglers who ended up forced to serve in the emperor's defense force in exchange for a prison sentence. She was the daughter of doctors. She held no formal education herself. She wasn't wealthy. There was no reason for de Maldane to keep her here at the palace. He could turn her away and she would resign herself to prison for desertion.

"And you wished an audience with the emperor to tell him your concerns," he said when she completed her tale.

"I…I know it was stupid of me. I assumed too much for my rank. I…I don't know why I did."

"You're in love with the dear major…aren't you?" de Maldane asked, a knowing tone in his voice.

At his words, tears shoved their way up through Tamara's throat, choking her on their way to force themselves from her eyes. Not trusting herself not to cry, Tamara gripped the cushions of the sofa and stared hard at de Maldane.

Not forestalled by her lack of vocal confirmation, de Maldane continued, "You are a recent recruit in the emperor's defense force. You have served less than a year in rank. Your service with Major Brolin has not been lengthy, nor particularly close. There is absolutely no reason anyone in so distant a working relationship should risk prison, and/or death for the major...unless love was in the way."

She stared at the major domo in fright. He was canny. He was candid. He seemed *all-knowing*!

"I-I don't! I couldn't...!" Tamara coughed.

"Don't feel so betrayed, Lieutenant. The major manages to create slaves of his admirers due to no genuine effort on his own. I once fancied *myself* in love with him on one occasion," he stood languidly and crossed to the door of the room, "it's simply who he is. You should not be ashamed to join the many who...fall at his feet." The door opened at the tapping of his finger and he turned back to face her, his robes trailing behind him delicately, "Stay here and rest. I'll have a few dishes brought to you. I shall return in an hour. Do not leave or you will find the guards interested in you once again."

* * *

"Well. You gave me a chase, didn't ya?"

Tamara jerked awake and squawked when she saw the man in riding goggles, leather helmet, and jacket bending over her. Her night ride pursuer! She pushed herself away from him, but she was already at the end of the sofa. Desperately, she felt for her belt...no knife! How did he get in here? Where were the guards? Tamara scrambled over the edge of the sofa and tumbled to the floor. Her breath came ragged and her heart felt ready to burst from her chest. She moved to keep the sofa between her and her assailant.

"Ah, Scolder. You have arrived."

"Boss," her pursuer said pleasantly as he turned to greet the major domo

156

who entered the room behind him.

Tamara, on the ground and startled beyond reason, struggled to stand quickly.

"He…! This man chased me all night!" Tamara blurted as she eyed the unknown man and edged nearer to de Maldane.

"You're fookin' right, I did!" the man said, in a heavy East World accent, "Gave me a right headache keeping up with you."

de Maldane stood watching the two of them with little expression. Tamara faltered once again, confusion wracking her mind.

"I'm so confused…," she breathed, leaning against the sofa. Weariness and sleep deprivation weakening her.

"I tell you, someone would have my hide if I lost ya and someone killed ya without me bein' around to stop it! I won't have it on ma record!" He walked around in a wolfman manner, bowlegged, arms waving constantly.

"Aye, he would." de Maldane agreed, then he turned to Tamara, "I've come to tell you that the emperor has agreed to meet with you, but not until the afternoon. I'll have a servant take you to a temporary room."

The relief and exhaustion overcame Tamara Fieldmarsh and this time, she cried.

Chapter Nine

After a full breakfast and a nap, de Maldane summoned her to her meeting with Emperor Sylvanus. She brushed at the wrinkles in her uniform, regretting the decision to leave her duffel behind with the hoverbike. She wondered if anyone had found it and sold it yet.

This part of the palace was cool in colour scheme and in temperature. A constant breeze refreshed her. Low ceilings and reflected light from windows set off and away from view of the hall made her feel secure.

She trailed behind de Maldane, flanked on either side by hypervigilant guards. She felt new appreciation for security in the palace. Anyone could be lulled into a false sense of security...until they reached he inner walls of the palace.

After multiple twists and turns that made Tamara dizzy and confused (which she suspected was another security ruse), they reached the hall to the emperor's quarters. The guards at her side stepped back to allow two guards in different uniforms to join their little group and escort them to the door. Wow. Choreography.

de Maldane stopped at the door and stepped aside.

"I go no further," he said, putting out a hand to gesture her to continue through the doors.

She nodded and stepped foot into the throne room.

The room was so peaceful. It was *thick* with peacefulness. The room was smaller than she had imagined. In fact, it was rather modest and humble. It was also dim. Across from her was a wall of windows with white sheer curtains drawn all the way across, filtering the light into a type of foggy shadow within the room. One large golden chair stood in the middle of the room, halfway between the door and windows. No one sat in the chair. Guards stood at different intervals against the walls on either side of the chair, as well as behind her at the door.

"Come this way, Lieutenant."

Tamara jumped.

A small, dainty woman stood in a narrow, light-filled hallway to the left of the door, beckoning to her.

Tamara gave an awkward curtsy before advancing toward the woman. She meant to smile and exchange a greeting, but before she got close, the woman pivoted and walked down the hall toward another room at the end. Feeling out of place again, Tamara followed, her hands clasped behind her back. The hall was glassed-in with a beautiful rain garden on either side. It was impossible to see out into the lawns from here because shrub trees, tall flowering plants, and various trees flanked either side. This must be another security ruse. No one could see anyone passing through.

"In here," the woman said.

Tamara ducked her head and passed her as she entered. She looked around at what must be an office. She assumed she was to wait here before being called in to see the emperor. She turned to thank the woman, but she was already gone.

"Most comfortable chair in the room, aside from mine. Good choice."

Tamara jumped at the voice that spoke without warning. Looking around frantically, she blinked in astonishment at the man—who was no doubt *Emperor Sylvanus*—materializing from inside a wardrobe. He turned to close the wardrobe door, which Tamara realized was a secret doorway from another room!

Lips moving rapidly, but soundlessly, Tamara stumbled out of the chair and into a low bow, then up into a salute.

"Your Imperial Highness!" She choked out.

"Lieutenant," he said in greeting. His lips twitched with humor. He nodded his head and released her from her salute.

Tamara smacked her saluting arm to her side, lifted her chin, and stared blankly at the wall. Her heart beat a violent tattoo against her chest.

"At ease, Lieutenant," His Highness.

Tamara blinked and forced herself to breathe slowly and evenly.

"Where *is* my sister. I told her to bring you in and stay to hear what you had to say. Is she returning?"

"Your-your sister, sir?" Gods. Would she never get this meeting right?

"Yes. She may not have introduced herself. She's like that with other women. She can be jealous of other beauties. She's aging and *highly* sensitive about her fading looks of late. Until her late thirties, she was the reigning beauty." He rummaged around in the drawers of his desk.

Tamara didn't know what to do but nod uncomprehendingly. Then, as if he suddenly remembered his business, Sylvanus looked around and waved her to a chair, "Sit! Sit! Where are my manners. Tell me…what has brought you here today?"

Tamara sat in the chair that looked the most uncomfortable, leaving the chair she chose earlier to the emperor. She wished this meeting was over. She wished she hadn't shown her stupidity by coming. She wished she had never met Major Brolin. She wished. She wished. She wished.

"Your Highness, I don't know how else to begin this than by saying I believe someone wishes to harm Major Vale Brolin. He was the captain aboard my airship. I know I should not have come, my lord, but I fear there are enemy agents operating on our soil. I didn't know who to trust." The enormity of what she was doing crashed over her. How dare she inform the ruler of the greatest empire on Earth that she heard someone wanted to harm the one she loved. She felt heat rising to her neck, ears, and cheeks. Shame drowned her in its unmerciful waves.

"Mm. I fear the same," His Highness said as he reached for a cigar humidor. He lifted the lid and pulled out the largest cigar Tamara had ever seen. He lifted a small bust of his father sitting on the desk, pressed an unseen switch, and a large plume of flame erupted from the mouth of the bust, startling her. He placed the cigar in his mouth, lowered it to the flame, and lit his cigar. Tamara blinked.

"Tell me how you heard of this plot to harm my dearest friend."

Again Tamara felt a fool, but again Tamara told her story of overhearing the cryptic one-sided conversation aboard the airship. She added her fear of sabotage upon the *Victoria*. She outlined the strange conversation she had with the old woman at the training grounds. She slowed down to a halting mumble as she realized His Highness was staring at her with dawning interest.

"Wait a bit...." he said, his nasal High Imperial drawl lingering on the vowels. "Are you...are you *Fieldmarsh?*"

Tamara sat back in confusion. Surely de Maldane had told him who he was meeting?

"I-I am Tamara Fieldmarsh, Lieutenant First Class...my lord."

"I am often hounded by citizens begging a meeting. I rarely pay much attention to names and causes. I sort of just do them for good will. de Maldane! I could wring his scrawny, elegant neck!" Sylvanus stabbed his cigar into the tray with force.

"Forgive me, Your Highness. I don't understand. Was I not supposed to come?" Tamara felt perhaps *she* would wring de Maldane's scrawny neck.

"It seems de Maldane neglected to tell me you are the Fieldmarsh personally handpicked by Brolin to serve on the *Victoria*. You are...how should I say this...an entity, Lieutenant."

Tamara gripped the arms of her chair tightly. As Sylvanus looked about the room and blew smoke rings, her world was blowing up, coming back together and falling apart again. Tamara thought only of how horrible the last several months were and how those months ended up with her in a strangely informal meeting with the ruler of all New Victoria where she was told someone handpicked her....and she was an "entity"!

"Yes. I have had my eye on your progress since we had you moved to the Defense Force. Dear Vale doesn't know it, but I have plans for you myself." He chuckled, stood and walked about the office. Smoke filled the room and Tamara's eyes watered.

The Emperor of New Victoria And Lands Beyond *had plans for her himself*?! She wondered if she were still sleeping in the room de Maldane had given to her. Perhaps she had never left her barracks. Yes, she was dreaming. Nothing that had happened since the time she overheard the plot to assassinate Major Brolin was true. She was still sleeping on the *Victoria.* Vale Brolin never came to say goodbye. She never became a Lieutenant First Class. She still aided smugglers. She still repaired air ships. Perhaps she had never left her parents' home. Perhaps she still slept on her enormous bed filled with stuffed animals and pillows. Soon, her nanny would come to wake her with a cup of warm chocolate and a muffin. Yes. She just needed to wait for Nanny to wake her.

"Hm. Interesting. Interesting." Emperor Sylvanus mumbled around his cigar. He stared out into the distance, blowing smoke rings. "You are a force to be reckoned with, Fieldmarsh. I know your father, but you, you are not your Father. He is an estimable doctor to be sure. But you. You were not content to submit to someone else's will. You're instinctive. Willful. Fiercely protective. Yes, I heard about your defense of your friend's honor. And now you are here to thwart a plot against someone…you hardly know. A good person to have in one's corner, hey?"

Tamara fought the twinges of impatience with My Lord Emperor. Was he merely a bombastic personhood, enjoying his cigars, giving only half-an-ear to citizens who came to him for help?

Sylvanus turned to assess Tamara, "Do you need something to drink, my dear? Perhaps something stronger than water?"

Tamara gulped, "There is nothing I would like more, Your Highness, but I must keep my wits about myself. I admit I fear for the major."

"As do I," he said, all levity in expression replaced with seriousness, "He came to me a month ago, telling me of suspected sabotage upon my new airship the *Victoria.*"

Tamara's mouth almost dropped open. So he *did* inform the Emperor!

"I sent him on a mission. I won't tell you where as it was a top secret mission. What he found was alarming. What you learned about spies on your base, he also learned from the horse's mouth."

Tamara's eyes widened.

"Yes, Lieutenant. You are not off base with your fears. However, while I know almost all things that operate within my empire, big, small, dangerous, benign, I will not be told all. And one thing I feared, but had no direct knowledge of, was a plot against my closest friends and advisors. I suspected. I *expected*, but I could not *know*. You understand?"

Riveted, Tamara nodded and then corrected herself, "Yes, Your Highness."

He returned to his desk and leaned forward to peer into her face.

"I also believe those plots to have originated *within* the circle of close advisors. I am between a rock and a hard place. I, like you, can not be sure whom to trust implicitly. You will be of help to me."

"Me, my lord?" Tamara couldn't believe she wasn't still dreaming.

"Yes." Without warning, he came around the desk and stood before her in the most informal posture, yet. He crooked a finger toward her, and she leaned toward him as he bent toward her ear. She heard a faint rustle of movement nearby. She knew a guard or two somewhere was ready to pin her to the chair she sat in with a broadsword if she blinked too fast or moved too quickly.

"Be my, as yet unsanctioned, Minister of Finding. Find out who is plotting against me!" He whispered, "Tell *no one* of this." He straightened and his gaze bore into hers with such intensity that she understood how easily someone could underestimate him. She had! He was cunning and quick. His girth could lull someone into believing he was soft, gluttonous, given to an extravagant lifestyle with little care for much else. Sylvanus Marananth was not soft. He was as strong as steel and just as impermeable. She felt the undercurrent of danger in his aura. She was sure that at this distance from him, Sylvanus Marananth would be the one to pin her to the chair with a dagger. He needed no one to defend him in close quarters. His guards were there as backup, not as a primary source of defense.

She nodded silently.

In a louder voice, he said, "Let me get my sister. She is my closest advisor. She'll help us navigate this situation. I applaud your determination in coming all the way here to risk death at the hands of the palace guards." He smiled as he spoke.

The door opened with no signal or button that Tamara had detected. A guard mumbled, "Yes, my lord?" She closed her eyes at the thought of how extremely foolish and fortunate she was at not being slain on sight. The palace guards were adept at not being seen, but being always present!

"Fetch Lady Marananth. I need her counsel."

"Yes, my lord."

Once the guard left to do his bidding, Sylvanus returned his attention to Tamara, "I take leave to tell you that Vale's return to *New Victoria* was most surely hastened because of you."

"Me?" Her heartbeat grew rapid.

"Yes. He didn't say so. He didn't hint at it, but I have never before seen him so agitated and overcome."

Seeing her confusion, Sylvanus answered her unspoken question, "Lieutenant, someone wishes you in the same place as the major."

Tamara's mouth dropped open, "Someone wants *me...dead?*"

Sylvanus' eyes darted toward the door, "Ah! Assandra. Come meet Vale's guardian angel." He gestured toward Tamara.

Although her senses were reeling at this knowledge of attaining a price on her head (she had only been the Minister of Finding for five minutes!), she hastened to stand to greet Lady Assandra. She remembered Emperor Sylvanus' remark about his sister's looks and jealousy. She wanted to appear less gauche than she must surely look. But, her mouth fell open at the sight of the beautiful goddess standing in the doorway, whose violet eyes were staring at her in shock.

"You?" Tamara blurted in surprise.

"*You!*" The goddess shouted in rage.

"What?" His Highness asked in confusion.

* * *

Tamara's mind raced. As she stood there in the office of the Emperor of New Victoria, she felt the blood draining from her face, down into her feet. Soon, she would fall to the floor in a faint. Could she disguise her outburst in a faint? That wouldn't work, His Highness had witnessed the meeting between his sister and the Lieutenant here to save Major Brolin. He would have questions and she didn't want him to ask them right now. She had to buy herself time.

"I apologize, My lady. I didn't recognize you at all when I saw you in the city. I apologize for the damage my hoverbike wrought on your clothing." Tamara held her breath.

Assandra Marananth's eyes narrowed, and her jaw clenched. Her large, heavily made-up eyes darted to her brother's face before moving back to Tamara's. "Oh. Well. You're forgiven." Lady Assandra said, entering the room hesitantly, her beautiful eyes wary and guarded.

"Ah." Sylvanus said, confused and thrown, "Well! Sit, Assandra. We have much to discuss."

Assandra's eyes cut to Tamara as she glided across the floor to take the seat beside the enormous desk. Feeling sick, Tamara avoided her gaze.

Assandra turned to her brother, her jewels and diamonds winking in the room's light. Her skin gleamed healthily because of a lifetime of expensive creams and lotions. Her perfectly formed jaw curved into a graceful neck encircled by pearls and gemstones. She put out a chiffon-drenched arm to brace herself against the desk, "What is happening, Sylvan?" She asked in a husky voice.

"The Lieutenant has risked life and limb to bring me the sad news of espionage and duplicity that has come to her ears," he said, smiling soberly at Tamara.

Tamara bent her head, her breath coming rapidly.

"Has she?" Assandra asked softly.

Tamara could hear the hard edge in her voice.

"Major Brolin is in danger," she said in a low voice. She feared if she didn't clarify His Highness' statement, Lady Assandra would get the wrong idea.

"Vale? Now, why would Vale be in danger, Brother?" She asked, barely able to speak through her rigid jaw. Tamara noted the extreme tension in Lady Assandra's posture.

Sylvanus shook his head at his sister, "He *is* one of my closest friends, *and* an advisor."

"Pooh. I am the closest advisor you have and no one wants to kill *me*."

Assandra said, waving a hand at what Tamara understood to be an attempt to appear nonchalantly dismissive.

Tamara sat rooted to the spot. She felt Lady Assandra's eyes on her as she pretended rapt attention with Emperor Sylvanus. The eyes bored into her and Tamara fidgeted.

Tamara wasn't sure if she would end the day alive after all. She felt immeasurably tired and weary with all she endured. To learn of faithless people who pledged undying loyalty in one day and plotted death the next toppled her faith in the world's good.

"Sister, I want you to use your resources to find who has plotted against Vale and have them stopped, or executed," Sylvanus said.

"Yes. Yes, of course. Anything for poor Vale," Assandra said absently as she fiddled with her earrings. "But," she continued, "you know this could take a great deal of time?"

"Time? Why a great deal of time? I've seen you move faster to move pearls from a bevy of smugglers in the mountain!"

Tamara couldn't take it anymore. She stood and spoke formally, "I must beg your humble pardon, Your Highness," she bowed low, "I fear I have suddenly taken ill. The night's journey and hunger have overtaken me. I beg leave to return to my rest."

"You're ill?" He asked, incredulous. "I didn't realize. You seemed in perfect health!"

"I apologize for my impudence, Your Highness." She kept her face trained to the lush carpet below her feet. She could feel Lady Assandra's gaze boring into her skull.

"Well...by all means. We dismiss you."

"Many thanks, Your Highness," Tamara said as she backed from the room.

Walking as quickly as Imperial decorum would allow, she passed back through the glassed-in hall, through the throne room and through the open golden door pulled open by the guards. Tamara couldn't swear that she would find her way back to the room, but she hoped to run into-

"Major Domo!" she exclaimed in relief, for he stood before her as if waiting.

"Lieutenant. I trust you relieved yourself of your mission to His Highness?"

"Yes, yes! Please, could you lead me back to my room? Immediately?"

He frowned slightly, "Are you ill?"

"Decidedly so!"

"Very well. Follow me."

The trip back to her room seemed to take hours. She took quick looks behind, expecting someone to rush up behind her and grab her, carting her off back to the imperial office. She wished de Maldane would increase his speed. Finally, they reached a hall she recognized and de Maldane gestured for her to enter her room.

Once she opened the door to the room, she grabbed de Maldane's arm and propelled him in with her, closing the door.

"Is anyone listening?" She whispered.

"I beg your pardon?" He said, outrage darkening his face as he removed her hand from his robes.

"Are there any guards hidden somewhere inside this room?" She hissed.

"The guards are for protection for the emperor. No one would concern themselves with a lowly lieutenant!" He said.

"I need to leave the palace *immediately.*"

"Explain yourself!"

"I...think I may be in danger and I need to go do something for the emperor. If I don't leave, someone will try to stop me by killing me!"

"Lieutenant, you're not making sense!" de Maldane stepped away from her.

"I'm sorry. I can't say why...I just saw someone I know is...please, I need to leave. Could you give me some food to take with me?"

"Do you mean to say that someone *inside* the palace means you harm? That's impossible, Lieutenant. Besides, the only one who need worry about his safety is Emperor Sylvanus and he has the guards to protect him."

"Will you just listen to me? I know what I know. *Please.* I need to leave, can you get the kitchens to provide a couple of meals for me?"

"How dare you assume the palace kitchens would...who do you think you are? You come here to the palace by illegal means, you *jump* the palace gate, you cause the guards to give chase-"

"Please, stop! I came here for an excellent reason! To save a life! To save several lives!" Tamara tried to calm herself. She felt herself panicking.

"You came because of a yearning in your pants! Spare me the moral high ground you profess to have! I will not embroil the palace in a silly scheme by a lovesick lieutenant who is chasing someone who does not know *she exists!*"

Tamara felt her lip curl and her eyes narrow. Then her hand was pressing de Maldane's jaw against the wall. She gritted her teeth as she spoke, her eyes glittering with suppressed anger, "If you value your job and your allegiance to the sovereign emperor of New Victoria, you will give me what I ask so you may *continue to keep them.*"

de Maldane's face struggled with shock, new respect, indignance, and a sprinkling of fear. Tamara released him and stepped back. She watched him warily. de Maldane brushed off his silken robes and patted his hair. He huffed with annoyance, but spoke, "I shall have the kitchens send a servant with provisions. They will be here within an hour."

"No. Have the servant bring it to me at the gate where I entered." She said.

"It's important." de Maldane's brow furrowed in confusion, but he nodded briefly.

"This needs to remain secret."

He nodded once more before turning and fleeing the room. Tamara wondered how much she could trust him. She wondered how easily she could leave the palace. Would the guards stop her? She ran to the doorway.

"de Maldane!"

He turned reluctantly.

"Will the guards stop me from leaving?" She asked.

"You. Guard. Escort the lieutenant to the Southeast Gate." Then he turned and disappeared down the hall.

A guard materialized from a wall and stood waiting for Tamara to command him.

"Well? *I* don't know how to get to the Southease Gate from here. Lead on, sir!"

He regarded her for a moment and then proceeded down the hall behind them.

The guard indicated that the other guards should open it. The large heavy iron gate moved noiselessly on well-oiled hinges, and Tamara passed through. She noted the irony of the previous manner by which she had gained entry onto the palace grounds. She didn't bother turning to thank the guard. He would either stare at her impassively, or he would have already left her to return to the palace.

She stood on the treed lane and looked around. It seemed like days had passed since she had hidden her hoverbike, hopped the gate, been chased by a million guards, and run through the imperial garden. Instead, it was only hours ago. She sighed.

The wide lane gave way to pebble stones and her boots crunched as she strolled down it to cross the road that ran along the gate's high stone wall and hugged up against the back lots of nobles' homes. She figured she had a little while before the servant bearing food came to look for her.

Heart beating rapidly with anxiety, she crept to the old farmer's shed to check for the hoverbike and duffel bag. She exhaled in relief, finding it untouched. She headed back to sit under a tree to wait for the servant. Willing herself to remain calm, she sat with legs crossed, looking around. The day was as silent and peaceful as when she arrived early this morning.

The tree she sat under was a large, sturdy oak tree. She inspected the others from where she sat. At some point, each of the oaks were planted at the same time in a straight and orderly line that extended from each corner of the palace wall to the next. The grass beneath was well-tended and lush, providing a serene place for the eye to rest. The Imperial City looked to be a marvelous place to live…so long as you didn't live in the slums at the outskirts. She wondered if the emperor knew his kingdom had slums in it. Was he an attentive ruler, or did some plights of his citizens fall beneath his notice. Did his advisors and officials inform him of the sad state of many of the provinces? She tried to keep her mind busy, but at several intervals she found herself resisting the idea of fleeing without food and planning to take some whereever she could find it.

Tamara fiddled her fingers on her legs and bounced around, leaning forward to peek through the gate, checking for anyone with a palace uniform—besides a guard—who looked to be delivering a package of food. She avoided lingering near the gate fearing the guards putting her through a chase again. She was sure this time they would either kill her on sight or cart her off to jail with no way for her to get help.

"Hey! Are you the person waiting for food?"

Tamara twisted around to peer behind the tree, startled. A girl in an imperial page uniform staggered toward her with a canvas bag slung over her shoulder. Tamara hopped onto her feet to relieve her of the burden.

"Yes! That's me. Is that *all* for me?"

"I guess. I was told to give it to a woman in a defense force uniform at the gate."

Tamara stared into the bag in disbelief, a mound of paper-wrapped food lay inside the bag.

"I can't...I couldn't possibly take all this food on my hoverbike!" She said. Pulling out package after package. Did de Maldane know all this food was coming to her?

"You have a machine?!" The girl asked, her face bright with excitement.

"What? Oh, yes. Yes. It's back there. But, I can't carry all this and my duffel on my bike. Do you want some of this?"

The girl made a rude noise with her lips, "And risk being beaten for stealing? No thanks. Can I see the machine?"

Gods. What would she do with it all? She couldn't just leave it here. The girl would probably get a beating for wastefulness.

"Sure," she said, answering the page's question. She hitched the bag up over her shoulder and led the way to the shed where she uncovered it for the girl's inspection.

"The gang will never believe I ever saw one with my own eyes! Can I get my friends to come see?"

"What? No. I have to leave immediately. Sorry, but it's an emergency." *I have to leave before she sends someone after me.*

"Oy!"

Tamara had just thrown a leg over the hover bike when she turned to see who was hailing her.

A bowlegged figure ambled over to her.

"You!" She yelled, "What do you want! I've had enough of you!"

"Yeah? Well, too bad sweet cakes! Ya can't get ri' o' me so easily!" He threw his duffel bag over his shoulder and stood waiting expectantly.

"Why?" She raged.

"Look 'ere, kid. I was hired to keep you safe like. I'm paid to stay stuck on you til he sees you with his own two peepers. Got it?"

Tamara slapped her fist against her forehead, "Arrgh! I can't…"

"Stuck like glue to ya, chickie. May as well make use of me!"

She cut her eyes to him, "What do you mean 'make use'?"

"I can tell when someone's on a mission like. You got the look! I'll help ya. You're a pretty little thing. Plenty of blokes wouldn't think twice of takin' ya and dumpin' ya. Right? Drop me off at my bike. You owe me that much."

"I owe you nothing!" She shouted.

"After that chase you gave me? I haven't had sleep in twenty-four hours! I never expected you to bolt like you did last night! "

"Who the devil hired you?! My father?!"

Scolder giggled. It was a high-pitched, unnatural sound that gave Tamara the willies.

"Naw! 'twas Major Brolin."

"*What?!*"

"Ya. Told me to keep watch of ya while he was away."

Tamara's legs gave way, and she slipped slowly to the ground like thick mud sloshing off a river bank.

"Aw, naw. Ya not gonna cry are ya?" Scolder asked in a whining tone. Why were the roughest-looking ones comfortable with every bit of mayhem but emotions? He shuffled over to her and poked her arm and then her knee when she didn't respond.

"Gods! Stop poking me!" Tamara shouted at him. She scrambled to her feet. She couldn't believe Brolin hired someone to keep watch over her.

She peered into Scolder's face, "He really told you to follow me?"

His bony face with its scars, divots, and lumps took on an almost earnest quality as he pounded his chest where his heart was. "Upon my ma, he did. Said you were in danger. Told me to follow you as soon as they released you from jail. He wanted to stay, but he couldn't. Are we gonna get goin'?"

Tamara felt like she could fly.

"Yes, Mr. Scolder, we'll go."

His face registered disapproval, "Just Scolder, Lieutenant. No "Mr", understand?"

What an odd man he was. Tamara gave him a brief nod and climbed aboard the hoverbike. She winced as he grabbed her shoulder as he climbed aboard. The hoverbike dipped to the ground. She started it up and it roared to fiery life, disbanding birds and small animals.

"Why do you have so many bags?" He shouted in her ear.

"One's got food!" She shouted back at him, "Where's your bike?"

"Its-here, let me drive," he shouted, tapping her shoulder, signaling she should leave her spot.

"No one drives this bike but me! Where am I going?" She couldn't hear his sigh, but she sensed it in his body posture.

Scolder jabbed a finger to show the direction of his hoverbike. They roared off into the evening.

Chapter Ten

T amara and Scolder rode for several hours before he gave the signal to stop. They left the beautiful green lushness of the Imperial City several hours ago. Now, they rode through seemingly endless terrain of brown and red sand, a continual wall of dead, flat-topped mountains on both sides, and small brush vegetation dotting the landscape.

He led them off the traveler's road a decent distance toward some large boulders. Once the bikes were "stabled", they sat to eat something from the food bag. The palace kitchens packed it full of wonderful foods, and Tamara felt sleepy and full at the end of the meal.

Scolder built a fire. Tamara lay beside it, relishing the warmth in the chilliness of dusk. Her head lay on the duffel bag and she perused the stars in the clear sky.

Scolder poked at the limbs and twigs, "I don't want ya worryin' yourself about if you're safe with me. I'm not so hard up I need to force it."

Tamara jerked upright and stared at him in astonishment. "Well, I wasn't *before!*"

He looked up at her from the other side of the fire. "Ya mean you're worried about it *now* after I told you you're ok with me?"

"Why'd you even bring it up?"

"Well…I had another job where I had to protect a girl and she was so frightened. I couldn't figure out heads or tails why she never, ever calmed down. I mean, I tol' her I was there to protect her, but she stayed scared." He shook his head. "I took her to stay with my lady friend til her parents came to fetch her and she got it out of her. Turns out, the men I rescued her from threatened to rape her. She expected the same from me…just 'cuz I was male, too. Fair hurt my feelings."

Tamara squinted at Scolder, unsure if he was making it all up. But, he stared moodily into the fire, his bottom lip protruding pitifully.

"Oh. Scolder. I'm sorry. I understand. Thank you for trying to put me at ease."

He mumbled something she assumed meant "forget it". Tamara had to smile a little.

"So, what mission are you on? And I'm guessing you don't have your commander's leave to be on it." Scolder said.

Tamara remembered his insistence that he could help her on her "mission" when he hailed her before they left the Imperial City. She felt she could trust Scolder. Carrying secrets takes a toll whether that secret is heavy, or light. She felt burdened by it.

"You're right. I'm out here AWOL right now. I'm in so much trouble unless I can somehow get Major Brolin or the emperor to speak for me."

He was silent.

"Scolder?"

"Ya."

"I'm afraid I'm possibly about to make your career a difficult one with what I'm about to tell you."

"My career? Difficult? That ride last night was difficult. Everythin' else is easy as pie."

Tamara smiled. "Well, I have to save my life and try to save Major Brolin's. And I suspect I'll do both at the same time."

"Saving lives is easy. You haven't told me the tough part."

"Who do you work for exactly?"

"Well, Major Brolin hired me as you know, but…have you ever heard of something like a "secretarial pool'?"

Tamara nodded.

"Well, in that case, people who can type, or file, or write letters and stuff sort of wait, til a businessman or businesswoman needs someone with their skill, right?"

Tamara nodded again.

"Consider me a secretary, 'cept I kind of have a permanent military attachment."

"Isn't the correct term for you 'mercenary'"?

"Oh, you. Never been called mercenary in my life."

"You know what I mean."

"Well, if I didn't have a military covering, I guess you could call me that. But I have dealings with the palace."

"I thought so. And to whom do you answer? Emperor Sylvanus? Lady Assandra? de Maldane?"

"Either." He said, regarding her curiously in the light of the flames.

"Well, one of your bosses is a traitor. I'm sorry to say." Tamara said, hanging her head and looking at her hands in the firelight.

"I see. And how do you know that?" He asked quietly.

Tamara took a deep breath, "Before I was a Lieutenant, I was an engine tamer for anyone who needed me to repair an airship-"

"But the only people who own airships are-" Scolder broke in.

"Yes. Smugglers and the military."

"Ah," Scolder said and relapsed into silence.

"I had to go to a client's mansion in the mountains to demand payment. It had been weeks since I completed the work. This was before I demanded payment before delivery of the repaired airship. I learned my lesson." She lay back down on the duffel bag and spoke to the sky. "But this time, knowing I was pushing my luck and I would probably die doing this—I needed the money—I asked people where he lived and someone gave me the address. I got there and talked my way into the house. There were alot of people there and I was pretty tense. I soon realized the smuggler was in another part of the mansion, making an illegal deal for something. Well, I'm not sure how it happened, but I sort of forced my way into the room. There were several people sitting at a table and there were maps, diagrams, drawings of machines...money! The smuggler started shouting at me. I started shouting back about him trying to stiff me on my money. A woman who was there working some sort of smugling deal with him started shouting at me about being there. She tried to threaten him saying she'd have him cut up if he didn't throw me out. She started threatening to kill *me!*"

Scolder's eyes remained on her face. She wondered if he understood what he was saying.

"She scared me. But, I had worked with this smuggler a few times. He's non-violent. He just wants to earn money for his family. Anyway, he started trying to talk her down. He didn't want blood on his hands. He got me my money fast. The woman was evil. She threatened to peel the skin from my face if she ever saw me again. She saw me again today."

She exhaled slowly. She would never forget those eyes.

"It was Lady Assandra, wasn't it?" Scolder asked quietly.

Tamara's eyes darted over to Scolder. He looked down at the fire as he poked at the twigs and limbs.

"...yes..." she whispered, "and I don't know what to do about it."

"Did she recognize you today?"

"Immediately."

"Ah." He said.

They were silent for a few minutes.

"How did you get out with nothin' happenin'?" Scolder said, asking the million dollar question.

Tamara sighed, "The only thing I could think of was to fake a misunderstanding. We were right in front of Emperor Sylvanus. What else could I do?"

"You're a quick one. Brolin was right." Scolder said, slipping down into his bedroll and closing his eyes.

Tamara's heart soared. Brolin made sure she was taken care of, and he spoke highly of her.

Scolder spoke again, "Ya know, before he left-that night you was in jail-he told me he'd found out something about some of the recruits. They weren't who they said they were. He said he would come back and handle it. Til then, I was to protect you."

"What did he mean?" Tamara asked.

"I don't rightly know."

"Do you know where he went? I was so…um…surprised that he left so soon after the dinner."

"I don't know. I'm not given a whole bunch of details when I get jobs like these. I expect he'll return to base soon."

Tamara thought about Brolin's words about people who weren't "who they said they were". Spies, she guessed.

"We only get a couple of hours sleep, then we ride again." Scolder said, before turning over and falling promptly to sleep.

Tamara didn't know if she *could* sleep. But when Scolder shook her awake two hours later, she felt refreshed and ready to travel more.

* * *

They reached the town by dawn the next morning. They pulled off the traveler's road to sit under some trees to eat breakfast.

"We can't take you to the base. They'll arrest you on sight and I can't do anything about it for a while."

Tamara nodded.

"I'll have to take you to Brolin's quarters."

Tamara shot a quick glance at him.

"You'll have to stay there under my keen eye."

"But, how will we know when he'll be back? The penalty of my AWOL increases the longer I'm gone."

"Why didn't you think of that first, chikkie?"

"Well, I-I don't know! I was trying to help!"

He waved a hand at her, "Ah, I'm just joshin' ya."

Tamara looked down at her food. Her appetite left suddenly. . Why *hadn't* she thought of that first! There were times she felt stupid and young, while other times she felt mistress of her life and 'all-knowing'. This was not one of those times. She thought about staying in Major Brolin's house. A thrill went through her and she chided herself. She couldn't act like a young miss. It wasn't becoming in this situation. She had made a horrible mess of things for herself. She wasn't sure how things would work out.

"So, he gave you a key to his house?" Tamara asked curiously.

"No," Scolder said, crumpling paper food wrapping into a ball and tossing it into the underbrush, "I'll just have to break in." He stood. "You done, Lieutenant? We need to get you indoors before the sun is up and we ride through town and someone recognizes ya."

"Wait! You will *break in*? As if I wasn't in enough trouble."

He raised his hands in a flurry of movement, "You're not in trouble with *him* are ya? He'll be happy you saved *him*. He's not gonna report ya, is he?"

Tamara cursed herself for her stupidity again. She didn't have another choice.

"We have to take the bikes to my rented garage. No one will look there for them."

"Well, that's lucky, I guess."

Tamara shrugged and started packing up her things. They reloaded her hoverbike and then started into town.

After stashing the hoverbikes in her rented garage, they skulked around town until the reached the buildings that housed military family members.

"Which one is his?" Tamara hissed at Scolder crouching behind some large rubbish piles in an alley. She raised her shirt over her nose the stench was that bad. Scolder pointed at a door on the second floor. She wondered how nosy the major's neighbors were and if the floors creaked.

At Scolder's signal, they raced like escaping rats along the back alley to the back entrance into the building. Scolder tried the door handle and it turned easily in his hands. Tamara grabbed his sleeve.

"We're just going to go inside like we live here? Why don't we just go in a window?" She hissed.

"I don't know about you, but I can't ruddy climb a sheer wall without equipment," he hissed back, "can you?"

Tamara settled back, resigned to stay quiet until she was inside. There was little she could offer up for suggestion, seeing how she ruined everything else for herself. Soon they were inside the building and creeping up the stairwell to the second floor. Even this early in the morning, they heard children chattering, mother's scolding, babies jabbering. The smell of cooking filled the stairwell, but not in a pleasant way.

"It's here," Scolder whispered.

Tamara flattened herself against the wall by the door as he fiddled with the lock. She stared around, desperate to be inside before someone saw them breaking into the major's dwelling.

"Got it!" Scolder said, yanking her into the dim interior.

Not sure what to do, she crouched onto the floor, trying to stay still and avoid alerting the family downstairs that she was inside. Scolder closed the door carefully behind him and turned to walk toward her. Too late, but she realized he didn't know she was directly behind him in the dim light.

"Oof!" Scolder wheezed as he tumbled over her, the fall jarring the floor boards.

"Shhhh!" She hissed as loud as the sound Scolder made.

"Well, don't stay so close under me, hear!" He said, annoyed.

Tamara crawled over to the window to peer outside, trying to get her bearings.

"Why ya crawlin'?" Scolder asked, no longer whispering.

"I don't want anyone to hear me," she muttered.

"Where dya think you are? Cheapside? These buildings is built sturdy like. Stone. Brick. No one will know you're in here unless you're screaming crazy."

"Oh," she said, standing sheepishly.

"Got anymore of that food in your kit? Need something to take with me while I see if his nibs is back on the base."

After he left, Tamara sat on the old sofa so similar to the one she had when she shared a flat with Neridette. She hadn't thought of her in weeks. She felt ashamed by her lack of attention to her dearest friend. She stood up to pace while waiting to hear from Scolder. She looked around the apartment in the dim light, not wanting to snoop, but wanting desperately to snoop! She ran her fingers over the low, nondescript sofa tables, and the odd chair set carelessly into a corner.

How do you live, darling? She thought, relishing the use of the endearment. Hands behind her back, she tiptoed from the sitting room into the separate area used for cooking and eating. She noted a clean set of dishes stacked neatly on the table, with a clean folded napkin, and a set of utensils. There wasn't a thing out of place. It seemed that her major was either a compulsive cleaner, or he used this place only to sleep.

She craned her neck to peer into the small bedroom at the back, seeing only a tiny bed, a table, and a small bureau. Standing at the door with arms crossed, she imagined him in this bed, shirt and trousers removed. Did he snore, she wondered. Overtaken by her imagination, she stepped into the room, her heartbeat growing rapid. That fleeting meeting of a few nights ago kept her in a heightened state of longing and awareness when she thought of him.

She sat on the bed and looked at the pillow. She bent to lay her head on the soft whiteness, closing her eyes, breathing in deeply. She didn't want ever to be this far away from him again. Feeling remorse for the way they parted on the airship, tears leaked from her eyes and she cried softly for love, in despair, in disappointment, in anxiety, and fear for her and the major's life. She hadn't thought of it before, but she missed the touch of someone who cared for her and wished for her. Would he ever know how much she longed for him? As she drifted off to sleep, the last thought she had was of his hand on her back as they danced.

She awoke to the sound of voices. For long moments, she panicked as she tried to remember where she was. The room was dim and her heart raced. Then she recognized a voice. Those chocolatey velvet tones; Brolin! She jumped up and ran lightly to the door of the room and just as quickly shrunk back. Curse her vanity! But she couldn't go out there looking like this! Actually, she didn't know what she looked like. She hadn't looked in a mirror in two or three...or four days? Gods. She hadn't bathed in almost that long. Tamara strained to look past the door frame to see if there was a bathing room near. Two closed doors greeted her inquiry, and she groaned to herself. She would have to sneak down the hall while the men discussed whatever they discussed.

She was glad they built this building sturdy; the floors didn't creak easily. She tried the knob of the first closed door and pushed it open slowly. The gamble paid off. Bathing room. She tiptoed in feeling like a fool. She closed the door and slapped her forehead and then cringed as she waited for the men to come to inspect the sound of her beating her own head in. She didn't hear a break in the conversation, so she continued her stealthy progression inside. The light was failing outside, but a pleasant pink hue of the sky filtered in through a long window above the tin tub at the far end. She could see well enough, but she couldn't make out her reflection very well in the mirror of the sink basin cabinet. She shrugged.

Moving as quickly as she could before one of them came to check on her, or, gods forbid, come *to* the bathing room, she slipped off her boots, trousers and blouse and readied herself to have an impromptu wash. Then she realized she had no washcloth. Cursing between her teeth as quietly as she could, she got on her hands and knees, looking for a place to store washing cloths. She opened the door at the bottom of the basin cabinet and stuck a hand in to feel around—she tensed herself against finding a stiff, dead rodent. The soft, plush she felt was indeed not a rat, but a stack of clean, folded washcloths. She cheered silently and stood. Breathing steadily, she poised her hands above the taps and pulled. An almighty commotion accosted her ears! The pipes groaned, shuddered, and squealed. Tamara cursed a silent, steady stream of obscenities into her balled up fists. She shoved off the taps and listened. The voices in the other room were silent. Tamara beat her feet against the tiles and slumped to the floor in a tantrum.

She heard tapping at the door. She froze. The tapping sounded again.

"Chikkie poo? Alright in there? I saw you sneaking in here."

Scolder.

"Does diddums need help?" He asked.

"Go away." She muttered.

"As you wish, doll," he said, sniggering.

She hated him profoundly.

After he left, she groaned. They must surely be laughing at her for her childishness. Gritting her teeth and cursing herself silently, Tamara wondered what was wrong with her. Perhaps a bath would restore her sanity…and hopefully the length of time would make Scolder and Brolin forget her silliness.

The hot water was heavenly. She had a wonderful soak with her selfishness, self-consciousness, and desire to be missed. But once the water cooled, and her burst of temper cold, she began to feel shabby.

"You are twenty-six years old!" She raged at herself. "Act like it!"

But there's no task so hard as making one act one's age when one has only seen maturity performed, yet has not actively participated. Reluctantly, and sure she had a tongue-lashing to look forward to, she drained the water and wrapped the towel around herself. She refused to put the old uniform on. She would walk out there like the grown woman she was, rummage around in her bag, find a clean uniform and put it on.

And so, armed with that silly thought, she marched out of the bathroom into the full gaze of those fiery-blooded men: Vale Brolin and Scolder.

"Aye," Scolder said, "I think I'm in the wrong room. Where've you been hiding that physique, love?"

A full-body blush flushed through her and she regretted her decision, but she said, "Thank you, Scolder. I'll accept that as a compliment."

"Oh, it is, Lieutenant. It is." He settled back into his chair, crossed his arms, and looked away.

She meant to avoid Brolin's gaze while she was dressed so, believing she could concentrate better when fully dressed. But when she turned to look for her duffel bag, she found it sat beside *him* on the old sofa. Trapped, she allowed her eyes to meet his. He leaned back against the sofa, one leg crossed over the other at the ankle. He looked confident and comfortable… and un-plotted against! What right had he to look so safe when she had worried so much about him, went AWOL to rescue him, pled her case with the Emperor of all New Victoria and beyond, and encountered a traitor for him! How could he?!

She felt her knees grow weak, but she forced herself to smile pleasantly, walk toward him, and say "I'm so glad to see you haven't come to harm, Major Brolin. I trust Scolder has given you a full report?"

She marveled at how steady and confident her voice sounded to her ears. She moved closer and reached out an uncertain hand to her duffel bag, unsure of what she thought would happen to it if she got too close to the major.

Her hand stretched further toward her bag, and her body sighed in relief as she felt it clasped in the warmest, most comforting grasp she had ever felt.

Vale Brolin stood and held her hand in both of his.

"You are the most brave woman I have ever met and I am the most grateful man on Earth. To know that you knowingly risked arrest, death, and prison to see me saved from an assassin's plot is something that can never be repaid."

And Tamara, the poor girl with her sometimes old and sometimes young mind said, "Oh, it was nothing." She could have cried. What she wanted to say was, "I will never let you leave me again." And she half-believed she would mean it if she did. She turned to look up at him and he smiled a heartfelt and grateful smile.

Vale Brolin turned her palm in his upward and he raised it to his lips, kissing it in the sweetest manner, causing a bittersweet tingle of sensation up her arm. She soon realized that her skin felt everything that touched her. She realized the towel she wore just grazed her legs at the thigh. She realized the towel was loosening where she tucked it in at her breast. She realized her body swayed ever so slightly toward the man towering above her. She realized she would stand here in front of him and let the towel slip ever so slowly down to the floor. She realized she was going to pull the major down with her to the sofa and she would-

Scolder cleared his throat.

In that moment, she hated him profoundly.

* * *

Fully dressed several minutes later, They sat around the major's small dining table to discuss everything that happened over the past few days. When Tamara recounted her twenty-four hours in the base prison, Brolin's face grew red with anger.

"I'm all right. No harm done," she said softly.

"But there *could* have been harm done," he said.

Scolder's eyes passed between the two of them from where he sat at his side of the small round table. "Izzere somethin' here I'm in the middle of?" He asked, jabbing a finger at both of them.

"I get your hint, Scolder. I'll tell you both what I learned while you were gone."

"But wait, when did you arrive? I've only been gone for two days." Tamara said.

"I was gone for the day you were in prison. Nord woke me with the news that you were arrested for treason. I knew this was a frame up as the search the night before turned up a windscreen from an airship...with a portion missing."

Tamara gaped.

Vale looked at her with a slow-smoldering anger in his eyes, "Yes."

Tamara wilted into her chair. How close she was to being sent to the emperor's prison for treason with that evidence!

"Where did they say it was?" She whispered.

"In a trunk in your rooms," he replied.

She leaned forward and placed her head in her hands. Why wasn't she on her guard? Why didn't she think of this?

"You couldn'tna known they'd do that, chikkie. Don't hammer on yourself about it," Scolder said. He poked her on the shoulder.

She looked askance at him with one eye and gave him a begruding smile, "Why must I tell you to stop poking me," she said, smiling. She sat back and took a deep breath.

"All right?" Brolin asked.

She nodded quickly.

"I'm afraid I have more unsettling news for you, Lieutenant," he continued.

"Oh, no," she said.

"One reason I'm positive it was a frame-up—and we both know it was—is because I received a visit the afternoon of the dinner. This visitor suggested—rather obviously now—that it would be in the empire's best interest for there to be a search conducted whilst everyone was at the mandatory dinner."

"Someone had the gall to *suggest framing me* to *you?*" Tamara exclaimed.

"...yes..." Brolin said. His expression concerned her. Why did he look so angry and sorrowful at the same time?

"Who was it?" She asked, her voice rising.

Brolin glanced at Scolder.

"May as well tell her, boss. Gotta hear it sometime."

Tamara's thoughts went to anyone who might want to cause her harm. She didn't know enough people, did she? But, then, she was rather unpopular for rising to Lieutenant so quickly when she wasn't even qualified for the rank. Who hated her so much they wanted to see her shot by the firing squad? She held her breath. Was it Thorncrist? It couldn't be!

"Weathermarker," Brolin said, watching her face carefully, "Fillip Weathermarker."

The blood drained from her face and she stared blankly at the table. Fillip framed her for treason? She glanced at Brolin.

"No. I'm not saying this out of some sort of jealousy over Weathermarker. He really came to me to suggest a search."

"No...it can't be. He said he...wants me...he wouldn't do this. Not Fillip..." Tamara said, her heartbreaking. In some, odd, uncomfortable way, Fillip was a friend. Then, she remembered his coldness during their last meeting when she called him names and he apologized for...how things would end. She turned a horrified face to Scolder and Brolin.

"Gods! He really set me up! That poisonous little rat set me up! I could kill him! I *will* kill him! I will-!"

Scolder reached over and grabbed her wrists and held them tightly. She turned furious eyes to him, but his face wasn't callous, or teasing. He was serious.

"We all want him. Especially the boss here, but, we want him for real." He released her wrists.

"He wanted me to die," she said in a small voice.

"As much as I despise him," Brolin said in his velvet voice, "I don't think Weathermarker wanted you to die. I think whoever he answers to will do

185

what they require eliminating you."

"As to that," Scolder began, "Chikkie's got some ideas about who wants that." Then he sat back and folded his arms, waiting for her to complete this thought.

"You do?" Brolin asked, eyebrows raised.

"Yes," she said, wary of his response, "but, I don't know if you can handle hearing it."

"What? Why not? If someone is trying to assassinate the empire's citizens, I need to hear it so I can alert the emperor and his advisors so we can-"

"It *is* one of his advisors who is doing this!" She blurted.

Brolin stilled and stared at her.

"She has a good story, boss. Hear her out before you yell at her."

Tamara looked at Brolin's beautiful face in misery. Major Vale Brolin wasn't an empire-sanctioned mercenary for hire like Scolder. He was an idealist, a loyal citizen, a military man. He wasn't crassly jovial, unlikely to take sides, like Scolder. This was likely to break his spirit.

"Tell, chikkie. He needs to hear it. He can't do his job to protect our emperor if you don't tell him what he needs to know."

Slowly and carefully, she recounted the same story she told Scolder last night in the desert. She watched his face, hoping he would come to understand as quickly as Scolder so she wouldn't have to tell him. He waited for her to finish, his face solemn.

"...and she recognized me yesterday. His Highness asked me to ferret out whoever was plotting against his advisors. I hope he came to understand that I took such an undertaking seriously, although for my life I had to leave immediately." She searched his face for some sign of his thoughts.

He settled back in the chair, elbows balanced on the arms, fingertips steepled. He closed his eyes as he spoke.

"I had my fears about his close advisors. It makes great sense what you say." His eyes opened again, "But his own sister is plotting? No one would suspect her. She's always charming. Always knows just what to say. Has a good word for you when she greets you..."

Tamara experienced a wave of jealousy.

Scolder piped up, "Former lady friend, eh, boss?"

Brolin jerked out of his reverie.

Tamara made the final decision to forget Vale Brolin. He was too far removed from her. Too elevated in imperial circles. Too well-known. She needed to forget him and concentrate on the task at hand.

"Scolder. It's the major's business. Not ours."

Scolder darted a knowing glance at her, but kept quiet.

Brolin avoided her eyes, "We need to find out how to stop her," he said.

"So, you do believe me? You don't think I'm just insane and making it all up?" She asked.

"I believe you. Everything makes perfect sense. You know, I have to thank you for so many things. Your quick-wittedness and attention to detail is what helped me understand why some things were so wrong on our soil.

Tamara nodded, unable to speak.

They spent much of the evening discussing details. The major decided they needed to arrest Thorncrist and Weathermarker (she explained her visit from the old woman at the park). If Thorncrist, or Weathermarker confessed that they got their orders from Lady Assandra, or if they could trace their orders to her, they would take their evidence in statements to the emperor and see how he would handle it. They knew they needed to work quickly.

Tamara told him she hadn't seen Thorncrist since before the dinner. She didn't know if she was still on the base or not. Brolin was afraid she was on a mission to create more mischief. They decided to sleep on it for the night and Brolin and Scolder would progress to the base in the morning. Tamara needed to stay where she was until Brolin created some sort of excuse for her absence to keep her from being arrested from the powers that operated the base.

"I have power, but even I need to find a way to override higher administrative powers."

"I understand." She said.

Brolin told her to sleep in his bed (how she loved hearing that), and he and Scolder would pass the night in the living room. Her night passed fitfully wishing she could find an excuse to convince him she needed him to protect her closer.

She woke up the next morning bleary -eyed and cranky.

Chapter Eleven

Tamara spent her time being bored around the house. There was nothing to do. She risked creeping outside the building once, but was so nervous about someone asking questions, she skipped back inside the apartment quickly. It was a moment of extreme joy that she remembered she hadn't unpacked her books from her duffel. Like a child on a birthday, she upended the bag and dumped the contents onto the floor in the major's bedroom. Two books tumbled out of the cloth she had wrapped them in before she left on the *Victoria*. She realized after a sickening thump that her little wireless radio was still inside too. Holding her breath, she inspected it, looking for cracks and dents, and only released it when it look in fine fettle. She turned it on to test it and sighed in relief at the small sound of a tiny orchestra flowing from the tiny speaker. She placed it on the bureau.

She turned the books over in her hands and read the titles. She opted for the book by J. S. Bean, prompted by the furor created over her scandalous writing. Several pages in, her mouth fell open, and she closed the book quickly. Was *that* the kind of book this was? She cracked the book open again and read the page with one eye. She covered her mouth and giggled. She didn't realize how much time passed until her stomach growled meanly. She raced to the dining table, carrying the book in her hand, rummaged for something quick and raced back to read. That's how they found her later that afternoon, curled up on the major's bed, the mess she left from her duffel on the floor, and crumbs from her hurried lunch scattered atop the blanket. She had been so immersed in reading she didn't hear them enter

189

the rooms.

"You look comfortable, Lieutenant," a warm voice said startling her and causing her to choke on cracker crumbs.

"Oh!" Her heart jumped about in her chest and she had a difficult time keeping her composure. "I didn't know anyone had come back," she babbled, "Oh, the mess I made! Oh, no, crumbs! You must think I'm an absolute slob, Major…" she said, the last declaration descending into a whimper.

"Not at all. It's a rather heartwarming sight seeing you warm…comfortable…safe," he said, bending down beside her where she was hastily shoving her items back into her duffel, the book between her teeth. "It's alright, Lieutenant. I'm not annoyed."

He placed a hand on hers to still her frenzied movements. His eyes crinkled at the corners as he took in the sight of the book in her mouth. He sat on the floor and leaned against the side of the bed, one arm on the mattress. "What are you reading? I didn't know I had any books around." He said, reaching for the book.

"Oh, it's mine. I'd forgotten I had them in my duffel." Tamara, still delighted by the book, despite her momentary discomfiture, launched into telling the major the risque nature of the book. She laughed and laughed telling him of the antics the book's characters got up to. She got comfortable on the floor and launched into a particularly funny retelling when she stopped at the look on his face. She placed her hands on her knees, a grin still pasted across her face.

"What is it?" she asked, "Did I say something wrong?" Tamara cocked her head to the side, wondering about what he was thinking. He looked different. But, yet, familiar. Like she had seen this face all her life, but never knew it.

He shook his head a little and smiled, "No. No! Not at all. I was just listening to you talk."

"Did I talk too much?"

He smiled, "Never."

She returned his smile. She felt comfortable here with him on the floor, a mess surrounding them, her book in his hand. She leaned forward, eyes on his face, no self-consciousness, no self-sabotaging thoughts. She kissed him lightly on the cheek, feeling the stubble of his beard, and relishing the light scent of his skin. When she leaned back, she saw his eyes had closed. A warm feeling of pleasure spread through her body.

His eyes opened, but Tamara had turned away hearing a noise outside the room. It sounded like someone scraping a blackboard angrily. She shook her head: it must be Scolder trying to get their attention as discreetly as someone like Scolder could.

She peeked around the doorframe and spied him sliding a chair across the floor repeatedly, while glaring at the door to the bedroom. When he saw her he sat down.

"Did you need something, Scolder?" Tamara said, arms crossed and lips pressed together. He really was such an odd man.

"I was out here by my lonesome. Wanted comp'ny. Tha'sall." He said, looking at her with wide, innocent eyes. "We have stuff to talk about. Stuff that happened today."

"Right," Tamara said, the warm glow of being in Brolin's presence dissipating into a warm mist.

She returned to the room and felt a thrill as she gazed upon the man in her dreams sitting on the floor, head back upon the mattress, eyes closed. With one knee bent and the other straight on the floor, he provided a picture of such leisurely sexual relaxation that she could have cried. He opened one eye and looked at her, startling her. His mouth formed a slight curve at the corner, showing how amused he was at having caught her watching him. She smiled sheepishly.

"Scolder is waiting for us," she said with an apologetic smile.

"Ah, right," he said, shaking out of the lethargy, "lots to discuss." He unfolded himself and stood, following Tamara back to the little table.

"Well, we had Weathermarker and Thorncrist arrested on suspicion of treason.

"That quickly?" Tamara asked, astonished.

"Yes, we had to move quickly before someone warned them. After your visit to the palace, I expect Lady Assandra—if she is indeed behind thier treason and not simply a smuggler—would put out a warning. Do you think she knew you left he palace so quickly?"

"I told de Maldane to keep my departure a secret, but I don't know how much he can be trusted...or even if someone else spread the word. I did have an unconventional entry, afterall. People would be interested."

"From the way I heard it, when she jumped the gate, she already had ten guards on her trail. Twenty by the time she made it to the inner garden! Flew like the wind!" Scolder said, beaming like a proud father.

"That many, Lieutenant?" Brolin asked, looking at her with admiration. His eyes held hers with a glittering light and Tamara laughed.

"There couldn't have been so many. I've never run so fast in my life. I'm sure there were only three or four."

"At the palace? Pssht. You saw how many there were on the inside. You just didn't see them all." Scolder said, shaking his head. "She risked all for you, boss."

"...I'll never forget it."

Tamara wished Scolder would leave. As much as she learned to love his brash and scraggly manner...he was just...always *there*.

"Lieutenant, how do you feel about going back to the palace?"

Tamara thought about it. Lady Assandra would be on the lookout for her. Considering her wide network of spies, and smugglers, she may have people posted on the road looking for her if she decided to return. Fear gripped her heart, and she turned miserable eyes to Brolin.

"I'll do it." She said, her voice thin and high. "When do I have to go? How will I get word to you?" She looked down at the table, reliving the first night she left, the first fear at believing someone was following her-

"Me and my man, Nord will be with you, Tamara," Brolin murmured. She adored the way he said her name. He favoured each syllable with delicate attention, resting lightly on the vowels and almost rolling the 'r'.

"Oh!" She breathed, relief flooding her. "Oh...," she continued, realization dawning over her face, "you said your man, Nord. Scolder? You aren't coming with us?"

"No, chikkie," he said tenderly. He reached across the table and clasped

her hands, "I'm only a mercenary, doll."

"Oh, you. You've never been mercenary in your life," she said. She felt a genuine friend was leaving her forever. She squeezed his hand and gave him a watery smile.

"Don't cry, chikkie, or I'll have to poke you," he replied, a tender smile softening his odd features.

She turned to Brolin, "When do we have to go?"

"How much rest have you gotten today?" He asked by way of an answer.

"That soon?!"

"Aye," Scolder said, "Lady Assandra can't be allowed to get the jump on anyone. But he's teasin' ya. Ya gotta leave first thing in the morning."

Tamara sighed in relief.

"I leave tonight though after I help the major with somethin'. Promise me you'll always fight and you'll never, ever, lose that beautiful physique, chikkie."

Tamara stood and squeezed Scolder in a hug so tight he squawked about never being able to breathe again.

Brolin stood up, "Scolder made a good point just as we arrived back here, and I agree its best if you travel out of that uniform-er-meaning, you should wear civilian clothes. Do you have any in your rooms in the barracks?"

"Yes...I need to go get them?"

"Scolder has agreed to help go with me to get them. If you didn't have any, he offered his services in breaking in entering."

"I'm sure he did!" She said, smiling.

"I'm sorry to leave you again...very sorry, but we shouldn't be gone for too long. Take this opportunity to rest up for the journey." Brolin said before turning away and following Scolder through the door.

She heard them descend the stairs, and then she was alone. Quiet at night differs from quiet during the day. She looked around the rooms, nervousness threatening to force her to sit huddled in the corner until they returned. She decided she wouldn't submit herself to such misery. She would take a bath. It may be the last one she had again for a while.

She winced as she turned on the tap at the bathtub, the shudders and bangs grating on her raw nerves. For one last bit of reassurance, she crept to the front door and swung it open. The sounds of the families in the building provided a sense of comfort. Life continued. She closed the door and returned to the bathing room. It was too quiet. She darted to the bedroom and grabbed her little wireless. Returning to the bathing room, she turned the dial to the beautiful classical music, shut the door and undressed. The water was pleasantly warm, and her nervousness drifted away. Soon, she started to feel sleepy and wondered if she should get out. The sound of Scolder and the major returning lifted her mind and she quickly exited the tub to greet them.

As she dried, she thought about what she would do if the major entered to find her still undressed and glistening with water. Her body warmed at the thought. The image of him lifting her up by her hips and carrying her over to the basin, leaning her against the mirror and murmuring how much he wanted her into her neck as she clutched his dark hair made her shiver.

Tamara shook her head, clearing her mind. She pulled on her shift and stopped at the sound of the bathing room doorknob turning. Was he looking for her? She braced herself for being discovered. Then, she stared in horror at the unfamiliar face that peered at her around the bathing room door.

Before she could think or move, a dark figure rushed at her with startling speed. He knocked her to the floor and her head smashed against the side of the tin tub. She heard the transistor radio fall to the floor and smash into pieces. The music stopped. She didn't know if she was up or down. Her vision grew foggy. All she knew was she would die if she didn't fight. She felt a hand around her throat. She felt the cool tiles of the floor. She felt her breath constricting.

In a rush of anger, Tamara didn't fight the hand at her throat, she turned on the floor, until she maneouvered herself to face partly away from her assailant. Struggling to breathe, she pulled her knees up to her chest and kicked. She kicked against the wall, shoving her backward into the stranger, throwing him off balance.

Coughing, retching, and clawing at her throat, she crawled to her knees. Her vision was still foggy and her body's need for air ignored the next big need to get away or maim the man! She crawled for the door, but she felt the man grab her by her feet and drag her backward to the full tub of water. Coughing violently, and gasping for breath, Tamara clawed the tile floor, searching for something, anything that would help her.

High-pitched ringing filled her head, making her retching and gasping sound faraway in her ears. She heard nothing from her attacker, only labored breaths as he fought to keep his hold on her. Her nails made tapping and scraping noises against the shiny tiles in the silence of the room as she scrabbled to get away.

The man wrenched her upward by her hair. Stars pricked her vision, and she screamed in rage remembering her fight in a brothel so long ago. He grabbed her beneath her arms and pulled her down toward the water. She writhed and screamed and kicked. She tried to pivot herself around, but the man had learned his lesson after the first time. He closed the space between his arm and the edge of the tub.

She would not die here!

Taking a risk and gathering all of her strength, she stopped fighting just long enough for her assailant to dip her head into the water. As he stood there, believing he'd won, she whipped her legs up from the floor, over his head and to the wall the tub sat against, then she pushed herself off with a surge of speed, propelling her *and* the man from the tub. As he crashed backward onto the tile floor, she jumped onto the sink basin and screamed as she wrenched the heavy mirror from the wall. The assailant looked up at her dizzily. Tamara lowered herself to the floor and glowered at him as she raised the mirror above her. Then she brought it down with surprising speed onto his head. He was still.

Tamara sank to the floor, wheezing, and retching.

"TAMARA!!"

Shapes, shadows, and voices whirled about her, and Tamara let the blackness take her.

"...we leave *tonight*..."

* * *

She awoke sometime later to the sound of a motor and roaring icy wind at her back. Her head felt funny and her throat hurt. Her head hurt, too. Something was jostling her up and down, and she just wanted it to stop. She tried to move her arms, but they felt pinned down. Panic rose. The man in the bathing room! She gasped and coughed and opened her eyes. She couldn't see! She cried out for help, but her voice came out in a hoarse whisper.

"Major, she's awake!"

Tamara didn't recognize the voice and panic overtook her. She wriggled and bucked.

"Boss! She'll make me wreck the bike!"

"Tamara! Sweetheart! Hold on!"

At the sound of Brolin's voice, she stilled her movements. What was happening? Darkness took her again.

* * *

She awoke again to the sound of Brolin's voice beneath her ear. She heard the sound of a motor again. She felt the chill wind. This time, she didn't move. She smelled the major's scent, and it calmed her. She listened to him speak to someone and slowly opened her eyes. Tamara saw the collar of a leather jacket and beyond that a sunrise.

Wiggling her fingers, she found them at the end of her arms crossed at her torso. As she gained more consciousness, she realized she was pressed against the major's chest and that she couldn't move her arms.

Tamara moved her head, but winced at the pain.

"Erm…" she murmured through dry lips.

"Don't move, my love, we'll be there shortly. Just sleep." Brolin kissed her forehead and Tamara closed her eyes, the pain in her head momentarily removed. She slept.

* * *

"Tamara..."

Tamara heard her name called.

"Tamara..."

She snuggled her head deeper into the warmth. One side of her face was freezing, and she wanted the voice to go away.

"Tamara. Love. I need you to let me know you're awake. Can you open your eyes?"

"Yesshh..." she whispered through thick lips and fuzzy tongue.

She heard a gentle chuckle.

"Open your eyes. Let me know you're ok."

She opened her eyes. Her vision was double for a second until she focused. She slowly raised her head to see Vale Brolin's concerned face close to hers. How she loved that face.

"Where am I?"

"You're on my hoverbike."

"But you're here, too." She said sleepily.

"Yes," he said, smiling.

"How? How did I drive?" She asked.

"Is she alright, sir?" That unfamiliar voice asked.

"Get a doctor, Nord. One we can trust...obviously."

"Yes, sir."

"Who...?" Tamara asked.

"My trusted man, Nord. He rode with us to the Imperial City."

Tamara gasped. Or rather, she tried to, but she coughed instead.

"Nord!" Brolin called, his voice carrying.

Tamara heard footsteps crunch pebbles.

"Yes, sir?"

"Help me?"

"Right."

She felt hands doing something behind her back, and she felt whatever had pinned her arms removed. Then she felt hands and arms lift her from Brolin's bike and carry her away from him. She put out a hand to grasp his arm as she winced in pain.

"To the guest room, Nord."

"Right, sir."

She looked up at the face of the man called Nord. He was such a nondescript character that no one would notice him if he weren't carrying them up stairs and into a house.

"You don't have to carry me...Nord," she whispered hoarsely.

He ignored her.

"I'm...*cough*...pretty sure I can walk."

No response.

She closed her mouth.

He pushed open a door with his shoulder, gently knocking her head against the frame, and carried her into a peaceful room. He sat her on the edge of the bed, observed her for a second to be sure she wouldn't topple over, and not trusting her, pushed her shoulder gently until she lay back onto the bed. He checked that she wouldn't roll off and left her.

Tamara's mind whirled and the fight of her life flashed scenes in her head. She felt a tightness in her chest and she swallowed hard to keep it there. But as the memory of her struggle to live accosted her senses, the tenseness in her chest tightened into a ball and it rose and rose to her throat. She shook her head, trying to tell it 'no', it couldn't rise, and her head shot dizzying flashes of pain, and she gasped. She lay there breathing forcefully through her nose, when she felt a light hand on her shoulder. She opened her eyes with a jerk and saw Nord standing beside the bed holding a tray.

"I apologize for intruding on a very personal moment, Lieutenant. But, I've seen my share of soldiers who experienced a life-threatening event that affected them for many, many days hence. I've brought you something to help you relax and sleep until you feel robust enough to face the memories."

Tamara stared at him with overflowing gratefulness. She raised herself carefully and accepted the small glass of warm, sweet liquid. It soothed her throat and warmed her stomach.

"Thank you, Nord. I'm grateful."

He gave her a formal little bow and left the room.

Tamara clutched the duvet and pulled it around her, bunching it beneath her chin. She turned over as the effects of the drink lulled her senses into a quiet place. She saw the major enter the room, and she reached out a hand toward him, but she never knew if he came to her because blessed sleep claimed her and she slept peacefully.

VI

Vale Brolin

Chapter Twelve

Bursting through the apartment door and hearing Tamara's screams and cries propelled Brolin into the darkest, most dangerous level of violence he had ever experienced. Nord had to pull him away from the unknown assailant before he converted his bones into powder. That bathing room was wrecked. Everything in there cracked, broke, tore, or disintegrated.

As he sat here in his room at his luxurious home in the Imperial City watching the sleeping beauty that was the love of his existence—Nord ignored his command to place her in the more feminine guest room—he tried to figure a way to coerce Tamara into giving up her independent life to stay with him in the Imperial City when all this was over. Should he threaten her with prison if she didn't stay with him? Did he bribe her with jewels, furs, travel, and babies? Should he tell her he needed her and couldn't bear to be away from her even a for a little? Did he drug her? Hypnotize her?

"Sir?" Nord intoned in his unobtrusive manner from the bedroom doorway.

"Yes?" Brolin replied, keeping his watchful eyes on Tamara as she slept in the massive highbed.

"You've been in here for hours. The doctor did say she would be fine with a little rest. Would you like something to eat?"

"I want to be here when she wakes."

"Yes, sir." Nord replied and disappeared.

Tamara murmured in her sleep and Brolin jumped up from his chair by the bed at the window.

"Are you all right, Tamara? Do you need…anything?" He whispered, stroking her hair from her face.

His face fell in disappointment when she didn't answer but continued to snore softly. He returned to the chair and settled in for another stretch of watching. As he sat, he took stock of the injuries and cuts to her face and hands that he could see peeking over the deep folds of the duvet. His face tightened in renewed anger. That Lady Assandra had sent an assassin to kill Tamara while he was away and without a protector had ignited a white fire in his heart. She would pay. He should never have left her alone. He didn't expect Assandra to move so quickly!

He sat on the sofa in the apartment's sitting room cradling Tamara after he took her from the bathing room and Nord went in to see if he could identify the assailant.

When he exited, Brolin knew by his face.

"Palace assassin?"

"Yes, Major. Secondary."

Secondary assassins worked the will of the advisors and other high-ranking officials of the palace. It was rare for them to go out to kill citizens. It was rare for them to kill at all.

He looked at Tamara's unconscious face. The evidence of her internal rage, determination, and instinctive skill showed clear in the aftermath they discovered when they raced in to rescue her, but what would have happened if they came a few minutes later? Would she have escaped? The assailant wasn't dead, but momentarily knocked unconscious and badly gored by the broken glass.

He was dead now, though.

Brolin handed Tamara over to Nord without a word and they tramped down out of the building to waiting vehicles. Nord being the lighter of the two, strapped Tamara to himself so their combined weight wouldn't weigh down the hoverbike too much. After she awoke and fought him, he thought it best for the major to ride with her so he could calm her, seeing she responded instantly to his pleas to be calm. And so, Brolin could have ridden to the end of the earth in the happiness he found simply by riding with Tamara Fieldmarsh, Lieutenant First Class, cradled and secure at his heart as they rode through the cold night.

It was with a bittersweetness they arrived in the Imperial City under cover of darkness. Of the two times he held Tamara Fieldmarsh, this was the longest and most memorable, albeit traumatic, of times. How he wished he could hold her through the night without the threat of death hanging over them.

Her funny sleepy face that turned up to greet his as they sat on the hoverbike before his Imperial home pleased him beyond measure. The presence of Nord placed limitations on how much Brolin expressed his emotions and regard for the petite female form wrapped securely in his arms. When Nord took her from him, he felt physically separated from his life-giving force.

He looked earnestly at her beautiful sleeping face. Yes. Something would need to be done to keep her in his bed forever. His head drooped back slowly and exhaustion overtook him.

* * *

He opened his eyes some time later to odd sounds and voices. He was immediately alert and on guard.

"Tamara-!" He uttered, propelling himself from the chair toward the bed. "Yes?"

He looked beneath his hands pressing against the bed's duvet—there was nothing beneath it but mattress! He blinked and sat back astonished.

Tamara sat propped against pillows with a tray topped with soup. She looked so shining and beautiful...and alive and awake! She looked amused. Nord stood on the other side of the bed turning on the lamp. He glanced over Tamara and the major like a godfather ensuring his godchildren were well taken care of.

"Did you need me?" Tamara asked, teasing.

Yes.

"For a moment, I feared for you. I am surprised instead, to find you awake!

And with an appetite!"

She giggled and his heart soared at the sound.

"Your shadow is an excellent chef, Major."

"Please. Refrain from calling me a shadow, Lieutenant. I am neither vapid, nor inclined to stay in the background," Nord said as he passed around the bed to exit the room.

Tamara looked startled and cast an alarmed glance at Nord. Brolin laughed.

"His sense of humor, you understand. He is wickedly funny, but chooses when and with whom to expose his wit. I believe he deems you worthy."

Tamara's spoon clinked into her bowl and watched Nord as he left, then she turned wary eyes to Brolin.

"Is...is that his wit? I felt very much reproved."

He wanted to wipe that look away and replace it with the smile. He scraped the chair closer to the bed and leaned against the mattress with his forearms, looking up into her face where she sat in the middle of the bed amongst the pillows.

"Nevermind him my darl-er...he didn't mean any harm. You'll see when he returns. Tell me, how do you feel?"

"I feel well. I am surprised, frankly. If I keep my mind occupied, I don't think about last night. Or was it a few hours ago? A day? I've sadly lost track of time."

"Last night. You've been asleep off and on since. It's near evening now."

Brolin noticed she had stopped eating. He stood to take the tray and walked around the bed to place it atop the large, deep bureau top across from the bed. He returned to his chair and settled in, enjoying his time with her.

She looked around the room with appreciation. "Where am I?"

"My home...in the Imperial City." He said softly.

Her face lit up and she snuggled back under the duvet and moved slightly closer to his side, and looked at him. "This is *your* home? I haven't seen the rest of it, but this room is heavenly," she said, a large grin spreading across her face. She turned her head as she spread her arm out to gesture at the rest of the room with its high ceilings and deep cream walls, "I miss sleeping in this sort of place. It reminds me of my childhood home. And this duvet is the clouds of heaven itself!"

As she looked around the room, Brolin saw the bruises on her neck where her assailant must have had his hands. His heart lurched.

"...Tamara..."

"Hm?" She flipped back to look at him, scooting closer, her eyes on his... his heart in her hands.

"Oh!" She said, sitting up suddenly, "when do we go to the palace? We can't let Assandra know she's failed before we surprise her!"

His mouth fell open, "But...Tamara...you've just endured an almost successful attack on your life...I..."

"I know!" She said emphatically, "That's why I want to go as soon as possible. She can't be allowed to get away with everything she's done!"

Words failed him. He didn't expect that she would want to make a foray into certain danger after her ordeal; the third in a week!

"Tamara...I don't think...I think you should rest and allow me and Nord to finish this."

"No."

"No?"

"*No.*"

"But-"

"NO."

He would get Nord to help speak some sense into her. He couldn't have her in harms way again! She was still weak. What if Assandra tried again in a brazen attack at the palace? What if they got separated and he couldn't save her this time?

"Nord!" He shouted.

"No!" Tamara stated again.

"No, hold on, hold on, Tamara. I need you to understand what's at risk. *Nord!*"

"Sir?"

"Nord, please help me tell the Lieutenant what the stakes are if she insists on going with us to the palace."

Nord blinked, "I don't understand, major."

"She *insists* on going with us. She has just been savagely attacked."

"I must say I understand her desire to see vengeance."

"Thank you, Nord," Tamara said, crossing her arms and glaring at Brolin.

Brolin stared at Nord. Why wasn't he cooperating?

"Nord."

"Major?"

"Come with me!" He hissed, brushing past him out the door. He strode down the hall and turned into the kitchen. He spun around when he heard Nord behind him.

"What was *that?*" He hissed.

"Sir, sir..." Nord held his palms up placatingly.

"What?" Brolin said, turning around and leaning against the kitchen island, arms crossed.

"I hesitate to say this, but, that woman in there is appropriately angered, traumatized, and desirous of justice and vengeance. She is entitled to each. But you, sir."

"What *about* me?"

"You are trying to protect her like...like...like..."

"Spit it out!"

"A lover, sir. You are fighting like her lover and not her major." He looked away discreetly, a red flush staining his cheeks. Brolin knew it pained him to speak thus.

He sighed. Nord was correct, as usual. He tried to stunt Tamara's desire to fight as she was most surely entitled. Rather than admit this, he huffed and brushed past Nord to stalk back to Tamara.

She sat glaring at him from the bed, arms crossed. He stood at the door, arms akimbo, glaring at her. Nord stood in the kitchen discreetly sighing his reproach. Suddenly, Brolin's defenses crumbled, and he walked toward the bed as if in a dream. Face expressing his misery, he climbed into the bed, boots and all. Giving in to all the reasons he flaunted the rules against impropriety and fraternization at the very beginning of their relationship...

indeed, when he saw her weeks and weeks before they met in her hangar, Vale Brolin, the highest and respected pilot in all of New Victoria and advisor to the Emperor closed his eyes and reached out for the warmth and steadying scent of the engine tamer of wide renown, known to tame the wildest, the roughest, the most degraded, and the most volatile. He buried his face into her skin, unconsciously echoing and reversing thier earlier positions during their night flight to the city. Tonight, she was strong, and he the one needing her comfort.

Nord tiptoed back down the hall, his cheeks a bright red.

Chapter Thirteen

T he next morning greeted an awkward Tamara. Sleeping in Brolin's embrace proved to be an eye-opening experience, but in the gloom of the morning, overcast and threating lightning and thunder, she felt shy. Brolin had always made her feel wanted, but she was so unsure of how steady his desire for her was. She looked at him sprawled on the bed, blankets wrapped up in his boots, pillows thrown to the floor. Part of her still wanted to guard her heart from the likely heartbreak she expected to experience in his presence. Tamara was sure he and Lady Assandra had a sexual history. Today, she was going to confront the enemy that was Assandra Marananth. Tamara knew she held no inhibitions about what she would do to the woman if they crossed paths. She sent an assassin to kill her. She was positive she was behind the plot to kill Brolin. Would *he* be as ruthless as she?

Tamara snuck from the room, looking for clothing. She found it outside the door that Nord must have closed discreetly sometime in the night. He was all things discreet. A direct opposite to Scolder. She missed him. Tamara scooped her belongings and tried the doors in hall until she found the bathing room and had a morning bath. Such a change from the other place! Quiet pipes, wood carvings and surrounds. It must be heaven to live here.

When she exited later, smelling of roses and lavender, and reveling in freshly laundered civilian clothing, she found Brolin had awakened in her absence and disappeared. She tried to repair the disheveled appearance of the room and then looked for the kitchen, rubbing her complaining stomach. Nord, ever resourceful, had left some quick-ready items on the table and she ate quickly, eager to be off.

She heard footsteps coming down the hall and tried to make herself busy, heat rising to her ears. She looked down and straightened her trousers, retied her boots...

"Good morning."

She turned around and smiled at the unlawfully handsome man. "Good morning."

"Sleep well?" He said, pouring himself a cup of coffee.

"I did. And yourself?"

He walked over to the table, set against an enormous window and sat down. He looked her full in the face and spoke, "I slept the best I've ever slept since I was a child."

Tamara blinked. The major sat back, opened a newspaper, and drank his coffee.

"We leave in fifteen minutes," Nord said, walking into the room.

Tamara nodded at him, "Good morning, Nord."

"Good morning, Lieutenant. I hope you and the major slept we....that is... ahem...I hope you slept well."

Tamara's mouth moved, but there was no sound. She heard a noise from behind the major's paper that sounded like a laugh, but she couldn't be sure.

"I slept marvelously, Nord. Thank you," Brolin said from the newspaper, a definite tone of humor in his tone.

"I need a knife," Tamara blurted.

Nord spun around. Brolin lowered his newspaper.

"For defense. At the palace," she explained.

* * *

The walk to the palace was tense. Nord had told them he went to the palace earlier that morning and spoke to de Maldane. The atmosphere was tense and de Maldane said he feared a coup was in the offing. When Nord asked who he believed was responsible, de Maldane either didn't know, couldn't say, or was behind it all hoping to appear innocent.

211

They planned to enter the palace through the usual means to prevent alarm spreading throughout the palace, should Lady Assandra and her mercenaries prompt an attack just by their presence.

Brolin walked ahead, Tamara behind him, with Nord drawing up the rear. As they reached the gates, they were astonished to see someone running from the palace, waiving their arms frantically and shouting.

"It's de Maldane!" Nord and Tamara exclaimed.

"Open the gates!" Nord barked at the guard in the guardhouse just on the other side. They darted through the gates as de Maldane reached hearing distance.

"She's done it! She's launched a coup! She has the emperor holed up in the throne room! Hurry! Quick!"

Adrenaline jumpstarted Tamara's blood and she raced to behind Nord and Brolin as de Maldane trailed behind them shouting details at them. They reached the golden door, painfully familiar to Tamara and rushed through to get to the throne room. Tamara had lost her bearings halfway through, but Nord and Brolin obviously knew it by heart.

They reached the hallway just before the throne-room door, when they stopped. It was dangerous for them to continue this way, as they would probably be shot on sight by Assandra's mercenaries.

de Maldane caught up with them and motioned for them to follow him. He raced down the hall and opened a door shorter than the rest set within an alcove. They stooped to enter.

"This leads to the guard's quarters below the throne room. We must see if anyone is here!"

"Who goes there!" A voiced roared from within.

Tamara jumped.

"His Highness's chief butler and houseman, Felix de Maldane! Major Vale Brolin, advisor to the emperor, his all-man, and...what are you? Lieutenant Fieldmarsh of the Defense Force! Is all well?" He called back.

"Enter," the voice said.

They entered an armory of sorts with a low ceiling.

"We are currently assessing the situation. The emperor has his private guards, but we need our reinforcements within to force them out.

"How did this come to pass?" Brolin barked, rage and impatience giving his voice volume.

The guard looked him over before answering, "It seems Lady Assandra wanted to catch us off-guard, so to speak, by launching her attack so early in the morning. We don't fortify our ranks until half-past this hour! So, she succeeded in that. But not all is lost."

"Is there a secret passage into the wardrobe in the imperial office?" Tamara asked.

All turned to look at her in astonishment.

"He showed it to me...sort of...when I was here before," she said, explaining herself.

The captain of the guard looked at de Maldane.

"Show them," he said.

And that's what led to Tamara Fieldmarsh earning her first battle scar.

VII

Vale & Tamara Together

Chapter Fourteen

T amara didn't know what to expect as the captain of the guard walked her around to the secret entrance to the emperor's wardrobe. Time slowed, a rushing in her ears deadening the clarity of her mission. Shouts erupted up and down halls as Assandra's mercenaries attacked the emperor's guards. She felt for the knife Nord handed her before leaving Brolin's house and its feeling of safety. Adrenaline hit her again and she moved like a ghost, feeling nothing, hearing nothing, seeing only the back of the captain of the guard rushing her to the emperor's hidey-hole. Tamara wondered where Scolder was. Was he safe? Did they find out about his part in her escape before?

Wait until you hear a commotion on the other side. Brolin had told her.

Rush in with caution. Nord had said.

The captain jabbed a finger toward a tall statue standing within the alcove and rushed away without telling her what she was to do with it.

Quickly, she looked for levers, or buttons, she pulled at the arms of the statue, no avail. Muffled shouts, cries, and the sounds of scuffle reached her. She scrambled to find a way to move the statue. Suddenly, it came to her: *push!*

She moved to one side of the statue and shoved with all her might. The statue spun on a turn table, revealing a hidden door. She pushed that, too, and it opened. That statue returned to his previous position. Unless you looked very, very, very closely, you wouldn't know she was there! Genius! But where was she?

Soon, she understood she was in a little passage that led into the room behind the wardrobe the emperor entered through at their meeting. A secret, within a secret, within a secret. She heard scrabbling and put out a hand. Her hand encountered a wall and she moved toward it listening. Someone was definitely in there. It must be the emperor. She didn't want to alert him to her presence knowing he had hidden guards even here, and he was a skilled man who could dispatch her into her reward quickly. Remembering what Nord and Brolin told her, she waited.

It seemed an eternity had passed before she heard the scrabbling inside intensify and a voice raised. Did she move now? She heard thumps, and bumps, and felt for her knife. When she heard two voices raised, one distinctly female, Tamara felt for the opening. It took her longer than she preferred. She *preferred* to kick out the wall and rush in like Nord told her to!

She pushed and shoved frantically as the sounds on the other side of the wall intensified. With a great push, the opening gave way, propelling her into the room. She stood before the astonished emperor.

"Wait! I'm with you, Your Highness!" She shouted.

The sight before her was of overturned tables, upended chairs, destroyed tapestry and paintings. She turned around to survey the damage and stared into the furious, purple glare of a crazed Assandra Marananth.

Assandra's hand flicked out like a viper, and Tamara gasped in shock. Blood— Tamara's blood—splattered into the air and came to rest on the ancient objects in the emperor's secret place.

A searing pain attacked the left side of her face like fire and her vacationing rage returned to her like a bucket of flesh-destroying lava. Tamara picked up the nearest thing to her; a bust of a previous emperor, and it flashed through the air, cracking anything that happened to get in its way.

Tamara advanced, seeing Assandra's face central in her haze of red. Assandra backed up to gain leeway, but Tamara didn't slow. She dodged Assandra's knife, depending on her speed to keep her off balance. She threw the bust at her and kept throwing things until she had her in a corner. All she needed to do now was to disarm her.

She noticed movement in her peripherals and heard someone shout to get the emperor out of there. Someone had finally broken through into the throne-room and made it down the hall! Assandra's coup had failed!

The guards guided Sylvanus through the hideaway to safety.

The blood drained from Assandra's face as she realized her fate.

"Assandra Marananth! This is the captain of the Imperial Guard! Surrender to the guard immediately!" A commanding voice called into the room.

"Never!" She screamed like a madwoman believing she could win.

Tamara watched her and her knife warily, because Assandra kept flicking it through the air to keep her at bay.

"Tamara? Are you in there?" her beloved's voice called to her.

"You call her Tamara, Vale?" Assandra hissed, "You've bedded *her? This whelp of a girl?!*"

Tamara blinked. Was she having a conversation in the middle of her own failed coup?

"Tamara. I'm here." Brolin said, his voice nearer, meaning he was inside the room. Tamara kept her eyes on Assandra.

"Stop talking to her, Vale! Talk to *me!*" Assandra screamed, flicking the knife at Tamara again.

Tamara's blood boiled.

"You and I meant more to each other than this *child* could ever mean to you!" Assandra ranted.

Vale spoke carefully to Tamara, "Tamara, you can come to me now. Let the captain of the guards take her."

"No one will *take* me, Vale Brolin!"

Tamara wanted to rush up there and shut her mouth forever. If it wasn't for that knife, she could, but Assandra had already sliced her face up pretty badly, she could feel the blood dripping down her neck and arm. It hurt like the fires of Hades.

"*You* could have taken me, Vale! But you treated me like you were better than me! Like I wasn't beautiful enough for you!" Assandra snarled, spittle and mucus flying from her lips and hanging from her nose. Any beauty she possessed had been effectively erased in her madness.

Assandra stood in front of a large, heavy tapestry affixed to the wall with a heavy, wooden rod. The room seemed to serve as a treasure vault of sorts, storing the emperor's favourite pieces of art and furniture in here for him to enjoy seeing. Praying he would forgive her, but doubting he would care that much considering the damage Assandra had caused already, she jumped onto an old-fashioned bureau and angled herself to grab onto the bar quickly.

Assandra, hardly noticing Tamara had moved, turned to face Vale, "If you had just given me what I wanted, I wouldn't have killed you! We could have been beautiful together! Me, the Empress of New Victoria, and you, my husband at my side! You've ruined everything!" Assandra advanced on a stunned Brolin.

"Assandra-" Brolin began, his tone attempting negotiation.

"Don't speak to me you traitor!" Assandra railed, "Why didn't you die? Why didn't your stupid child bride die?" She wailed, "I told them to kill you both. Why didn't you die and save me this misery?"

The captain of the guard peered out of the wardrobe to assess the situation and stepped out, another guard following his lead. His eyes flew to Tamara standing on the bureau.

"Nobody come any closer!" Assandra shouted, waving her knife around, "I'll kill him if you touch me!" Her hair, usually perfectly coifed, was wild.

From her perch, Tamara waited for the prime moment. Assandra continued to advanced on Brolin, who stood on guard, but mentally thrown off-balance by the insane words of his emperor's sister.

Tamara steadied her breath. As Assandra moved closer to the center of the room, and thus toward the jumble of upturned pieces of furniture, she poised herself to jump.

"I am the Lady Assandra Delavine Marananth and I order you to leave!" When she received no obedience, she advanced further onto Brolin and Tamara jumped! She grabbed the bar, turned and jumped off the wall, pummeling Assandra into the pile of furniture and sending her knife flying out of her hand.

Tamara saw stars and gasped for air. Brolin darted for her, and lifted her off Assandra, pulling her to a safe distance. The guards poured into the room, pulling an unconscious Lady Assandra to her feet.

Brolin spun Tamara around into his chest and crushed her as he held her. He moved toward the wardrobe, to get distance from the madwoman and the guards who must now do their jobs.

They stood in the Imperial Office, silent, waiting, when a commotion erupted from inside the wardrobe room. Shouts of "Get it away from her!" and "Help me!" came to them. A high-pitched, blood-curdling scream filled the air and wouldn't stop. Tamara covered her ears and squeezed her eyes shut. Brolin gripped her tighter.

She heard the Captain of the Guard shout.

"Gods! She's dead!"

Tamara and Brolin gasped. He released her and rushed to the wardrobe, stepping inside. Tamara followed.

Guards stood staring down at the floor in shock and horror.

"What happened?!" Brolin shouted.

"She grabbed my knife! I don't know how! We tried to get it away from her!"

Brolin rushed over, shoving guards out of the way. He kneeled down and placed his hand over her heart. Then he stood slowly.

"She wouldn't be taken by us. She chose her way out," The Captain of the Guard muttered.

Brolin returned to Tamara.

"Let's go. The Captain of the Guard will inform Emperor Sylvanus. He'll call for me later."

#

They walked slowly out of the Imperial Office into the glassed in hall. Tamara stumbled slightly and Brolin took her arm to steady her. She felt immeasurably tired. She placed a hand over her throat, feeling the pain from last night's attack coming again. Then she stopped in consternation as her hand touched wetness. She looked down at her hand: blood. Her mouth went slack. Assandra's knife slash to her face. She had forgotten about it.

Brolin turned to see what was wrong, and he blanched at the sight of the blood on her hand. He held her hands in both of his, glancing over the wound. Tamara winced, not wanting to know how bad it was.

"We'll find de Maldane to have this treated…if he hasn't turned coward and run," He said. He looked deeply into her eyes. "You are a brave and a fierce warrior, Tamara Fieldmarsh."

He released one hand, held on to the other and led her through the hall, navigating through yet more Imperial Guards streaming through toward the ghastly scene behind. Above their helmets, Tamara saw the sky dark with roiling clouds. The sound of thunder vibrated the glass. Heavy winds bent the trees and rustled the leaves of ornamental plants. She saw the rain cleanse the air of contaminants and swirling debris.

#

de Maldane led them into his richly furnished pristine quarters. Intensely coloured wallpaper filled with drawings of plants and trees covered the walls in deep greens and aquatic blues. The storm outside cast the room into deep shadow, heightening the atmosphere of intimacy and refined tastes.

"Call the physician." He murmured to a man inside dusting the lamps. Then, he spun to face Brolin and Tamara. "Come with me," he said. They followed him into a small room at the back of the small apartment. Wood and glass cabinets filled with bottles, jars, and other medicine boxes lined the opposite wall. It was a narrow room, with the light coming from the same wall of windows as the principal living area without.

"I assist the physician when he cannot tend to someone in a timely manner. I keep my own potions and notions in here. I find it inordinately useful to have my own room for patients." He said, guiding Tamara to an old-fashioned doctor's examination chair. He motioned for her to sit.

He dipped a small flat wooden stick into a jar of ointment and then applied it to her cheek.

"There. That should control the bleeding and pain until the physician arrives. I do hope the scar doesn't disfigure your face too much," de Maldane said, glancing over her face and figure before glancing at Brolin.

Then he left them to wait.

"I think de Maldane hates me." Tamara said.

Brolin climbed onto the examination seat behind her and stretched out, closing his eyes. His right hand reached out blindly for her.

"de Maldane is disdainful of all." He murmured.

Tamara felt her cheek gingerly and then pulled her hand away. She felt her body relaxing under the mesmerizing touch of Brolin's finger trailing lazy circles on the back of her hand. What would happen with them now? The time would come when she must return to her post at the training grounds. She had to complete her five years or face prison. She didn't know where he would go. Would he tire of her as much as they say he tired of the other women in his life? She protected her heart by reminding herself of the gossip. Imagine her becoming so uncontrollably besotted by him that she became another Assandra Marananth.

She understood the effect of Vale Brolin on the nerves and emotions. He made you feel worth more than gold. He spoke to you with sincerity. He caressed her with such sweetness that you felt you had no alternative but to fall madly for him.

Behind his seemingly calm demeanor, Brolin was frantically searching for a way to end his or Tamara's posts to keep them together. He schemed relentlessly. He would ensure Sylvanus pardoned her AWOL standing at the training grounds. He wondered how quickly he could get Tamara moved to the Imperial City. He thought about the shameful way she was coerced into serving, exchanging prison for simulated freedom.

He remembered the first time he saw her as he and Nord investigated the smugglers. Undercover, they had observed the smuggler's trade routes, mules, machines, and supply men. They encountered one T. Fieldmarsh. They bribed men to give them information on this so-called "engine tamer". Getting directions to T. Fieldmarsh's usual places of work, they were astonished to find Fieldmarsh was a woman! They observed her in her trade of receiving airships, repairing, and sending them out. Her magnetism and fierce independence drew his interest. Women rarely worked in her chosen field of work. What made her do it?

As he continued to investigate the smuggling rings, he kept encountering her work. Tamara was the first engine tamer owners of airships looked to for repairs. She had an uncanny ability to coax everlasting life from a machine. In a time when women chose the safety of home and conventional work, he couldn't understand how such a feminine woman continued to thrive in this field without a man trying to end all of her work and reputation with violence.

He learned why when one day he and Nord observed Tamara smashing a thug's hand with a heavy engine wrench when he tried to caress her bottom. It was a delectably rounded bottom. He had noticed it several times himself. Time passed and it was obvious that although Tamara didn't delve into direct illegal activity herself—and he allowed that she may not even understand precisely what she was doing—she had a large impact on the successfulness of the smugglers. Without Tamara's work, their airships didn't fly over the mountains and into the next territories. She had to be stopped.

He couldn't bear the thought of her languishing away in an Imperial prison, or facing the firing squad. He had to save her. He reported his findings to His Lord Emperor, leaving out his immense attraction to the little outlaw. He suggested moving her skills to the Defense Force. Sylvanus agreed.

Brolin opened his eyes and gazed tenderly at Tamara's face as she looked at the various glass containers in de Maldane's examination room. He admired the firm line of her jaw, her deep curls, the gold highlights of her deep skin, and the way she accepted his caresses leading him to believe she would accept his love and devotion for once.

Before he left her on the airship, he decided he wouldn't give her his heart again. He would bottle up his love and watch over her from afar. After seeing her asleep in his bed at the little apartment at the training base, he knew he would annoy and anger her to distraction before he ever gave up being in her presence. He would make himself indispensable to her. Everything she needed, big or small, he would provide.

"Ah! The brave major and....his Lieutenant!" A jovial voice boomed about the small room, causing Tamara to startle. Brolin clasped her hand in a reassuring grip, then he sat up and greeted the palace physician.

"Doctor Eisle, thank you for coming."

"Not at all, not at all!" His accent was wonderful to Tamara. It clipped the ends of his words and created a lilting tone to his speech. He dropped his medicine bag onto a table and walked over to Tamara to inspect her cheek, *tsk*ing away.

"Tell me, dear, how did you get this?"

"She was defending the emperor," Brolin murmured.

Doctor Eisle's eyebrows raised to his hairless head, his small round eyes growing comically rounder. The light glistened off of his round onyx cheeks.

"Whew! My girl! Any higher and your eye would be gone!"

"Is...is the scar..." Tamara ventured.

"Oh, don't worry about that. I have a miracle working cream that will make it seem you ran away a coward and sustained no injury!" He cackled merrily at his joke.

Tamara smiled and then sucked in her breath as the movement angered her wound. Brolin's face tightened into concern.

"Oh, tut tut, you won't be smiling or laughing very easy for at least a couple days. But you'll be right as rain soon enough!" Eisle chuckled. He dug into his bag again, rummaging and tut-tutting. "Here we are, my girl! Morning, afternoon, night! Don't miss!" He handed Tamara a small, wooden jar with a metal cap.

"Oh! Infection...take these drops with breakfast and before bed. We don't want you becoming ill. Although, I wouldn't be surprised if a small fever came upon you." He smiled at her, then his face transformed into a frown. "What's this?! Who has done *this* to you?" He abruptly lifted Tamara's chin with his fingers, and he turned an accusatory eye to Brolin. "What do you know of this?"

"She was attacked last night in the south. A palace assassin," Brolin muttered, anger staining his voice.

"Mmm....I've heard horrible things just today of plots and schemes. Does it make you cough?"

"Not anymore," Tamara said.

"Mm. Good sign. Come to me if you have trouble swallowing. Okay?"

"Yes."

"Take care my dear. I have other wounded people to tend to." And he was gone.

Tamara slid down from the examination chair and turned to Brolin. "Well, I suppose now I don't know what to do." She shrugged.

de Maldane looked in, "His Highness wishes to see you both."

They looked at each other and followed de Maldane out of the room, out of his little apartment, and to the emperor's private quarters which Tamara had yet to see. A guard rushed them into a small estate within the palace. The floors were marble and everything looked covered in gold. They passed through room after enormous room before ending at the imperial bedroom.

Sylvanus Marananth lay in an enormous bed in the center. His eyes were red-rimmed. He looked utterly devastated and unlike a royal personage. Two ministers of state stood on either side of the bed, hands clasped. Brolin and Tamara bowed and approached when he waved them over with a weak hand.

"I owe my life to you, My Lady Tamara," he began.

Tamara's heart jumped. He called her "my lady"! Hiding her astonishment, she bowed again slightly, showing deference.

"Without you, my poor sister would have injured me, or killed me as she intended. I did not understand she suffered so poorly in her mind. You have my eternal thanks."

"It is my honor and my duty," Tamara murmured.

He acknowledged her statement with a nod of his head.

"Vale Brolin, my close friend and confidant," he said, turning his attention to the major.

Tamara stepped back.

"I am most pleased to see that you still have your life and that the assassins failed."

Brolin bowed.

"I hear you and the bravery of your man-at-arms helped turn the tide of the attack against me?"

"It is true, Your Highness," Brolin answered.

"You also have my undying gratitude."

"Please, you must help me understand my sister's madness. Why did she do this? Why did her life have to end so tragically?" His voice died away as he fought a spasm of tears. An attendant poured a sedative and handed him a silk handkerchief. Another attendant brought forward two chairs for Brolin and Tamara. Brolin told him the entire sordid tale.

Assandra Marananth, sister and advisor to Sylvanus Marananth, Emperor of New Victoria and surrounding territories grew tired of her status of advisor. She wanted to rule on her own. Struck by the change in her features, no longer having men fall at her feet and give gifts for her wiles, she grew dissatisfied with life. Three years before, she disguised herself and visited the cities, speaking to those who operated below the law. She looked for men unsatisfied with Sylvanus' rule. She promised them wealth and power if they helped her. She amassed a following of men including smugglers, assassins, thugs, and mercenaries who traveled regularly across the mountains into the enemy territory.

Finding favour with certain men in power in the enemy's land, they gave her money and supplies to help overthrow Sylvanus. The enemy sent spies into New Victoria to gain information about new technology. Assandra helped some spies get into the defense force to destabilize the country. At some point, her mind deteriorated further, and she felt threatened by Brolin's advisership. She attempted to seduce him, hoping to gain power over him and get him to her side. Brolin resisted, and she planned against him. She combined her thirst for power and her insecurity of her looks to create a violent case against the ruler of New Victoria.

She bribed gambling cave owners and other men in the underworld to find vulnerable men and women to join her cause. One such man was Fillip Weathermarker, sent to sabotage and frame Lieutenant Fieldmarsh because Tamara knew Assandra from her work with the smugglers—although Assandra wasn't sure Tamara knew, she couldn't take that chance.

Fillip's father, a magistrate in the courts, had cut off his generous allowance because of his wastrel lifestyle and constant debts. Fillip craved respect, and they convinced him to join the defense force and rise through the ranks so Assandra could promote him to her courts at the right time. When Assandra discovered Brolin and the emperor's favour of Tamara Fieldmarsh and her brother's desire to have her moved into the palace for a lofty position, she panicked. She knew Tamara had to die or she would recognize her and spread the alarm about her own duplicity. She tasked Fillip, and another spy sent from the enemy country, to frame Tamara Fieldmarsh for treason so she would stay in prison or die by the firing squad. The other spy was one Tabitha Thorncrist.

Sylvanus Marananth was silent following Brolin's revelation. He lay back upon the pillows, one arm thrown over his eyes, tears streaming down his face. The room was silent. No one moved. The earlier storm and thunder had cleared and a warm sunlight streamed into the towering windows. This contrast of light during the emperor's emotionally tragic day seemed cruel. His sister formed a coup against him, tried to kill him herself before she died by her own hand.

At last, he lowered his arm from his face and gestured for the attendants to help him rise. Brolin and Tamara stood in deference as the emperor stood and a large, enveloping robe thrown about his shoulders. He moved toward them holding a handkerchief to his face.

"Vale Brolin, Major in my Defense Force and advisor within my court, I wish to award you the seal of advisership and wish you to serve as my leading advisor. You shall receive the accompanying salary, living quarters, honors, medals, seal, undermen, servants, property, governing contracts, and personal allotments as the law demands." He stuck out his hand wordlessly and an attendant approached with a silk lined box. Sylvanus removed a golden seal attached to a ribbon.

"Bow, Vale," He said affectionately.

Brolin bowed and Sylvanus placed the ribbon around his neck. Brolin straightened, his face contorting and working. Sylvanus placed an affectionate hand on his shoulder.

"I know, Brother, I know." He said. "You balk at the award of the position so recently vacated by my poor sister. My heart is broken, but I am most pleased to have my closest friend at my side in a stronger capacity. Thank you for your service."

He shook his hand and returned Brolin's bow.

"Lieutenant Fieldmarsh." He turned to Tamara and saluted her, then he smiled a watery smile.

"Your preparation to do all to save your emperor's life shall not go unrewarded. Will you come tomorrow at the notice of the Palace's butler. I shall have something for you."

"Of, course, Your Highness," Tamara replied.

"Then I shall see you tomorrow. Good day." He said and turned away.

They rushed Tamara and Brolin from the imperial rooms.

Chapter Fifteen

That night, celebratory wine and champagne flowed in the major's home. Tamara felt shabby without formal clothing as she stood in the impromptu gathering with friends and neighbors cramming inside. Brolin was ecstatic.

Tamara wondered where Nord disappeared to. She hadn't seen him since that morning's rush to defend Sylvanus. She pushed through the crowd looking for a familiar face other than Brolin's. She smiled as a drunk couple congratulated her and muttered jovial salutations. She didn't know who anyone was and couldn't understand where everyone had sprung from so suddenly.

Tamara wanted to sleep long and hard. She wanted Brolin to cradle her in his arms as she slept, the way he did last night. Her enemies bruised her body, bruised her mind, and bruised her emotions.

Unable to take much more of the body heat and drunken voices, she walked out into the chilly night to sit in the small garden at the back of the house. She heard footsteps crunch the pebbles in the walk behind her and turned a glad face to greet who she thought was Brolin. Instead, she saw Nord.

"I see it wasn't me you wanted to see," he said as he sat in the opposite garden chair.

"I'm sorry. I didn't realize you were here. Where have you been?" She asked.

"Brolin sent me on a mission."

"Oh."

"Are you alright, Lieutenant?"

"Please. Call me Tamara."

"All right, then. Tamara. Can I do anything for you?"

"I'm...I'm tired. My body hurts. My...my heart hurts."

"Tell me," Nord said, placing a small wrapped package she hadn't noticed to the side of him on the chair.

"I heard everything about Fillip and Thorncrist today," she said softly.

"Oh...I see," Nord said, sympathetically, "The major finally told you?"

"No. Emperor Sylvanus asked him to tell him everything while I was sitting beside him."

"Ah. I know that's not how the major wanted you to find out. He wanted to tell you privately."

"It's not his fault. I just can't help feeling...worthless."

Nord sat forward and peered into her face as she fought tears, "Ohhhh, no...no, no don't feel that way, please. Tamara, you aren't worthless simply because one or two people try to make it so." He reached across to grab her hands. "Please believe me. There are people I know who believe you are worth more than gold."

She looked at him, desperate for him to go on.

"But...," he returned to his seat, "that's not for me to explain. You must hear it from...let's go inside. Looks like a party." He pulled her to her feet and picked up his package.

She allowed him to lead her to the house.

"What *is* happening?" He asked.

"I thought you knew!" She said.

"I do *not* know." He said, guiding her up the stairs.

"Your boss has a new position in the palace," she replied, passing him to push open the door.

He gasped, "You don't say."

She spun to face him in confusion. Then she laughed and slapped his arm playfully.

"You *did* know, Nord. You just wanted to distract me, huh?" She said gratefully.

"I don't know what you mean, my lady," He said with a wink.

#

"And here are the two people I owe my life, my thanks, my gold, and my heart!" They heard Brolin before they saw him. He pushed through the crowd of well-wishers in the large sitting room, arm outstretched.

"Thank you…thank you…thank you…" Brolin said, catching Tamara by the arm and tugging her to him. He kissed her forehead with pleasure, pressing her into his chest in delight. Tamara giggled as she listened to his joy at the moment. The kisses he placed on her forehead made a ridiculous "smack" each time, and Tamara couldn't contain more giggles, louder giggles, from pouring from her.

Brolin turned to express his good news to Nord "Nord! My man! Guess who I am today!"

Tamara's face creased in an amused smile, her hands clasped under her chin as Brolin gave Nord the news he already had.

Unable to handle reveling, joy and drunkenness, Tamara grabbed a glass of champagne, walked to the bedroom and closed the door. She kicked off her boots, drained the champagne in one gulp and climbed into the bed and slept.

#

The next morning, she awoke to Nord shaking her gently, but urgently.

"Hm? Is something wrong with the major?" She sat straight up, almost smashing Nord in the face, "Where is he?"

Nord smiled, "No, Tamara. The palace has sent word requesting your presence."

"Oh! So early! I'll get up right away."

"It's midmorning. I hope you slept well."

She frowned and looked at Nord, sure he was lying. She looked at the window blazing full with light. She looked beside her, slightly disappointed to find she was on her own. She jumped out of the bed and Nord left.

She bathed quickly, attempted to tame her hair, wondering all the while where Brolin could be. She wanted to tell him where she was going. But in a rush, she dressed in a pristine uniform, regretting she didn't have her formal tunic and then she ran out of the house to meet the carriage waiting for her. Then, she was on her way to the palace.

It was a novel feeling driving up to the primary gates of the palace in an official carriage and not hopping over the gate to enter through the garden. She exited the carriage and met de Maldane who escorted her this time to the throne room. A crowd of officials, attendants, palace servants, and other richly dressed bystanders stood inside around the throne and she quailed when she saw them.

"Don't be afraid, Lieutenant Fieldmarsh," His Highness said kindly.

She bowed low and then approached.

"Tamara Fieldmarsh, Lieutenant First Class in the Imperial Defense Force, I hereby pardon you for infractions undertaken in your quest to save the empire from forces that wished her harm."

"Thank you, Your Highness."

An attendant crossed to her and affixed a pin to her collar. Tamara bowed her head. She was so relieved. She had been sure she blew her chances to stay out of prison, sure they would force her to return to hear sentencing. She was also sure the Emperor was often insincere in his promises to inconsequential citizens. She looked up when he began speaking again.

"Tamara Fieldmarsh, Lieutenant First Class in the Imperial Defense Force, I imbue you with the powers legally given to the new position of Imperial Seat of Captain in my personal army (Tamara gasped). Accompanying this position is all the salary, property, and seals relegated to such a position." And as he did the previous day when he awarded the major with his seal, he held out a hand to an attendant.

"Someone is here who wishes to perform the honors in awarding this seal."

Tamara's mouth fell open, then she shut it again quickly. Looking tall, heartbreakingly handsome and severe in his court clothes, Brolin separated himself from the crowd at the fringes carrying a box affixed with the royal seal. He didn't look at her, but wordlessly handed the box to the attendant standing by. He opened the top and removed the seal attached to its ribbon carefully. The attendant signaled she should bow again. Heart pounding, tears pricking her eyes, she bowed and blinked rapidly, determined not to cry before the emperor. Brolin placed the ribbon about her neck and she stood. Unable to resist, she stole a glance at his face and he met her eyes with pride. He reached up and wiped away the lonely tear that escaped her eye, and then stepped back, clacked his heels and saluted her with military precision. Swallowing hard to keep herself from disintegrating into tears on the throne room floor. She snapped out her best salute in return.

"You are aware of my undying gratitude in the part you played to save my life and the empire. This new position of honour and service begins at the beginning of the coming month. I wish you complete and speedy healing from the wounds you received during your battles. ..." He cut a glance to Brolin who now stood out of Tamara's line of sight, but she knew, "and I wish that everything you seek in life and all that you deserve presents itself with speed and accuracy. Blessings on you and your life." He stood and bowed low in deference and the crowd erupted into cheers.

Emperor Sylvanus departed the room with his personal guard, the guard she would oversee in a month's time! Hardly able to contain herself, she accepted the congratulations of strangers in a fog of shock and over stimulation. She felt she would faint. She looked over the heads that mobbed her, looking for Brolin. Then, she felt something pressed into her hand and she found a scrap of paper with a message.

I can't wait to celebrate with you. Please, wait for me at home. -V

She didn't know the correct way to leave the proceedings, and so Tamara Fieldmarsh, newly appointed captain of the new imperial personal guard suffered for an interminable amount of time until de Maldane rescued her from overly zealous well-wishers and sent her on her way in a carriage.

Chapter Sixteen

She awoke with a start. Hot and clammy, she sat up gasping for air. Her throat was dry, and she was desperate for water. She hastily unbuttoned her blouse and threw it across the room. Stepping out of the trousers, she sat panting. Clad in her chemise, corset and drawers, she half-stumbled down to the bathing room.

She stepped into the room, relishing the feel of the cool tile against her toes. She made her way to the water basin cabinet and turned the tap, waiting a second for the water to flow and then she hungrily splashed her face, neck, and chest with the cool water. She leaned against the cabinet and let the water run over her hands while she leaned her head against the attached mirror. She sighed as she turned off the tap. She felt better.

The light from the small window above the bath cast moonlight into the room. She looked into the mirror and almost laughed at her reflection. Her face was glistening with water and the hair framing her face shone with water droplets. She didn't care; she was finally cool.

The day's events…the entire month's events… left her drained, depressed, upset, directionless, and listless. She lay on the bathroom floor and breathed deeply. Then she cried. She cried for the false friends who wished her harm. She finally cried over the jolting change of life that took her from being her own woman. She cried for the gradual acceptance of her life in the service and the feeling she betrayed herself. She cried for losing her innocence in life. She cried from the heaviness of love and her desire to protect herself. She cried from a broken heart that realized life is not always what you make it, but sometimes a composite of what others help make it become. She cried in gratitude for those who helped her. She cried in despair over those who worked to break her.

Soon, her body calmed, and the tears lessened.

She looked up at the night sky shining through the small round window above her. Her thoughts turned to Vale Brolin. She thought about his heavy dark lashes, his sultry eyes that crinkled at the edges when something amused him. She thought of his dark hair that he wore in an informal pompadour, his hair consistently glistening and full. Her hands strayed to her belly as the thought of his hands roving her body shot through her mind. She closed her eyes and wondered what it would be like to experience being naked in his presence. She removed her half corset and threw it in the corner. The moonlight streamed down onto the tiles and shone on her skin.

Thoroughly frustrated and annoyed with herself, she stood to splash her face with more water.

As she stared at her reflection, her eyes caught movement at the doorway. She stilled as she watched a shirtless and powerfully muscled Vale Brolin drift into the room. His eyes held hers intensely as he gazed at her reflection. He reached her at the basin and she watched as he stood behind her, dwarfing her with his broad shoulders. His dark hair was tousled and the stubble on his chin glistened with light hairs among the dark.

Tamara held her breath as she watched his reflection lower his head to the curve of her neck and breathe in deeply. His right hand circled around her and cradled her head, turning it toward him so he could kiss her temple. Tamara's eyes closed, and she held onto his firm and massive forearm for stability.

His left arm cradled her against him, his arm around her waist. Tamara's head felt light, and it whirled as she stood against him. He kissed her earlobe. She sank further into his chest. He caressed her bottom lip with her thumb. She sighed deeply in her throat.

"Never let me leave you again," he murmured into her ear, his chest rumbling and vibrating her spine, sending pleasant shocks into her stomach.

He spun her toward him and lifted her to sit on the basin cabinet and he rested her against the mirror; the coolness providing a pleasant contrast to her heated back. Leaning forward, Vale murmured into her neck, "I left my heart behind with you when I left the airship all those weeks ago." Vale straightened slightly to gaze into her eyes, and Tamara's heart fluttered at what she saw in his eyes. "I haven't been right since." His eyes rested briefly on the brand new scare she gained in the battle, then he closed them and rested his forehead against her mouth. She kissed him tenderly, raising her hands to run her fingers through his hair. How could she have resisted him all those times before? What sort of person had she been back then? She was powerless against him now.

"When Scolder found me at the base, I was tearing the place apart, demanding to know what had happened to you! I thought the enemy agents had kidnapped you and taken you away from me." He placed his forehead against hers and closed his eyes. His long lashes rested against his cheeks, creating a deep shadow.

"I will ride to the death to find you," he continued, "but I feared you were gone forever and my world turned dark and meaningless. I was in a dark, mindless rage."

Tamara's heart cried out for him. She never thought he would return and believe the spies had taken her and experience such awful misery.

"Then Scolder found you..." she prompted.

"Then Scolder found me." He lifted his head and looked deep into hers again, and her heart wrenched for him again. She saw his helpless sorrow as he remembered.

"When he told me he had taken you to my quarters, I thought he was lying to me. I plied him with so many questions, he grew irritated with me and shouted at me to go home and see for myself."

Tamara smiled.

"I think I knocked over a woman and a small boy on my way up there. When I opened the door, for a moment, I knew Scolder had lied to me. When I think of you, I think of light, and I must have thought light would fill my rooms if *you* were here. But it was a dark as I had left it"

She watched his face as the remembered emotions flitted across it in the retelling.

"I raced around the rooms and when I saw you curled up in my bed, I-"

"You what?" She asked softly.

Vale straightened and pulled her toward him so her legs straddled his hips. He bent his head and murmured against her lips, "I knew I always wanted to come home and see you that way."

Tamara pressed her lips against his and breathed in deep. It was hardly enough. She was left feeling cold when he broke the kiss.

"Tamara, love of my existence," he began and her heart met his words with a thrill, "It nearly broke me to hear your screams when the assassin attacked you." He closed his eyes in a spasm of painful memory. He laid his forehead on hers. Man and woman relived their individual pains of that night. With an impatient sound, he pulled Tamara to him and carried her, hands beneath her buttocks, to the bedroom.

He sat holding her on his lap, his head beneath the curve of her jaw. He sighed and Tamara traced the outline of his neck and shoulder in the moon's light. She caressed his skin, memorizing each hill and valley. She smiled.

Suddenly, he fell backward, carrying her with him.

"Never let me leave you again. Bad things happen when I leave you," he murmured nuzzling her neck.

Her spine shot sparks as he slid his hand between her chemise and her back, tracing figure eights at the hollow of spine. Tamara fought and fought her wish to protect herself. Her heart said "keep him". Her mind said "he's playing with you". She grimaced and uttered a helpless sound.

"What is it? Are you giving in?" He whispered teasingly.

"Ohh..! I...think...I want to." She said, squeezing her eyes shut and burying her face in his chest.

"Why don't you?" He asked.

"...I really want to...!"

"So, do..."

She snuggled closer into him.

Brolin leaned on one elbow, "My love. What's holding you back?"

She peeked up from his chest to look at him, playing with the silken hairs on his chest, "Well…you can't guess?"

He threw up a hand and sat up, "I can't imagine why beautiful, seductive Tamara Fieldmarsh would deign to resist such as me."

"Seriously," Tamara said, scrambling to sit up and look him in the eye, "You really don't know?"

"I'm fast beginning to change my mind on wanting to know."

"It's…all your other women." She replied, shrugging.

"Women? Are you referring to Lady Assandra?!"

"Nooo…the others. They told me you dabble with women and leave them soon for another."

"Please tell me which other women I have so I can run to them instead tonight and get some tender loving care."

She smacked him on the arm, "You know who I mean!"

"I *don't.*"

"Third Mate Kerrigan? The different women I saw you with at the state dinners? The physical arts instructor?"

Brolin stared at her.

"How on earth-? *Kerridan?* 'Harridan' Kerridan? The most acerbic woman in the defense force?"

She grinned and got on her knees, placing her arms around his neck, admiring his eyes, "Well, is she the only one you abhor? What about the woman trying to get into your pants the last time I tried to warn you?

He threw back his head and laughed, "Dyva Windcage! The largest prattle-mouth in all Victoria. She's sixty If she's a day."

"Don't laugh at me," she said, drawing close and grabbing his bottom lip between her teeth.

Vale groaned and pulled her face closer to his treating her like a lifeline.

"I'm not going any further til I sort this out," he said, laying back again. He put his arm behind his head, one leg bent, the other stretched out. Tamara collapsed onto the bed, unable to hold herself up seeing his bare chest in all its magnificence. She lay on her stomach and took secretive darting glances at his physique.

Brolin noticed and smiled in his heart. "Who told you these things about me?" He asked.

"I can't remember."

"Was it Kerridan?"

"No."

"Weathermarker?" She heard his voice grow chilly.

"It was Thorncrist…" she whispered. "Stupid of me to believe it."

Vale turned on his stomach and matched her position. He looked at her earnestly, chin resting on his arm.

"I take heart that you believed her."

She stared at him, "You do?"

"Yes. Ask me why."

"Why?"

"Because what she told you is the only thing holding you back from allowing yourself to be here, in my bed, every night."

Tamara felt effectively outmaneuvered. Left with no rejoinder, she turned on her side to face him, her head cradled on her arm. He copied her posture.

They lay among the tangles in the duvet in silence. Wind roared outside the window and leaves tapped against the window. Moonlit shadows of swaying branches moved back and forth on the bare floor and walls.

"When I arrived home earlier, I saw you asleep, and I wanted to crawl in and pull you into my arms and sleep beside you."

She brushed his closed eyes with her fingertips, "I'm sorry. The day just… just wore me down."

"I know. You've a had a horrible time of it," he said. He caught her hand before she withdrew it and kissed her fingertips before placing her hand on his heart. "Feel that?" He whispered.

"…yes…"

"You're the only reason it's beating."

"Will it stop if I'm away from you?"

"It's a guarantee."

"Well, then I just can't let you leave me then."

Tamara looked at him feeling fighting the urge to draw away and hide her heart again. She watched his grin start as he looked at her uncertainly. Then she watched it grow larger and spread across his face. His arm reached out, and he scooped up toward him. His kisses were sporadic and frenzied and she laughed for him in his joy.

"Well, I will definitely sleep with you now!" He said, laughing and pulling her up to the pillows, lifting the duvet and pulling it over them both.

"Why did it take so long to get to this point, sweetheart?" He murmured, pulling away again to look into her eyes.

"Really, just all your other women. There can only be one," She said, meeting his lips again.

"So…" he said through the capture of his lips in hers, "Will you be my 'only one'?"

"Always."

"I have something to seal this moment forever," Vale whispered, kissing her forehead, "I'll be right back."

Tamara lay among the dozens of pillows, watching the pattern of moving tree shadows on the wall. She heard the autumn rain tap the window pane and watched the shadow of a lone leaf sliding slowly down the window in a rivulet of its own. She replayed the memory of their conversation over in her mind. The only thing holding her back was what someone else said to her. Her heart was always ready to accept Vale Brolin, she just didn't know it. Her heart knew it from the beginning in that old hangar all those months ago when she saw him walking around her hangar. She smiled to herself and a sweet lethargy moved through her limbs. She stretched, and that's how Vale found her when he returned. He held something behind his back.

He approached the bed and kissed her and then said, "Close your eyes for a moment."

She closed her eyes, listening to his movements curiously. She heard him open the window, and she heard the relaxing sound of soft wind and rain. Then, she heard paper rustling, and she cocked her head, trying to discern his movements.

"No peeking," he said, placing a hand on her outstretched arm.

"Ok." She murmured.

She heard a sharp *ting* of metal against the dull *thud* of wood, and then a few seconds later she heard the sweetest, familiar sound. The sound of a waltz. Her eyes popped open, and she looked at Vale in the moonlight. She felt her bottom lip tremble and tears prick her eyes. She sat up and looked at the small, metal object he had placed on the bureau.

"A radio…!" She began, but she couldn't finish the sentence around the thump in her throat.

Vale reached for her and she stepped off the bed into his arms, words failing her.

Seeing the tears threatening to overcome her, Vale smiled tenderly and wiped her eye.

"Your old one was smashed that night in the apartment. I had Nord search for another like it." He gathered her into his arms and moved to the steps of the waltz holding her tenderly. "I wish you music and my love for always, Tamara Fieldmarsh," he murmured into the rioting mass of coils on her head.

The engine tamer and the airship pilot moved together to the music in the night…for always.

Fade to black.

Miscellaneousness

"Tamara Fieldmarsh With Companions" Sketch Copyright 2020 N. Annette
Knight

"Tamara Fieldmarsh in the Cafe" Sketch Copyright 2020 N. Annette Knight

Upcoming Title In This Series

The Servant Girl
Coming 2022

Did you have a fun time reading this novel? You did? Awesome! Go to Amazon and leave me a review! I look forward to reading it!

About the Author

My personal history with books began with frequently getting in trouble for reading instead of cleaning, or reading in the bathroom, or reading at the table, or being irreverent to books my mother felt were too serious to be found funny. My father read to us until we were high-schoolers and my most vivid memory is of him reading *Don Quixote* and pronouncing the name—and everything else within—with *razor-sharp precision.* These memories and having felt *so many things* when I read as child makes up the voice and tone I use when I write: emotion, humor and precision. These do not always appear in the same story together, but when I use them, each has its root in my history.

Thank you from the bottom of my heart.

N. Annette Knight

You can connect with me on:

🌐 http://www.nknightwrites.com

Also by N. Annette Knight .

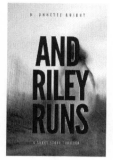

And Riley Runs: A Short Story Thriller
Danger stalks 12 year-old Riley as she maneuvers through the harsh, red landscape of the Utah wilds alone. Her crisis is worsened by approaching night, an injury, and a phone battery that will soon die. As the nameless danger begins to take a very real human shape, will the deepening darkness bring the chase to its inevitable end, or will Riley escape the clutches of a hunter?

Feverish Rainfall: A Romantic Short Story
Stranded in a foreign country, Quinne struggles to earn enough money to return home. Taking a job as a flutist with a local band, Quinne encounters distant, distractingly sexy, and out-of-reach Farrell. When an unexpected incident forces them to share a living space for a night, true feelings, and long-held assumptions rise to the surface. Will Farrell learn the truth about Quinne, and will Quinne finally act on her desires?

A Varied Merry Christmas
Originally produced as stand-alone works for social media, this anthology of short holiday stories comes to you Holiday Season 2021.

Made in the USA
Middletown, DE
16 April 2021